PRAISE FOR THE HOT BLOOD SERIES

The Original Anthologies of All-New Erotic Horror Fiction

HOT BLOOD

"Read *Hot Blood* late at night when the wind is blowing hard and the moon is full." —*Playboy*

HOTTER BLOOD

"A worthy successor to *Hot Blood,* taking an even more aggressive and daring approach to erotic horror . . . Riveting." —*Gauntlet* magazine

HOTTEST BLOOD

Winner of the Horror Writers Association Bram Stoker Award for Best Short Story: Nancy Holder's "I Hear the Mermaids Singing"

"Twenty envelope-stretching stories . . . Check out *Hottest Blood.*" —*Rocky Mountain News*

DEADLY AFTER DARK

"It's good to see the *Hot Blood* series continuing. . . . Recommended." —*Afraid* magazine

Books Edited by Jeff Gelb and Michael Garrett

Hotter Blood
Hottest Blood
The Hot Blood Series: Deadly After Dark
The Hot Blood Series: Seeds of Fear
The Hot Blood Series: Stranger by Night
The Hot Blood Series: Fear the Fever

Books Edited by Jeff Gelb

Hot Blood (with Lonn Friend)
Shock Rock
Shock Rock II
Fear Itself

FEAR THE FEVER

EDITED BY JEFF GELB
AND MICHAEL GARRETT

POCKET BOOKS
New York London Toronto Sydney Tokyo Singapore

This book consists of works of fiction. Names, characters, places and incidents are products of the authors' imaginations or are used fictitiously. Any resemblance to actual events or locales or persons, living or dead, is entirely coincidental.

An *Original* Publication of POCKET BOOKS

POCKET BOOKS, a division of Simon & Schuster Inc.
1230 Avenue of the Americas, New York, NY 10020

ISBN: 0-671-53765-2

First Pocket Books printing July 1996

10 9 8 7 6 5 4 3 2 1

POCKET and colophon are registered trademarks of Simon & Schuster Inc.

Cover art by Gerber Studio

Printed in the U.S.A.

Copyright Notices

To our sisters,
Sharyn Diamond and Linda Garrett,
who endured our childhood aggravations
and encouraged our talents anyway,
no matter the direction in which they took us!

CONTENTS

INTRODUCTION

Welcome to the seventh volume in the *Hot Blood* series, *Fear the Fever.*

The seventh digit conjures up myriad thoughts and images. The number seven traditionally has been considered lucky, as in "I hope I get lucky tonight." There are, of course, seven deadly sins. And who can forget the infamous seven-year itch?

Well, if you've got the itch for alternative adult entertainment, we'll provide the scratch in this collection of erotic horror stories, or as we sometimes call them, "The XXX Files"!

Even as editors, we find it remarkable how many horror stories reflect new sexual themes. Just when we think we've read them all, we'll get another batch of gems like the ones you're about to read. Discover for yourself the tingling of sexual awakening within these pages, as writers new and established pull out their most erotic stops to please you.

If this is your first visit to *Hot Blood* territory, strap on your seat belt or other safety device (condoms and dental dams are not mandatory here!) and get set for a wild ride. We know you'll enjoy the trip. And if you like to get a little behind—in your work, that is—we hope you'll take the time from your busy schedule to sample the first six *Hot Blood* volumes for more chilling delights. If you've been with us before, we're proud to have you come again, so to speak.

JEFF GELB
MICHAEL GARRETT

FEAR THE FEVER

THE FIVE PERCENT PEOPLE

Lucy Taylor

One-fifteen in the morning at the venerable Kenberry Arms Hotel in London.

The phone on Caleb's side of the king-size bed jings.

I'm already wide awake, waiting for the call.

I knew it would come.

I knew she wouldn't leave us alone.

Caleb has driven her crazy. Over the edge.

I'm close to that same edge myself, holding on by my chewed fingernails. How can any woman not go mad who gets involved with Dr. Caleb Masterton? I found the lusty postcard from the Giselle person only two days ago and have been working off my rage in the hotel gym ever since. Another five percent person for me to worry about. But more about Giselle and her hormonally charged missive later.

Caleb has already spent hours today trying to pacify Gwen the madwoman—first lunching with her in a little bistro away from the hotel, so his fellow psychologists here for the convention wouldn't get more fodder for the gossip mill if the pathetic creature made another scene, then strolling with her in Hyde Park while he explained in a dozen different, convoluted ways a concept I had condensed for him into three simple sentences: "I don't love you anymore. I love someone else. It's over."

But with Caleb, nothing's ever over.

The phone yips like a stepped-on terrier.

I clutch Caleb's shoulder. "Don't answer it. You know it's Gwen. You'll only make things worse if you talk to her."

But he grumbles and gropes for the phone, mutters a sleep-garbled hello, and flops back onto the pillow. His wavy blond hair fans out across my shoulder, his hand cups and caresses my breast, while his voice shifts into his therapeutic best—alert, solicitous, conciliatory: "Please, Gwen, don't do this. Don't cry. Come on, you're exhausted. We're all exhausted. We've talked about this so much. Please try to get some sleep."

I lie with my head on Caleb's chest. I can't hear all of the words, but I can hear Gwen Boston sobbing, screaming into the phone like an animal being tortured. It's unbearable. I've despised this woman for so long, but hearing her scream, my heart breaks for her.

For myself, too, wondering how long it will be before the same sounds issue from my throat.

Oh, Caleb has a way with women, yes, he does.

Even though Gwen has been among my rivals, I hate Caleb for reducing her to this pleading, pitiable creature. I hate myself for putting up with Caleb's adolescent egotism, for not grabbing a cab to Heathrow and getting myself back to L.A.

Even though Gwen is only a five percent person and I'm the ninety-five percent person. That's how Caleb, the noted psychologist, darling of the lecture circuit, explained it to me. But how long will these percentages hold? I ask myself.

"Nothing for you to worry about, darling," Caleb once said to me when I'd broken up with him after finding out he'd slept with the wife of one of his colleagues. "*You've* got me. You're the one I love. Surely if you have ninety-five percent of me, you're not going to quibble about the other five percent?"

He was talking about his little side dishes, his flings. It sounded almost sensible coming from his sculptured lips.

Psychology is only Caleb's second career—his first is making women fall in love with him. Because he knows what women want, he lives up to every fantasy, when the affair begins. He makes each one feel that she is the most special, the most desirable woman in the world, that he adores and appreciates her as no man ever has. And after his conquest is thoroughly devoted to him, he lets her find out about the others, lets her know that she has fallen in love with a man too terrified of love to do anything more than gingerly, squeamishly, stick the tips of his toes into its rushing current.

Caleb has been listening to Gwen rant, trying to calm her now for almost an hour. I'm groggy, dazed, but unable to sleep, because I know before long Caleb will leave our bed and go to her.

Only a matter of time. Caleb the knight in tarnished armor riding a swaybacked steed. Off to save the damsel he's driven to distress.

* * *

How did it come to this? My lover on the phone in the middle of the night comforting a woman he claims he never loved, a woman he made love to only as insurance against "that staleness of libido brought on by an excess of monogamy," as he put it.

Caleb and I flew from L.A. to London for the conference on Group Dynamics in the Workplace that started two days ago. Caleb read a paper, presided over a panel of distinguished guests, and signed copies of his latest pop-psych book to gaga-eyed aficionados of the psychobabble circuit. We've made plans to fly to Zurich for some skiing tomorrow afternoon, then back to L.A. four days later.

Gwen, who works in administration at USC, where Caleb teaches, must have pulled up Caleb's itinerary from the computer so she could fly to London to intercept him. I don't think she was counting on me, though. Even though Caleb and I have been lovers for almost four years, Gwen always seems astonished to see me with him at these academic gatherings. Doesn't she realize by now that I may not be his only woman but I'm his primary one? Does nothing discourage her, humiliate her sufficiently that she will give him up?

She threw a scene while Caleb and I were checking in, clutching his arm, demanding in a high-pitched, mortifyingly shrill voice to know what I was doing here. People stared, and Caleb squirmed.

I suspect, however, that underneath his veneer of embarrassed concern, Caleb relishes this. *Sturm und drang,* after all, is his milk and honey. Being at the center of the tempest gets him hard. A drama queen in tweed and wing-tipped Guccis.

I get up and pace around our plushly appointed suite, peer out the windows, peruse the contents of the mini-bar. My fingers drift across the top of the suitcase in which Caleb has packed our toys: lengths of strong nylon rope that won't chafe wrists or ankles, a blindfold and a gag, a darling little cat-o-'nine-tails we picked up in an L.A. sex shop. The bondage gear is used on me alone; I've offered to tie Caleb up, but he only makes a joke of it: "You know you can't tie a decent knot, darling."

I stroke the leather whip, imagine cramming the handle down Gwen's throat until her face turns purple.

On the phone, Caleb is purring, "No, no, Alicia doesn't hate you. She's concerned for you. She's genuinely worried."

I remember Mama warning me when I was a kid that you could never trust a woman. They'd lie to you, stab you in the back, talk as if butter wouldn't melt in their mouth when they met you face-to-face but choose their adjectives for strychnine content when they talked behind your back.

I never understood why Mama said that. She was a woman, and I was growing up to be one. Why did she think so little of her own sex?

Later, of course, I learned that Mama was Daddy's second wife. She'd stolen him away from his first wife while she was working as a legal secretary in Daddy's office. So naturally she viewed women as sharks, being of the marriage-wrecking sort herself.

But I know not all women conform to that ugly stereotype. I think about my women friends, caring and supportive women who understand the sad reality that male usefulness and comfort often extend no further than the end of the man's dick. If only women would stick together, I think, not put men up on pedestals we polish with our tongues while we destroy ourselves and each other like wild dogs fighting over scraps.

What about me? Am I ready to offer sisterly support to Gwen?

Oh, God, I want to but . . .

I crawl back into bed, find Caleb has stroked himself erect. His azure eyes meet mine. Lust thrills through me like electric shock. I slide down between his legs. My lips close over his cock and vacuum it down my throat. Sucking Caleb's cock, one of life's little ecstasies. His fingers close in my hair. Compassion melts. I want to shout at the phone, "Listen to these slurping noises, Gwen. Do you know what I'm doing?" But my mouth is too full of Caleb to speak.

I admit Gwen Boston was the last thing on my mind while Caleb and I were flying to London. I had other worries then. The night before we left L.A., I'd found a postcard lying atop a pile of graduate theses on Caleb's desk. It showed a gauzy-eyed, zaftig nude lounging on a brocade-covered couch. "Caleb, darling, I miss you fiercely," read the flowery, curlicued script. "What serendipity that you should have called the other day—when I was lying on a couch very much like this one." It was dated the month before and postmarked Albany, New York, where Caleb was guest speaker at a convention on codependency last month. He said I shouldn't bother going. Wouldn't be any fun, he said. No time to play.

Is that what you said to Giselle, I wonder, to make her miss you fiercely?

When I confronted Caleb about the card, he only lifted up my hair, nuzzling the back of my neck while murmuring, "You're the one I'm with, the one I love. Remember how we've talked about that other five percent? Nothing for you to be jealous of. Less than five percent, really. Never even had sex with the woman, not *real* sex. She's phobic about germs. Just blow jobs. Truly, that was all it was."

The hell of it is I can't even pay Caleb back by making him jealous. He protects his ego by insisting he does not feel jealousy which, to my mind, is akin to lepers who can poke a finger in the fire and not feel pain: no sign of health, this, but quite the opposite, the numbing out of something vital. He claims he doesn't mind if I indulge in my own peccadilloes. Sauce for the goose and all that tommyrot. But when I tried to ease the hurt of Caleb's infidelities by cheating on *him,* I found it only made things more painful. The words "I made love with so-and-so" sound so tepid, so pristine, leagues away from the moaning, rutting reality of a lusty, sweaty, musky, penetrating fuck.

Leave him, I think. Punish him, make him pay.

But whenever I've left Caleb in the past, the only one who seems to pay is me.

Because the good times with Caleb are extraordinary. He's lusty and witty and generous; he attends to all the little things, both in and out of bed; knows how to fuck a woman forty-seven different ways. And add to that all the little erotic garnishes that he's proficient in, all those little things I crave—the scarves and knots, the sting of leather now and then. He's past forty, but still blond and tawny, sleek as Secretariat in his prime, the eternal adolescent, rock star bronze. He's Peter Pan, and, yes, I know, a book was written about that type of man. Look what happened to Wendy!

Caleb shoves the phone into the pillow as he spasms into my mouth. He takes a deep breath, puts the phone back to his ear, and resumes his soothing patter. I rest my cheek on his flaccid cock, inhaling the sultry musk of come.

I understand Gwen's obsession.

I weep for her at the same time that I hate her.

He will destroy us both.

Caleb hangs the phone up and hoists himself out of bed.

"Only be a few minutes," he says, climbing into his pants. "Got to go calm her down."

"You've spent the whole goddamn night calming her down!"

He leans over, takes my face in his hands. "Please try to understand. We don't want a scandal. Those tight-asses in the department back in L.A. would adore a scandal."

I can barely hear his words for the sharp static of fear sizzling behind my temples. Caleb is leaving me to go to Gwen. *Caleb is leaving.*

"Don't go. Don't give her what she wants. You'll only make it worse."

He pats my cheek. "Got to, love. Only be a few minutes. Just going to meet her on the mezzanine. Have a little chat, hold her hand. There, that's a dear."

And then he's gone.

The ticking of the clock sounds like the timing device on a bomb. Ten past two. Now ten past three. Three-twenty. I've tried watching late night TV—CNN and wacky British sitcoms. I've even masturbated twice to orgasm, but sleep is still as unlikely as lunch with Princess Di. I get out of bed, go to the windows and open the middle one. Gaze down at the occasional taxi passing below, then yank it shut. I dial the all-night coffee shop on the mezzanine. The gravelly voiced woman who picks up the phone says no one is there. I hang up.

Where is he, then?

A terrible thought rocks me. He wouldn't have, he didn't. Surely he wouldn't be so foolish as to— I pick up the phone and dial Gwen's room.

She answers, sniffing pitifully.

"Put Caleb on," I tell her.

He answers.

My adrenaline is pumping as if I'm about to rush into a burning building. I'm almost stuttering with rage.

"You're really pushing it, Caleb. Get out of that woman's room. Get back here now."

He agrees.

A triumph—I have never talked to Caleb like that. I rather like myself for doing it, but I'm scared, too.

I get more scared as the minutes pass and Caleb doesn't return.

I call again. This time no one answers.

Visions of Caleb and Gwen in one last carnal meltdown fill my head, a final bounce, the sexual equivalent of that last drink—"just this one for the road"—that the alcoholic says before every bender.

I put on my nightgown and Caleb's silk robe, grab the room key, and head for the elevator. Gwen is on the fourth floor, seven floors below ours.

I pound on the door, bracing myself for what I may find. Caleb finally opens the door.

"Jesus, Alicia, what are you—"

I rush past him into the room, which is empty, then investigate the bathroom. And stop. Gwen is in her bra and half-slip on her knees by the commode. Blood streams down her forearms. A pool of blood rubies around her knees.

"Dear God."

Caleb grabs me by the shoulders, pivots me away from the bathroom. "Christ, Alicia," he hisses "there's no need for you to see this. Get back to the room."

"My God, she tried to kill herself. We ought to call an ambulance."

"No, no, it's not serious. Not very, anyway. She's done this before. She only cuts enough to make a mess, look like she's bleeding to death. More for effect than anything."

Gwen overhears this diminishment of her injuries. She howls.

"Why now?" I ask. "What happened?"

"I said I never really loved her. I told her I only said it to get her into bed."

"Let me talk to her."

I go in the bathroom where Gwen has wedged herself between the toilet and the sink, stanching the flow of her blood with one of the hotel's plush terry-cloth towels. There's blood on her bare feet, on the tile, blood dappling her thin stubbly calves. This is not the way I think of Gwen: defeated, demolished, destroyed.

I squat beside her. "He isn't worth it, you know."

She looks up through bloodshot blue eyes. "I know."

"So why don't you give him up?"

"Why don't you?"

"Because I'm the one he's with, darling."

She rallies enough to sneer at me. "Your turn will come. He does this to everyone. He'll do it to you, too."

As if I'm so inebriated with desire that I haven't realized this. It's part of the ongoing despair I live with, part of the turmoil that wakes me in the night with the feeling that the sword of Damocles has turned into a giant penis about to smash down on my head.

"Do you want a doctor?"

From the other room, Caleb calls, "No, no doctors. She doesn't need a doctor."

"I don't need a doctor," echoes Gwen.

"But you're still bleeding."

"I don't care. He doesn't love me. I want to die."

"That's nonsense." I want to slap her till she wakes up from this trance of despair, this hideous bewitchment. "He isn't worth this, Gwen. Can't you see?"

She looks at me with haunted, yearning eyes. "He is, he is. I'd die for him."

Christ. Sprawled bloody and disheveled on the tiles, she looks like the heroine of a bad bodice ripper. Caleb comes to the door. "Let me talk to her, Alicia."

I stand up. "What's left to say? You've been talking to her night and day ever since we got here, and the only thing that's changed is that now she's slashed her wrists."

"Cut her wrists, Alicia. They're only cut."

"Dammit, she opened up her flesh with a razor blade. I don't give a shit what verb you use to describe it."

"Keep your voice down."

"Damn you."

He touches his fingertips to my cheeks, brushes his lips to my mouth. I can feel his kiss all the way down to my clit.

"Only a few more minutes," whispers Caleb. "Just to make sure she doesn't try it again after I leave. Please."

Caleb returns to our room an hour later, looking as drained and exhausted as a man who's been standing on a scaffold waiting to hang.

"How is she?"

"Better now. She's sleeping."

"What did you tell her?"

"That everything's going to be all right."

I sit up on my elbows. "But everything's not going to be all right. She's obsessed with you. And as long as you go running every time she calls, it's never going to end."

"No, she'll calm down. I told her I'd see her when we got back to L.A. We'd talk it out."

"What's left to say?"

"Please, Alicia, I've heard enough bitching for one night."

"But what can you possibly say to her? Either it's over or it isn't. There is no middle ground!"

His eyeballs dart around in their sockets. "She only wants to maintain our friendship."

"Meaning a platonic friendship?"

"Well, no, not exactly."

"God damn you!" I hurl myself against him, flailing with my fists. He throws me back onto the bed, pins me down. The rage empowering my muscles goes between my legs. This is how it feels when Caleb ties me to the bed. How can hatred and desire merge so easily?

"She'll never mean anything to me, darling," he murmurs. "She never did; she never will."

His legs pry mine apart. He slides inside, a perfect fit. I feel the temporary, blissful merging of the boundaries that should define us, an end to the separateness of our skin.

"I love you, don't you know that?" he whispers, and, oh, I want to believe him. I *need* to believe him, because I love him, too.

Four-fifteen: the phone.

I roll over, tears springing to my eyes. "Jesus, I thought you were going to ask the operator not to put through any more calls."

"If I had, she'd just come to the door."

"Then you call the police."

"Alicia . . ." His tone of voice suggests that I've just advised him to toss gasoline on Gwen and light a match.

Caleb picks up the phone.

At first I can tell she's talking calmly, Caleb making his reassuring little hmms and uhhs. While he listens to her, he puts his arm around me, strokes my hair. His hand feels so good, I want him to slide his fingers through my skin and caress the slippery, soft interior of my heart.

"No," says Caleb. "I don't think that would be a good idea."

The noise that comes through the phone is enough to make me jump and burrow my head in Caleb's armpit. Raw screaming, sobbing. As if she's being flailed.

"No, please, Gwen it's so very late, and Alicia and I are exhausted. Please, can't it wait till tomorrow? There'll be time, yes . . . I'll see you before we leave for Heathrow. No, Gwen, what would your coming to our room solve?"

I bolt up on my elbows.

"She wants to come *here?* No, absolutely not. This is my room too."

"No, Alicia isn't upset. She's only . . . she's just tired. I told you, no, it wouldn't be a good idea."

But I know it's only a matter of time. Caleb won't hang up the phone. Gwen will continue sobbing. With or without my permission, he will allow her to come to our room.

"Ten minutes," he tells me as he hangs up the phone. "That's all she wants. Ten minutes."

"To do what? To say what? Jesus, this is driving me crazy."

"Just to make sure she doesn't hurt herself again." He takes me in his arms.

A timid knock.

She slinks into our room wearing a fuchsia Chinese nightgown and tangerine slippers. Her wrists are bandaged. She clutches her arms across her chest and shivers as though she's entering a freezer. She looks at me sprawled naked on the bed and quickly turns away.

"What did you think, Gwen," I say, "that we slept in separate beds? Did you think we were just sharing the room to save money?"

Caleb winces. "Alicia, please . . ."

I get up out of bed and stride across the room. Let her get a good long look. Whatever else she does to deal with her pain, she doesn't exorcise it with barbells and StairMasters. I meet her gaze and then slide into my robe.

"I love him," whimpers Gwen.

"But don't you understand?" I do something odd then, something that surprises even me. I stroke her hair. Stroke it like maybe her mother should have done, or her father, somebody who cared about her, who could have taught her to respect herself back when it would have mattered. I know all this, because no one did those things for me. That's what brought me to Caleb. "You have to give him up, Gwen. He doesn't love you, sweetheart."

"He doesn't love you, either."

That's something I loathe considering, but it's definitely possible. The postcard from Giselle of the baroque script. Plump, pink-bosomed nude reclining like a purring cat: "Miss you fiercely."

Oh, Caleb, why? If you've got to have multiple women, then why not hookers, who wouldn't love you, wouldn't care? Why not well-married women bored with their husbands and looking for a lark? Why not a bold but straightforward ad: "Unavailable male seeks same in woman for frenzied bouts of uncommitted lust."

But Caleb only desires women whom he senses are needy, lonely, empty at their core, women who will fall in love with him and not be able to let go. Something about their hopeless, yearning love, makes him feel worthy, powerful.

Gwen collapses in a chair by the bed, dabbing at her puffy eyes. She stares at me with venom. "I don't see why we can't share him. You one night, me the next."

An arrangement I'm afraid Caleb might actually consider.

"Because he doesn't want you anymore, sweet thing. You were only a five percent person to begin with."

Before Gwen can ask what I mean by that, Caleb interrupts, asking if she'll have a drink.

"It'll help you relax, love. Scotch?"

"I hate Scotch." She turns to me. "What did you mean by five percent?"

"Vodka, then. I think I saw some Smirnoff in the mini-bar."

But Gwen won't be deterred. "Five percent? What does that mean? That I'm only five percent of your love life, Caleb? That I'm of so little significance? Did you really *say* that?"

"Will you please lower your voice, Gwen?"

While Caleb pretends this is a cocktail party, I feel a monster headache surging up behind my forehead. I go into the bathroom, erase the smudged mascara from below my eyes with baby oil, and gulp some aspirin.

Coming out of the bathroom, I feel cold air swirl around my knees and feet, a chilly exhalation slightly tainted with exhaust.

The bedroom looks empty. No sign of Gwen. The middle window is wide open.

Oh, please, I think, please, but I don't know if I'm praying for her safety or her death.

I look down first and see nothing but the solid blackness of the street eleven stories down. Then I hear her. She's sobbing softly, about ten feet away.

Out on the ledge.

"Oh, Jesus, Gwen what have you done?"

"If I'm only five percent, then I'd be better off dead. And if you call the police, I'll jump. I swear it."

Caleb pokes his head out the window beside mine. "Holy Christ, Gwen, get in here." He extends his hand, but it doesn't even begin to close the distance between them. "Don't do this, Gwen."

"I have to. You don't love me. I want to die."

I wonder if the others on this floor can hear this fervid discourse, but then, we occupy a corner room and those in the adjacent rooms, quite sensibly, surely must have their windows shut on this chilly night. I wonder if I should call the police anyway. I wonder if she'll do it. I wonder if . . . Oh, Christ, I wonder if Caleb will love me better if she's dead.

"Now listen, sweetheart," I hear Caleb saying in his best soothing, avuncular, Daddy-comforting-little-girl-with-skinned-knee tone of voice, "Nothing is worth this. *I'm* not worth this. You don't want to die."

"Yes, I do."

"I don't want you to die."

"I don't give a shit *what* you want. You don't love me."

"Gwen, honey, what have I been doing all evening? What have I been doing all weekend? Trying to reassure you that everything's going to be all right."

"But it isn't! It won't ever be all right! You don't want me, you want *her.*"

Yeah, he wants me, I think.

And he wants Giselle, of the overheated postcards, and he wants the waitress with the kewpie doll mouth and vacuumed-looking eyes who brought us tea and toast this morning, and he even wants the pear-shaped journalist with a nose so juttingly ethnic that it would be un-p.c. to even mention it, who clucked questions at Caleb over her pudgy belly at the airport the other day.

He wants them all, because they're all Erections, past, present, and future, the Muses of his preening masturbation, the proof that he's not invisible, but *loved.* He's bulimic about love. He sucks it up, then pukes it out, finds another lover, and repeats the cycle.

"Look, darling," I hear Caleb coaxing as he leans far out the window, "I promise you something. Word of honor. If you'll come in right now, we'll go to your room. We'll spend what's left of the night together and tomorrow, too. I love you, Gwen. I'll make this up to you. I'll—"

I grab Caleb by the arm, pull him away from the window.

"What the fuck are you telling her?"

"Jesus, Alicia, surely you can't think anything I say right now means anything. I'll promise to have her name tattooed on my dick if it'll get her back in the fucking room. Think of it, Alicia, if she jumps. Think what people will say."

"But do you mean it? Do you love her?"

"Christ Jesus, no. If she were standing out on somebody else's ledge, I'd be down below yelling 'Jump!' Believe me, there's nothing for you to worry about. She means nothing to me. She's a pain and a pest and doesn't even give good head."

Why is it this doesn't reassure me?

Oh, Gwen, you little idiot, why are you out there on that ledge? You don't deserve to die. Come in, come in, come in.

"I hate you," she's sobbing. "You don't love me, you never did. All you've done is tell me lies." Her sobs are like the keening of women I heard once in a funeral procession in Mexico.

"Just listen to me, darling. You're terrifying me. I love you, Gwen, I truly do. I was only trying to appease Alicia when I said I didn't. Believe me, won't you? Come take my hand. Come inside."

She sniffles, coughs, then mumbles in a tiny voice, "I don't want to die."

"Of course you don't, and you aren't going to. You're going to inch closer, very, *very* carefully. Slowly. You're going to take my hand and—"

"I'm afraid to move."

"Take my hand."

"I'm so afraid."

"You're going to be all right, my love," Caleb says. "I'm going to step away from the window now, but—"

"No," she screeches. "You're going to call the police."

"No police," says Caleb. "Word of honor. Two seconds, darling. Two. I'll be right back."

Caleb seizes my arm. "She's almost close enough to grab. I'm going to try to pull her in. I'm going to get her hand, to—"

"No! It's a trick! She'll jump and pull you down with her. She wants to kill you both."

"I'm not going out onto the ledge. You think I'm demented? I'm not going to die for that bitch. I'm going to lean out the window and catch her hand. But first I want you to tie me to the headboard of the bed with the ropes, just in case you're right, in case she tries to pull me down with her."

"Let her come in on her own, Caleb."

"I've got to do something. What if she jumps? How will it look?"

"Who gives a shit?"

"I do. My career—"

"Fuck your career."

"I'll pretend I didn't hear you say that."

Gwen moans, "I'm getting dizzy! I'm going to fall!"

"The ropes! Go get them—hurry!"

Caleb's suitcase is a mess. I frantically rummage through it, throwing things out onto the floor. I find the nylon ropes, but something else as well—an airline ticket and a card. I can barely read the note that's scrawled inside the card, for the tears blurring my vision, but when Caleb yells, I grab the ropes and run back to the window.

"Here." He loops the rope under his arms and twice around his chest, staying beside the window so Gwen can see and hear him as he tries to talk her in. I run back to the bed and tie him to the headboard, which looks sturdy enough to support the weight of a small car.

Meanwhile, Caleb is leaning out the window, one knee on the ledge, reaching toward Gwen, whose pale hand is now extended toward his. Not making contact—yet.

Gwen, my enemy.

I see Caleb's back and torso, leaning out the window. Into the void. Trusting his weight to the rope. Leaning away.

Farther and farther.

The man I want. The man I love.

"Caleb, wait!"

But my cry does not come soon enough.

He doesn't reach Gwen's outstretched hand. He teeters, spins, tries to regain his balance, can't, then bellows as the rope lets go, flies past him out into the dark like a cracking whip and drops, with Caleb plunging after it.

Gwen doesn't scream as Caleb plummets. For a moment I think she's fallen, too.

Then suddenly she tumbles in through the open window, shaking, sobbing. She collapses into my arms.

"He fell," she gasps. "He fell trying to save me."

"Yes, he did his best," I say. "He fell."

I could have shown her the plane ticket from Albany to Caleb's next conference, in Jacksonville, and the note accompanying it: "To my dear Giselle. You're the only one. I'm going to prove it to you. Soon."

I could have told Gwen that he died because the rope that was meant to anchor him came loose—because, as Caleb always said, I can't tie a decent knot, especially when my hands are quivering with rage.

But I say nothing.

Gwen stares up at me. Her blue eyes are glassy, manic, like circles of bright crayon. "He loved me, you know. He said he did. He loved me."

"He loved you," I repeat. "He loved us both."

Then I stroke her hair and hold her, smelling Caleb on her skin, while we wait for the police to come, while I pray that in time we may be free of him.

FEEDING THE BEAST

Bruce Jones

Trisha was killing her mother again—this time in the farmhouse kitchen with the old broken-handled steak knife—and in a little while killing her sister Dolce, who grunted like a pig and bled liberally. . . .

Then, free of them, free of the knife, free as the wind lashing her tawny locks, Trisha came running fierce and proud, heedless and grinning, over the rolling meadow, Shep nipping and barking delight at her bare heels—the fair-skinned girl with the banner of summer hair and the bounding, yelping German sheperd—alive and free and safe at last among fields and endless fields of undulant, sweetly perfumed yellow grass. . . .

Until the warm breeze shifted sour, grinning Mojo abruptly there, gold-tooth contrasting midnight skin, glistening now with the sweat of death, rough, callused hand sharp and shocking across her tender face, starting blood there at her lip . . . and Shep—brave Shep, try as he might—could not sink eager teeth into the skinny black legs because they kept disappearing which meant they weren't real and neither was Shep, Shep long dead now like this half-forgotten meadow . . . and this was now, not then, and Mojo was her pimp, and she—Trisha—was a hooker, and these peeling walls could never be the lovely yellow field . . . as she came up, up, and finally out of the dream to the dreary little room and the man sleeping beside her.

Amazing, she thought, yawning.

Not that she had dreamed of killing—this was old hat. Amazing that she had fallen asleep at all here on the job next to her john. *They* did that sometimes—the johns—passed out and snored blissfully if she gave them an extra good ride, especially the fat ones, the smelly ones, though this one had been neither. This one had been quiet and gentle, tender—even nice-looking in a dark way.

Which is why Trisha was so startled, there on the tired hotel sheets, turning in shafts of brassy afternoon sun, to find what her john had become . . . to find the far darker, more terrifying thing that had replaced him while she slept. . . .

Not a man at all, this misshapen shadow that shared her bed, but a thing of black hair, cruel pointed muzzle, pink lolling tongue guarding bone-white incisors as deadly sharp and long—longer than Shep's . . . so that for a moment Trisha actually thought the dream was real and it was her long dead pet there beside her on the pillow come to comfort and sleep with her while Momma was busy with the men.

But no. This creature was far bigger, far more terrifying than anything strictly canine, or strictly human either—a savagely insane juncture of the two, a great, dark sleeping beast from childhood nightmares, midnight matinees, but all too real, all too here and close, its hot breath against her bare arm, its great shaggy head so near she could see the corona of coarse hairs along the sleek, swept-back ears.

The eyes, mercifully, were closed; had they been open, red (Trisha was sure they must be red), and full of blood lust, Trisha Kincaid would doubtless be a dead whore, not a recently dreaming one.

Carefully then, not breathing, moving in a slow-motion haze of terror, she pushed herself up gently, hitching breath as the ancient bed sagged creaking resentment, lowered her legs over the edge of the mattress, found the cold floor, turned to see if the thing had awakened, was watching. It was not. Though now, at this angle, she could glimpse more of it in the dying ochre light—the broad matted chest, the massive arms, muscular sweep of thigh, placid but fearsome phallus. This too was swathed in hair, as were the testes, fat and shiny as a seed bull's. It was the power there, between the thing's legs, that was perhaps the most fearfully awesome of all.

Heart and knees knocking, Trisha just made it to the lump of her skirt and blouse, just made it to the old glass doorknob, twisting it silently . . . the voice behind her spinning her, gasping.

"You're leaving?"

Back against the door, throat constricted, heart slamming painful ripples to her fingertips, Trisha faced not the terrible dark beast, but the pale naked man of before; only his eyes and the hair of his head were dark now, as a sad wistful smile tugged tender, remembered lips. He caught her look, returned a knowing one of his own, nodding. "You saw . . ."

Trisha, trembling against the door, could but nod terror.

He came to her, reproachful, but for himself. "I'm sorry. It happens sometimes, when I sleep. You've nothing to fear from me. I'm sorry."

And twice amazed this day, Trisha found herself wholly unafraid . . . so much that she wondered absently if it was the creature itself she had truly feared, or something else. "You won't . . . kill me?"

His smile was as disarming as his winsome, weary expression. "Never. Never in daylight." Young eyes hollow, haunted by dark memories, perhaps decades of them.

Trisha, marveling, dropped her eyes to find further changes. The naked man stepped back, his smile rueful now, regretful? "Yes . . . that goes back to normal too. All of me back to quite ordinary and normal. Will you keep my secret?"

Trisha, her mind on other things, slipped thoughtfully into the Wal-Mart blouse, her trembling gone. "Have you ever . . . while you're that way, I mean?"

This made him assess her with new eyes, searching eyes. "No. That would bring death. I change to feed, not for love."

Then he turned, showing her his pale buttocks, and retreated to the bed, to his own clothes. Retrieving the little automatic she thought she'd hidden beneath her pillow, he placed it to his own chest, smiled into her eyes, and fired, the slug knocking him back but not entering, falling flat to threadbare rug. "I can't be harmed in the normal way, you see." He smiled that sad smile again, then said reflectively: "Will you betray me, Trisha?"

An anxious pounding at the door. Worried, muffled cries.

The tall figure strode to the ancient knob, twisted it, opened the door.

A beefy red face peered in anxiously. "Is everything all right, sir? We heard a shot."

"Yes, we were wondering about that too. Perhaps down the hall . . ."

The beefy face glanced once Trisha's way and retreated apologetically.

The tall figure closed the door, turned back to Trisha.

"How did you know my name?" she whispered.

"Will you? Betray me?"

She turned, ran a hand absently across the still warm sheets. "Will I see you again?"

Which made the smile falter curiously. "Whatever for?"

At home—a refurbished Ninth Street penthouse—Mojo slapped her hard for falling asleep on the job, slapped her again for forgetting the money, took her silver automatic—Trisha on her knees—stuck it in her mouth, and made her suck, suck hard until she'd summoned the weapon's load, the slug crashing through the back of her skull . . . except Mojo, laughing and gold-toothed, jerked free before this last, making her only imagine it, warning that the next whore who showed up without money was a whore who was dead. He and Angela—Mojo's current pump, a pretty Mexican who had recently usurped

Trisha's position—both getting a good laugh from this.

Trisha killed her mother again that morning—threw her from a cliff—forgot about sister Dolce and ran once more wild and free with Shep, yellow grass whipping her ankles.

That night, having made up her mind, she hit the streets searching, found his big dark car, and leaned close to his window. "Hello again. You forgot to pay me."

"Yes, I've been looking for you. Here . . ." He paid her double—paid her triple, counting the warm smile.

Which Trisha returned, then stayed his hand before he could pull away from the curb. "What's your name?"

"Franklyn."

"That's a nice name. Old-fashioned. I'm Trisha."

They shook hands.

"Franklyn, I have a . . . well, a proposition. Will you be in town for a while?"

"I sort of have to keep moving, Trisha."

"Stay another night. One more night . . ."

Trisha had read little in her life; movies had been her education, and these were enough.

She had exercised caution all her life, had come this far because of it. She exercised it now: melted down the silver crucifix at her neck, took the glistening lump to Fast Freddie who owned a gun shop on Third Street. Freddie smiled, flashing gold teeth at her, and asked: "What you up to now, woman?" but asked no more; he nodded and told her to come back on Thursday. When she did, with fifty bucks, he had the silver rounds all ready for her. "They soft, but they work," he said. Trisha loaded them into the shiny automatic, just in case, and sought out Angela.

Told Angela she'd scored a date, a "doubles," and for a lot of money, more than she'd ever seen. Then led her up to the little hotel room, let Angela—who looked not unlike her sister Dolce—enter first into the little room, the darkened room, quickly shutting and locking the door behind her.

"What—" from Angela inside. Alone with shadow and full moonlight and something else . . . then a quick, sharp scream—the kicking sound an antelope might make—and quiet.

Give me fifteen minutes, he'd said, and Trisha did, before unlocking the door, pushing into a room full of streaming moonlight, the silvery gun weighting her small purse.

He awaited her on the bed, muzzle yet dripping, eyes glowing red, as she'd guessed, so powerful, so dreadful an apparition that Trisha thought at first she must flee, though she did not. She undressed quickly instead, temples pounding, purse close at hand, came to the bed, and, unable to face eyes so soul-piercingly bright, presented him her pale buttocks.

It was the words she wanted most, had never known. Her johns had spoken them—shouted them—many times, accompanying their too-eager discharge, words usually curiously religious in nature—words like "Jesus!" "Oh, Christ!" or sometimes merely "Fuck, fuck!"—hissed sometimes vengeful, sometimes oddly tender, vaguely forlorn, more prayer than epithet.

Trisha had never spoken them, never experienced a mind so cleansed white with passion that unbidden words could find voice . . . never known fulfilled love, sexual or otherwise.

While mounted here, in full glorious moonlight, the beast's talons at her flanks, hot stench of blood-breath in her ear, the words came . . . at first a guttural gasp in the seemingly futile attempt to accommodate him, then, in a moment—face red, eyes and mouth bulging like a pond frog's—Trisha cried out, felt the savage tide catch, lift—let herself go with it at last, be carried away high and higher, screaming now the words . . .

And he, lost in animal grunts, animal thrusts, emptying his soul in her, filling her—filling the small room—with a high, lovely long-buried howl of completeness. . . .

Afterward—both of them changed into something else—they lay together listening to each other's breath, marveling that, amid such crimson carnage—Angela's twisted remains still lay beneath the bed—they could discover such long-sought need, such exhausted relief.

"Stay with me?" he breathed hopefully. "I have plenty of money, lots." And she nodded, snuggling, having sought long and finally found this treasure no power on earth, she'd make sure, would wrest from her.

"We'll have to travel," Franklyn said, "quite a lot, sometimes in hot, lonely places."

"Not lonely," she murmured, "never again lonely. But first . . . one more night . . ."

"The honky did fucking *what!*" from an inflamed Mojo.

"Refused to pay me," Trisha repeated, all innocence and fluster.

"Uh-huh." Mojo packed his slender stiletto and his Colt Python. "We just see about this shit!"

Knocking at the hotel door ten minutes later, impatient with chest-puffed bravado. "Open the door, motherfucker. Mojo want a word with your white ass!"

"It's open . . ." from within moonlit walls.

Opened, then locked a moment later, Mojo's "What the fuck—?" followed by two quick shots, a frenzied wheezing that exuded bright terror, a clawing at the wooden door that Trisha, from the hall, thought must be Franklyn . . . then a light popping, like a twig wrapped in wet cloth, snapped—a visceral grunt from Mojo as if he'd just come . . . and no more.

She faced Franklyn this time, lay beneath him, supine and triumphant, looked up into the vacuous face, the flaming eyes, the dreadful gnashing fangs and reveled . . . let him mold, pinch, let him scratch tender breasts with great curved talons until she came, yelping . . . held his fluttering hugeness within her, gripping the black-furred loins until he'd made her come again, shout the lovely Words—rear back his own shaggy head and make the little room echo with his plaintive love-howl . . . Mojo, trunkless and blood-crusted, watching, canted from shadowed corner with dead, yolky eyes.

"We're alike," Franklyn said later, changed and lightly stroking her, "outcasts and hungry. Alike."

They traveled the desert states, hot clear days, chill, restful nights during which she never again dreamed of Shep, his cool muzzle thrust in her palm, his trusting head against her lap.

In Arizona, in an enormous stucco chalet Franklyn had rented, they knew sweet peace. For a time.

She brought him boys sometimes, but mostly she procured young women.

"They all look like the same girl," he commented once absently.

She said nothing, and it seemed fine.

Until the emergence of Franklyn's great rival, his jealousy over the one person he could never exact vengeance upon: himself.

She found him wandering the desert beneath black, moonless night. "What is it, love?"

At first she thought he wasn't going to respond. Then: "It's not me, is it? It's not me. It's him—the beast—you covet."

And she took his arm, pressed against his shoulder. "Can't it be enough?"

He watched the ebon sky, sighed. "I want to hunt alone from now on."

She searched his face, hugged the arm again. "One more, darling . . . just one more."

Some of the young women were lesbians, overtly . . . some merely lost souls not unlike her former self. Some delicate to shattering, some abrasive with rebellion, steeped in the hatred of family abuse, like this one tonight, this reedy blonde who looked so much like the others.

"And this is the guest room." Trisha showed her.

The girl, Janice, ever pensive, clearly jealous, shrugged indifference. "Can that window be closed? I can't sleep with the moonlight in my eyes."

Franklyn came to see the girl just past midnight. To his shock, Trisha was still there, with no apparent plans to leave. She stood, back to the door, and watched.

Franklyn changed swiftly, with none of the protracted lassitude of the late-night movies. A shadow passed over his face, his smile became ghastly, the clear eyes red and burning—and it was done. He dropped panther-silent to the floor, not a panther, nor any longer a man . . . something dark and feral that rumbled throatily and urinated pungently in the small room, then advanced. . . .

Janice—imperious demeanor crumbled, face a rictus of disbelief—could but run . . . in a place where running could not be done.

Thus the chase, across moonlit bed and fallen chairs, was brief, though long enough to remind Trisha of the neighborhood tomcat of her childhood, the one next-door that used to trap and play with fat field mice. Janice, who was not fat, did not turn and fight at the end the way the mice had; she screamed instead and clawed at the wallpaper, leaving brilliant red and most of her fingernails there before the dark thing pulled her down.

Behind the bed, between brass rail and wall, the beast dragged her, kicking, pinned her with a satisfied whuff of black flared nostrils, bent dripping jaws, and ended the screams, the struggles, with a single bite, eliciting a nearly sexual grunt from Janice, a final spastic flutter of limbs as the big incisors broke something deep down, spraying blood and piss.

Trisha listened absently to the feast . . . came finally to Franklyn's hunkered form, stroked the shaggy head, and kissed it. Lingered to tongue his still streaming lips, sit atop him in scalloped gore and shout her words—her glory, her vengeance and triumph—to the moon's mindless eye. She yelped, startled, while coming when Franklyn drew her suddenly down, nipped her throbbing neck, lapped tenderly what trickled there.

Later, on smeared, rumpled sheets, lazily sated, pleasantly logy, Trisha reached for and caressed the huge hairy phallus, felt (with disappointment) it retreat, shrink away with the rest of him to become slender and pale and white as the bone-colored moon. She found, turning to kiss his face, that he was smiling at her.

"You bit me." She smiled back.

"My gift to you."

And, a distant chill plucking at her, she ventured: "Gift?"

"What you wanted, have been asking for all these nights. Death."

She turned a naked, red-streaked hip to appraise him. "Have I asked for death?"

Smile in place, he stroked her slim back. "Asked for it, demanded it, shouted it with every climax. 'Kill me!' And now I have."

"I said that? I said, 'Kill me'?"

"What did you think you were shouting?"

Trisha, genuinely awed, considered it. "Something more . . . erotic."

His smile broadened tenderly. "It isn't love you've been seeking, sweet, it's peace. Release from your guilt."

"Guilt?"

"Over your mother. And sister."

Trisha, abruptly chilled, glanced at the twisted thing on the floor, withdrew a fraction. "How did you know?"

"We know."

No one was more surprised at the sudden tears than

Trisha, nor more relieved. "They . . . hurt me," sobbing, "Mother gave me to the men because I was the pretty one. Dolce . . . Dolce laughed. I hated them."

"And loved them. They were killing you. You were killing them. I didn't know what to do. And then I did." He touched the still tender mark at her neck. "You're one of us now; the infection has passed. Forever dead, forever living . . ."

She pushed herself up, heart hammering alarm, finger tracing an invisible line at her carotid.

"You'll never know guilt," Franklyn told her. "Guilt is not to be found in us."

A cloud passed over Trisha's face. "Will we still be able to . . . ?" She nodded, imploring, below his belly.

He laughed. "More than ever. More explosively atavistic, lubriciously primitive. And nothing can ever harm us. You're invulnerable now. Watch . . . and trust." He pulled the silvery gun from her pillow, fired casually at her, naked in her surprise.

She would wonder in her last moments why she had left the silver rounds in the gun, why she had kept the gun at all. That old cautionary guard again, fearing the beast even as she trusted the man?

Wondered, too, in the fleeting breath of time between his last words and the white glare of the explosion, if she might somehow have warned him in time . . . or if, in fact, she had deliberately hesitated . . . if Franklyn, in his sweet ignorance, had not perhaps done her the greatest favor of all: gifted her—the silver slug tearing her chest, summoning bright blood—with that which she'd sought all along.

Dying there in strangled moonlight, the bed a pool, a lake, the approaching wail of sirens souring the peaceful night, she found no breath to explain with

. . . could only listen in descending darkness to his agonized scream, his tortured, high-pitched howl, wholly human now, of despair, chasing her into the final night.

Hear a moment later the familiar joyful bark, feel Shep's cold muzzle against her palm, the two of them laughing and truly free, racing through the yellow undulant meadow in the soft summer breeze. . . .

PURPLE HEARTS AND OTHER WOUNDS

Stephen Woodworth

PFC Billy Barnes stalked through the chaos of Tu Do Street, the humidity pasting the shirt of his civilian outfit to his chest. Sweat soaked and deflated the tissues padding the crotch of his underwear.

Stately French-style porticos and grillwork gave way to contemporary storefronts and garish bars. Street vendors and prostitutes, seeing a well-dressed American, pressed in upon him as he passed, making him offers in an incoherent mélange of English and Vietnamese. He scanned each female face for a certain set of Asian features, a distinct pair of brown eyes.

Feverish steps brought him to the Golden Flower, the massage parlor Cochrane had told him about. A svelte woman in a red satin gown leaned in the doorway, her mouth a jaded pout. Billy approached her, and she smiled languidly. "Hep you, sir?" she asked, running a finger down the buttoned front of his shirt.

"Vu Thi Tien." He wiped the sweat from his mouth. "I was told she might be here."

The woman's expression cooled. "No, she not here. But we have many other girl—"

"I really need to find her." He held up a twenty-dollar bill.

The woman smiled again.

After having her repeat the directions twice, Billy set out on the tortuous course through the Saigon streets. With a wave of giddy revulsion, he felt another erection stiffening at his crotch.

But the fly of his pants didn't bulge at all.

The last time Billy had seen Tien was his last night as a whole man.

He had waited an hour for her in the storage shed that night, lying on a bedroll surrounded by crates of grenades and ammunition.

She was late.

Exhaling a sigh of smoke from his Lucky Strike, he had stubbed the butt out on the floor. Maybe Cochrane hadn't been able to get her past the guards at the perimeter. They'd tightened security at Long Binh since Tet. Still, the guards wanted the services of Cochrane's ladies as much as Billy did.

She had to come, he told himself. Tonight. Tomorrow his unit would go on search-and-destroy in the forest northeast of the camp, and God only knew when he'd be back. Out of habit, his hand brushed at his cheek, where he'd felt the sticky cling of blasted meat that struck his face when Spider stepped on a VC mine.

Billy hadn't gone to Cochrane till then. He'd been saving himself for Marlene, for the promise that gleamed in her cheerleader's smile and in the diamond ring on her hand. But after seeing what happened to Spider, he wasn't sure there'd be anything left to save. He was nineteen when he came to Nam, and he'd never slept with a woman.

Until Tien.

A "shave-and-a-haircut" knock had sounded on the door of the shed. Billy had leaped to open it, and Cochrane stuck his smiling face inside. "Fear not, Mr. Happy is here!"

"It's about time." Billy swallowed. "Is she—"

"You have your donation to the base recreation fund?"

Billy had fished a five-dollar bill out of his fatigues and slapped it in Cochrane's open palm.

"Better have one of these, too, Billy-boy," Cochrane had said with a grin, holding up a condom. "Don't want to catch that bad Oriental strain that's goin' around."

Billy grunted and dug out another grimy bill to buy the rubber. With Marlene waiting for him back home, he couldn't take a chance.

Cochrane took the money and winked. "Enjoy." He left, and Tien stepped inside and shut the door behind her.

The light in the shed was so dim that he saw little more of her than the outline of her skinny limbs and the gloss of her long black hair. But he knew it was her from the plain, prim cotton dress she wore and the scent of strange spice about her.

She didn't look like a prostitute. Billy had insisted that she not look like a prostitute.

"Hey." He embraced and kissed her, pulling her down onto the bedroll with him. "I missed you."

"I miss you too." She felt tense, tentative in his grasp. "You have for me?"

He lifted his arms as if to be frisked. "You'll have to find out for yourself."

With a faint sigh, she searched the pockets of his jacket and pants, giggling as he groped and tickled her. It was a game they played. She would find her money in one of those pockets, plus maybe a Hershey bar or a pack of cigarettes. It let him pretend, let him maintain the illusion.

But not tonight. Tonight she found Marlene's last letter, folded and stuffed in the back pocket of his pants. "In here?" she asked, unfolding the page of flowery script.

"That's nothing." Billy snatched the paper from her and crumpled it. "From my sister." He leaned close and licked at her ear.

She rested against him as he slid the dress off her thin shoulders. "Your sister? She live in California, too?"

He tongued the nipple of her left breast. "Mmm-hmm." Tien's English had improved remarkably in the short time he'd known her, and he didn't like to think about how and where she practiced it.

"You take me there?" She pulled up his T-shirt and kissed the pale skin of his chest, just above the dangling dog tags. "You take?"

He stroked her cheek and looked into the brown eyes he couldn't see. "Sure."

"I be good to you." She lowered his pants, placed her lips against his erect cock.

"Yeah." He ruffled her hair. "Yeah, you would."

They made distracted, melancholy love. As he gripped her waist to thrust into her, Billy could feel the bone of her pelvis, the ribs that stood out beneath her skin. He tried to ignore the striations on her belly.

After thirty minutes, Cochrane knocked again. Tien left with her money, and Billy returned to his unit to try to sleep.

His platoon left Long Binh just after dawn the following morning, and they were deep into a forest of mangrove trees before the sun had fully risen above the horizon. A listlessness lingered over Billy, which even bitter breakfast coffee couldn't dispel, and he scanned the vegetation on either side of the trail with an unsteady glance.

They marched through the woods for three hours, and nothing happened. Billy's eyes ached from enforced alertness, from scrutinizing every leaf and lump in the path for traps.

"Was she good?" Jack, the grenadier, whispered, his gaze never leaving the trail.

"Shut up, Garrity," Billy answered with a smirk, letting him know she was.

"Quiet back there!" Scat, their team leader, scowled at them over his shoulder. "Don't make me come and kick yo' ass!"

"Good job, Jack," Billy muttered. "You'll have us on latrine duty by the time we get back."

Jack didn't have a snappy comeback. His body pitched backward as the report of the rifle caught up with the bullet.

"Sniper!" Scat yelled. He sprayed the trees ahead of them with gunfire.

Before Billy could react, another shot sounded from behind him. The VC had them in a crossfire. As he spun around and lifted his M-16, Billy felt a scorching impact at his crotch, which sent a white-hot ripple of pain to his skull. He collapsed, screaming, clutching at the blood that spurted from between his legs.

A medic bent over him, trying to pull his hands away from his groin long enough to stanch the bleeding. Through the sounds of gunfire and his own raw moans, Billy heard the radio-telephone carrier calling for choppers. Then he went into shock, his senses shut down, and the world turned black.

He awoke on a cot in the hospital back at the base, groggy but alive. When he tried to sit up, however, he became aware of a dull twinge of pain from his groin.

A bald black doctor attending to another patient's I.V. noticed that Billy was conscious and hastened over to check on him. "How you feeling, son?"

"Fine . . . little weak, maybe." Billy propped himself up on his elbows.

"Not surprising. You lost a lot of blood." He put a firm hand on Billy's shoulder and gently pushed him back down on the cot. "You rest now."

Billy pulled aside the sheet that covered his waist and found his crotch swathed in gauze, a plastic catheter jutting from it like a soda straw. "What . . . ?"

The doctor grimaced and patted Billy's back. "I'm sorry, son. We couldn't save it."

"Save it?" Billy repeated, numb. As the meaning of the doctor's words meshed with the sight of the bandages he wore, Billy let out an agonized howl. The doctor finally had to administer a sedative to get him to stop crying.

Billy drifted in and out of consciousness over the next few hours. Medics appeared and vanished each time his eyes rolled open. A small figure in baggy, ill-fitting fatigues swept past him, clutching something in the folds of its oversized jacket. It cast a furtive glance in his direction, and Billy thought he caught a glimpse of glittering brown eyes and coppery skin beneath the brim of its military cap. An aroma of spice seemed to filter through the atmosphere of sweat and disinfectant for a moment. Billy tried to focus on the figure's face, but another wave of exhaustion dragged him back into sleep.

After a week in the hospital, Billy was transferred to Saigon to await a flight to Hawaii and, from there, home to California. The army apparently decided that Billy had given enough for his country. "Pecker's a small price to pay for getting outta this place, man," Scat muttered as Billy packed to go. "I almos' think you lucky." He figured Scat was making fun of him until he saw his expression.

But I'm not lucky, Billy thought as he stared at a yellowed snapshot of Marlene on the flight out of Honolulu. I'd have been better off coming back in a body bag. He pictured Marlene rushing up to him as he descended from the plane, blond hair billowing, almost leaping to wrap her arms around him. He imagined her smile wilting as he whispered in her ear. His head lolled against the airplane window, and a tear seeped through his shut eyelids.

Somewhere over the depths of the Pacific, he had a dream.

He was in the back seat of his dad's Chrysler, fumbling with the buttons of Marlene's cheerleader outfit, pulling down her pleated skirt to reveal wet pink panties. But when he pulled her close for a kiss, the hair he clutched was black, the face Tien's. She pressed her tongue into his mouth and unbuckled his belt. To his amazement, he discovered that he still had a cock, healthy and hard as a baton. He shuddered as it penetrated the slick suction of her labia. The climax shook his entire frame, jolting him awake.

Billy sat up, hyperventilating. His bladder felt as if it were about to burst. The other servicemen on the plane stared at him, some with amusement, others with contempt. Face burning, he rose and lurched down the aisle to the lavatory.

With the lavatory door locked, he lowered his pants, reminding himself to sit down to piss. The rush of his dream orgasm lingering in his mind, he glanced down in disgust at the nub end of tissue where his dick should have been, the tatters of tender skin cinched together with sutures and scabbed over with scar tissue. Below, his scrotum clenched his one remaining testicle in a tight, shriveled fist.

As he looked more closely, though, he noticed something else. A drop of pearly white fluid hung on the rim of the tiny puckered hole through which he pissed. Billy wiped it off with a scrap of toilet paper and examined it with concern. The tissue exuded a recognizable chlorine odor.

Semen.

Marlene wasn't at the airport when he landed. Billy didn't see her until three days after he got home. She met him for lunch at a Bob's Big Boy, greeting him at the front door with a tepid hug, her mouth closed when he kissed her. Her blue eyes flicked from the window to the salad in front of her as they made pointless small talk.

"I missed you," he said as he strolled beside her in the park afterward, hands in his pockets.

She stopped to watch some children play hide-and-seek among the trees. "I missed you, too," she murmured, a distant echo. He waited for her to turn around. She didn't.

"I guess my folks told you."

She made a small sound, and her blond ponytail bobbed as she nodded.

Billy swallowed the saliva that had pooled in his lower jaw. "It's okay. I wouldn't expect you to—"

"I'm sorry. I'm so sorry." She put a hand over her unseen face. "It's just . . . I want to have kids. I want . . ." But she stopped short of saying "I want a man." With downcast eyes and smeared makeup, she faced him, took hold of his hand, and dropped a cold circle of metal into it.

When he got back to his parents' house that afternoon, Billy found that his Purple Heart had arrived in the mail with a letter commending his service and sacrifice. His expression blank, he tossed the medal and the engagement ring in the jar of loose pennies that sat on his dresser.

That night he twisted in sleep, his lips moving as if in prayer. Sweet, impossible kisses showered upon his invisible erection.

At first the dreams were a comfort, a refuge from the futility and powerlessness of his waking world. By day he tortured himself with dirty magazines and X-rated movies, sat on benches in shopping malls and stared at passing women who bowed their heads to avoid his dark glare. By night he moaned in ecstasy as Tien caressed his dream penis, healing him, restoring him.

Then he got a hard-on while sitting in an office of the Veterans Administration at three in the afternoon.

Eyes glazed, he was listening to a portly man in horn-rimmed glasses seated behind a large desk. On the wall to the right hung framed military decorations and insignia and black-and-white photos of a much younger and thinner version of the man standing beside a tank in Korea, as if the man wished to assure his visitors that he was indeed one of them. "Well, Mr. Barnes," he said, "the bad news is I don't think we can get you a greater disability benefit. Painful as it may be, your . . . injury doesn't really prevent you from earning a living."

Billy shivered and straightened himself in his chair. His nonexistent dick stiffened, massaged by soft, unseen fingers. He looked down in his lap and saw only the slack, zipped fly of his pants, vacant air where he felt the pulsing head of his cock.

"The good news is there are plenty of jobs out there for an able young man like you."

A tongue flicked over the glans, teeth scraped lightly down the shaft. Billy drew a sharp breath and crossed his legs.

"Now let's talk about what skills you . . . Mr. Barnes?"

Billy hunched forward in his chair, gasping, as his imaginary dick slid deep into the viscous tube of an open throat. "P-pardon . . ." He stood and hurried from the office, the man gaping after him. He came just as he shut himself inside a toilet stall in the rest room.

It happened to him again that evening during dinner with his parents. And again the following morning while driving down the freeway. And again standing in the cereal aisle at the supermarket. Seven times that day and ten the next, including once in the elevator on the way up to his family doctor's office.

"What the hell's going on?" Billy asked, his face drawn, as he sat naked on a table covered with sterile paper.

The doctor peeled off the rubber gloves he'd worn to examine the remains of Billy's genitals. "Well, I think we can safely assume that you did *not* experience orgasm." He threw the gloves in a waste can and rubbed his graying beard. "I'd say it's a phantom limb."

Billy squirmed, the paper rustling as it clung to his ass. "What?"

"Amputees often claim to have sensations in the place where their limbs used to be."

"Like right here?" Billy put his hand in the empty space at his crotch where his invisible cock jutted, tender and sore from overuse.

The doctor nodded. "The brain isn't used to the fact that there's nothing there, so it projects sensation where it thinks the . . . organ should be." He cleared his throat. "Obviously your case is more unusual than most, possibly complicated by certain . . . psychological factors. A sort of wish fulfillment, if you will," he added with an apologetic look.

Billy stared past him. "But what if . . ."

But what if someone stole my cock and was fucking herself with it right now, jamming it down her throat and up her ass and licking and sucking and screwing, over and over and over?

A crooked rictus of a smile stretched across Billy's face. "I guess you're right, Doc. It's all in my head."

He laughed as if that were the funniest joke he'd ever heard.

The doctor frowned and stepped away from him.

As he quivered in bed that night, Billy pictured Tien with his severed dick in her hands, kneading and rolling it in her fingers like putty.

In the next week he begged, bribed, and connived his way back to Vietnam, back to Long Binh. He learned to control his facial expressions during the unexpected orgasms, reducing the spasms to a nervous tic. Still, the effort wore on him. He lost weight, and his body ached with fatigue.

"You look like hell, buddy," Cochrane said, slapping Billy's shoulder as they met. "No wonder you're back here."

"Where's Tien?"

"Tien? Oh, yeah, the skinny one." Cochrane shook his head. "Gone, man. They evacuated her village. Think she ended up in Saigon."

Billy twitched. "Know where I could find her?"

"Try the Golden Flower. When she heard about you, she probably figured she'd need some new customers." He grinned. "Funny, though, I thought she would've told you herself."

Billy's hands closed into fists. "What do you mean?"

Cochrane chuckled. "Hell, she paid me twenty bucks to sneak her into the infirmary—"

Billy ran, and the rest of Cochrane's words were lost in the sound of helicopter blades cutting the air.

He moved down Tu Do Street in the direction the woman at the Golden Flower had indicated, a hand tugging at his invisible erection as if it were a leash.

He turned several corners in succession and threaded his way deep into a knotted avenue in Saigon's slums. An emaciated man and two little girls picked through the piles of uncollected garbage that lined the curbs. Across from them, an old woman washed her clothes in the brown water of the gutter, faceless beneath her conical straw hat. On either side of the lane stood ill-constructed wooden houses with roofs of tile or corrugated tin.

As instructed by the woman at the Golden Flower, he counted the doorways on the left until he reached the seventh from the street corner. He rapped on the flimsy wooden door with the restrained impatience of a traveling salesman.

The unseen fingers abruptly stopped toying with his hard-on.

Having expected her to hide or to refuse to see him, Billy was dumbstruck when Tien opened the door and greeted him with a disarming smile.

"I knew," she murmured. "I knew you come back." Bowing her head like a gracious hostess, she motioned him inside. He shuffled across the threshold as if sleepwalking.

The house consisted of a single room, small and bare. Clothes hung from nails hammered into the walls. The only real furnishing was a simple altar to the family ancestors. The scent of spice suffused the air but failed to mask the odor of urine and sewage emanating from a wooden bucket in the far corner. A small cooking fire crackled in the center of the floor, surrounded by assorted pots and utensils and two straw mats.

A withered crone sat cross-legged on one of the mats, her parchment face inscrutable. In her lap she cradled an infant girl. Beside her stood a boy of about three with spiky black hair, who stared at Billy with one finger in his mouth. Tien gestured toward them. "This is my mother, and my first husband's childs, Chau"—the boy—"and Thu."

She chattered to her mother in Vietnamese and pointed at Billy. The old woman grinned at him, revealing teeth lacquered black.

Billy's eyes darted around the room. "Where is it?"

Tien either ignored him or misunderstood the question. "First husband, he kill by VC before we meet—"

Billy grabbed her wrist. "I know you have it. *Where is it?*"

Irritation flickered across her face, and she twisted free from his grasp. Then she gave an impish smile. Kneeling on the mat beside her mother's, she picked up off the floor a stick that Billy had mistaken for one of the cooking utensils. She held it up like a scepter, and Billy's legs turned to water.

His mummified penis sheathed the point of the stick, stretched taut into a wooden erection. Its flesh had turned a bruise-colored purple; its skin was shriveled and leathery.

"I save it for you," Tien said, tittering.

Billy staggered forward a step. "You . . . you give me that!"

She shook her head and giggled. "You see. I be a good wife for you—good mother for your boy." She patted her stomach.

Mother? Billy pressed his palms to his temples, straining to think straight. She couldn't be . . . He'd always worn a rubber. . . .

"No," he croaked. "I can't—"

"Good family. You see." Her eyes twinkled. "I know what you like."

She licked the dead cock as though it were a Popsicle. He let out a groan, his eyes rolling up in his head.

"Give me that, you bitch!"

He lunged toward her, arm outstretched. With an insouciant air, she relaxed her wrist and let the impaled dick dangle among the flames of the cooking fire.

Billy shrieked at the searing pain and clapped his hands over his crotch, dropping to his knees.

He looked up, whimpering, at Tien. Her smile had disappeared. In its place was an expression of cold resolve, of ruthlessness born of desperation, her eyes shiny and hard as glass buttons. She brushed some soot off the singed phallus, and he realized why she had stolen it, why she had preserved it and prayed over it night after night, willing it back to life.

Pecker's a small price to pay for getting outta this place, man. . . .

Billy opened his mouth to speak, but his tongue felt thick, sluggish. His hands dangled at his sides, useless.

Tien smiled affectionately at him. "Happy family. You see," she cooed. "My mother, she like you too."

She placed the mounted penis in her mother's palsied hand, and the old woman gurgled in delight.

THE SINISTER WOODS

Wendy Rathbone

In the Sinister Woods, misty arms beckon. Murdered ghosts whisper, or it could be the wind, saying to the little boy who takes the long path around, 'Don't be afraid. Come into our land. Let us take you into our arms forever.' "

The young man standing on the ornate wooden porch stopped speaking and smiled at a second man, who was leaning against a perfectly polished redwood column.

The second man reached out, touched the first briefly on the chest. "Sounds like poetry."

"No." The smile faded, the soft tone of his voice airy with regret. He drew away, turned toward the front door with a nervous glance, then crossed his arms.

"Why can't I touch you? Why won't you let me? I want you. You want me."

"Shh. This is a true story. You have to listen." The

young man closed his eyes for a moment, then opened them, the porch light turning his brown eyes pale, frosting his dark hair white. "I was once that little boy, skirting the edges. Warned to stay away from the woods—what we called the sinister woods, especially, because they were dripping with darkness and lined with No Trespassing signs. But we didn't always listen. Or, rather, *I* didn't, my desperation strong enough to overcome outside authority. And friendship.

"Listen to me, my friend. I can't love you. All my heart wants to love you, I admit. But it won't happen. It can't. And you deserve better. You deserve a man, at least, with some soul left.

"Let me tell you about the sinister woods. And about Daniel, who was made of light. And then you won't want to love me. And you'll understand why I have to leave you alone for your own well-being."

I was twelve when it happened.

Boys will be boys, everyone knows, but this is no excuse. Not anymore.

What I did . . . I will tell you.

I was the youngest of four boys. My mother died when I was born. Infection of some sort. My father, a rich businessman whose hard hand and uncompromising power instilled a kind of cold and a kind of love in me, was my very god. All I wanted to do was please him.

He was a strong man. Big. Very dark. He wore dark suits that were altered to fit his tallness, his thickness. His eyes were slits of dark blue. His mouth was thin and white. He had muscles like heavy wind-polished tree branches. The veins crisscrossing his forearms stood out blue and strong. He always smelled of wood dust, of distant fires.

I thought he was handsome. I loved that about him most.

In his study, he'd be reading. I'd bring him coffee. "Father, what else can I do for you?"

"Stop fawning over me, boy. Get out."

He never thanked me.

At meals, I copied him, eating what he ate in the same order he did.

"Are you mimicking me?" he'd ask.

"No, sir. I just want to be like you."

"Of course you do." But instead of smiling at me, he sneered.

I jumped to do any chores he ordered. I called him "sir."

"Are you afraid of me, boy?" he'd ask.

"No, sir!"

"You should be."

Whenever he was around, I always felt a fluttering in my stomach, a tension. I felt guilty with every move I made. But I longed for him. The meaner he was, the more I loved him.

He did not approve of the novels I read, so I got other novels. He did not like my friends, so I got other friends. All except for Daniel, whom my father tolerated but rarely spoke to.

Daniel was everything to me. Almost as important to me as my father. He was my other half. White hair to my brown. Blue eyes so pale they were almost silver. His arms and legs were long and slim. They never seemed to tan. He always smelled of wheat. Summer wheat ripening in the fields. He glowed like light. When we spent nights together, which was rare and always at his house because my father didn't like guests, no matter how dark it got, I could still see him; he was so bright. He had a voice like wind. He was always breathless.

He'd come over in the summer afternoons and we'd go running through the fields and meadows beyond my house, getting lost, falling, laughing.

"You ever go into those woods?" Daniel asked one day, pointing across the field to the darkness beyond.

"I'm not allowed."

"Me either." He rubbed at his silky white hair. Always a habit with him, especially when he was thinking hard. "My mom says there's animals. Maybe even bad people. Hunters who will tie you up. Shoot you through the head." His pale eyes got big. He was not as easily frightened as I, though. Not quite as sensitive. Never guilty of anything.

But, like good kids, we always avoided the woods—especially that one patch of the woods at the back edge of Mr. Farmer's field. Mr. Farmer was my neighbor. He didn't care if we played on his property. But beyond the meadow, the property was not his.

And it was that little forest that Daniel and I called the sinister woods. It was always darkest there. We pretended it was haunted. We told each other we could see eyes staring out at us from gnarled trees. All the plants there were different. We made up stories that they came from a different world and had an evil intelligence all their own. Then when we got good and creeped out, as boys do, we'd laugh.

"Hey, Jack," Daniel would yell, his voice whipping the air. "They're coming to get us." We'd turn and run away from the forest's eyes. It would always turn into a race. I could run faster. Soon he'd be hollering, "Wait up! Wait up!"

I can still hear him.

We played every game. We overturned rocks and found lizards, beetles, centipedes. We caught bees and held them buzzing in crystal jars. We ate wild berries on the edge of the forbidden woods. We played double dare.

But sometimes we didn't do any of that.

Sometimes we'd meet and simply look at each other, as if what we shared was too important for words or motion. Those days, we were uncommonly solemn for boys our age. We would kneel and take our pocketknives, make cuts in our palms, then press them tight together. I would feel a stirring inside me unlike anything I'd ever felt, including my love for my father. It embarrassed me. It scared me. It also made me feel big and important.

After the blood ritual, we'd flop onto our backs side by side, fists still joined.

One day, our palms still bloody, we were lying in the field, staring up at pale summer skies and trying to see to the other side of the sun. Boys do this. Lean into the earth and try to float up out of their bodies. You've done it, I'm sure. Shared twin scars with another. Pressed them tight together even after the wounds have healed, smearing dirt and sweat and heat . . .

Side by side, in the dirt, our hands clasped, we were trembling. Both of us. It was hot that day. I was feeling languid, good. Then Daniel leaned over and kissed me. His mouth on mine pressed like silk, the taste like liquid sun. I couldn't move. I thought I would shatter into a thousand pieces, lost in the field forever. I thought I would never breathe again. But then he took his mouth away, and air filled my lungs. Sweet air, like his breath. Before I could get my bearings, he did it again. Then he touched me through my clothes. Here. And here. He touched me in ways boys are not supposed to, and I was thrilled and shocked and impressed that he was less than awkward about what he was doing.

All the time, the sinister woods were behind us. And I swear I felt eyes from those trees on us.

Watching what we did.

And we did a lot. I can't say more for the shame I felt.

Shame. God. I was red-faced when I came home. It wasn't because of Daniel, whom I really loved, but because of my father, who would surely take one look at me and know what I had done. With another boy.

My father. I felt I'd betrayed him.

I went to my room and sat and sat, staring at my model airplanes, my old stuffed bears, my books, which I'd replaced with my father's favorites. I skipped dinner. My father came up afterward.

"Are you sick, boy?" voice cold, nonchalant.

I wouldn't look at him. "No," I said. "Just not hungry."

"Where were you today?" he asked. He held an unlit pipe. I could see it in his big hand out of the corner of my eye. His head was tilted up, looking at my fluorescent star-pocked ceiling. His black hair billowed out behind him.

"Nowhere. In the fields."

"With Daniel?"

I nodded.

"You didn't go into the woods, did you?" he asked, fingering his belt. It was a threat. Though he'd yet to use it on any of us boys.

My stomach clenched. Much worse, I thought. "No."

"That's good. I don't like it that you missed dinner. That you are behaving in such a distracted manner. Perhaps Daniel is not good for you. I won't have dreamers in this house. With proper schooling, reading proper books, raising you properly, that shouldn't happen."

"Yes, sir," I said. And I kept thinking, He knows. He knows.

"I'll expect you at eight o'clock sharp for breakfast."

"Yes, sir."

"Are you afraid for some reason?"

"No." But I was.

"All right then. Good night, Jack."

See, my friend? Never any approval. Never compassion, even when I wouldn't eat, or when I was acting sick. I had to think—I could *only* think—that he knew all. He saw all. And he thought that I was very, very bad.

He closed the door, and I could hear his footsteps thrumming down the hall. My eyes were warm. I stared at the back of the door for a long time. I thought about Daniel and got hot and cold at the same time. I thought about how, when he'd touched me in places that were both sweet and bad, I had turned my head and stared at the tops of the trees in the sinister forest, watching them sway in a high breeze. Wondering how they seemed to so fully absorb all light.

The next day I was downstairs on time, eating breakfast with my brothers and my father, copying my father, eyeing him with the careful precision of a guilty twelve-year-old. What did he know? What did he think?

I had not slept well. I could hear my father's voice all night in my head: *Perhaps Daniel is not good for you.*

Daniel was the type of boy who got straight A's, was polite to adults, knew manners, wore fairly clean clothes. His family was not as prominent as ours, but our fathers knew each other peripherally. Daniel never got into trouble. He too always called my father "sir." Always lowered his eyes when shyly speaking to adults. Always offered to hold open a door, or pick up dropped items adults were too lazy to retrieve. His behavior was emulated by other boys in mock seriousness. The kiss-ups, my father called them, kids who put on airs around adults so they could get whatever they wanted. Only Daniel's "airs" were genuine.

This was why he, of all my friends, was the only one my father hadn't disapproved of, or told me never to see again.

Until now.

In summer we had no school, not like now, my friend, where they have school year-round. But I still had lots of chores. We boys had to keep up the house and yard. My afternoons, if I worked hard, were usually free, though, and that was when Daniel showed up.

My father was there to meet him at the door. "Jack can't come out today," he said sternly. I was hiding on the curve of the shadowed stair. I saw my father reach out and place his big hand on Daniel's slight shoulder. Daniel's white hair looked like snow. My father said, "There is a reason. Come out onto the porch."

The front door closed. I raced up the rest of the stairs and to my room where my window looked out on the front yard. My room was to the side of the porch, and several feet up. I could see part of the porch unobscured by the roof. I could see Daniel standing very still, arms at his sides. Nodding. I could see my father's legs, his hands touching Daniel's shoulders. He never touched me!

There was a heat in my chest as I watched this.

"No, sir," I heard Daniel say. And "Why?"

My father's voice rumbled. I couldn't make out any words.

Daniel backed up two steps, body stiff, almost shuddering. "You don't know!" he shouted. And then like a bird he flew down the porch steps, across the front lawn, along the dirt road. Into the fields. I could see his white dandelion head bobbing through the wild oats. Then I couldn't see anything because I was crying too hard.

I came down to the kitchen later that afternoon for a glass of milk. I heard my father in the kitchen. One of my brothers—I think it was George—was in there with him. And my father was saying, "I will not have a pansy in this house. He is fey. Weak. I'll see him on the streets first."

My brother said, "Father, what do you mean?"

A snort. "You know what I mean. They should all be killed."

And it was then I knew: my father had spied on us. He had! There was no other answer. I'd never done anything, anything, to make him think of me as bad. I had tried so hard. So hard!

You must understand. It was at that moment that I longed for something I could do to make it right.

The next day I asked my father if Daniel would be back. He shook his head. "You and Daniel spent too much time together alone. I told you I disapproved. He knows that too, now. You are not to see each other anymore." His eyes narrowed. He stared at me with glittering eyes. As if he hated me. It was like being pierced through, stung. I almost wished he'd hit me with his belt instead of giving me that look.

I could only nod.

I took long walks in the afternoons when there was nothing else to do, hoping I would meet Daniel taking a walk himself. I approached the edges of the woods. I looked deeper into them now than I ever had. I studied them. I felt as if I had broken the rules and gone into them, or their essence had come into me.

And my father knew it, too.

Without Daniel there, the dark forest was closer. The shadows. The long silences. The moisture that could only be made of tears. The forest was dark. Full of wolves. Full of bears. In the winter, sometimes I heard shots from hunters' guns.

One day, after many weeks, I saw a flash of white across the field. Like iridescent pollen. Daniel's head, then his face, then his body, emerging from the tall grasses of Mr. Farmer's land.

I quickly looked around. Was my father spying? I could only imagine that he always was. But I was glad to see Daniel, even though I knew I should turn away.

"Jack," Daniel said.

"Danny."

He held up his hand. The scar on his palm was white rimmed with pink. I held up mine.

Twin scars. We were brothers still.

The sky was eggshell blue. The air smelled like ripe grass. And cool leaves.

Daniel stepped forward and embraced me. Tight. "I missed you."

I stood there, dumb, guilt-gripped. I shook my head. "My father . . ."

"Is insane," Daniel finished. "He said terrible things to me." He was still touching my arms.

"I'm sorry." Warm streaks of pleasure traveled from my arms, where he touched, through my entire body. I thought I would start to cry.

He said, "Don't." And kissed me.

I felt the thrill and the guilt again. The pleasure. The shame. He moved his hands under my clothes. He kept saying, "It's okay, Jack." And stroking me. I couldn't stop the feelings. I wanted them. I wanted his hands on me. My whole body shuddered as he opened my jeans, as he kissed me again and again. The sun blinded me. I was sure we were being watched.

I pulled back, looking across the fields for my father's figure. The meadow was deserted. But I knew. I knew he was watching. He always was.

They should all be killed, my father had said.

I turned away. The woods were before me. "I can't! My father knows everything."

"You told him!"

"He spies. Somehow." I continued to stare at the woods, hands fumbling at my zipper. Could it be? Had my father gone in there? Into the place that was forbidden to everyone else? No Trespassing. But could my father be stronger than those signs?

Daniel moved closer. Close enough to breathe on my cheek, a hot fluttering like wings. "He can't know, Jack! No one was there. No one's there now. He can't know anything."

"He does." The woods were so still, so silent.

"You must've said something, then." He leaned his head forward again.

I pushed him away with both hands and backed up. My other half stood mute. It felt strange, unnatural, to be really angry with Daniel. He was the one friend, the one person in the whole world, who was like me. We were twins. We used to joke that we were practically telepathic. So how could he not believe me? Why, then, couldn't he see how this hurt me? My father's voice again: *He is fey. Weak. I'll see him on the streets first.* It was as if my heart had been ripped from me to hear that.

"Jack, your father is wrong."

But my father was all I wanted. I didn't say that out loud. I would be just like him.

You know how it is, with boys and dads. Don't you? Daniel knew how hurt I was. How couldn't he?

"Jack, please." He moved closer again. I moved away. He grabbed at my shirt. "Listen!"

"Don't touch me! Get away!" My voice was raspy, stopped up.

"No! You have to listen."

I walked away from him, pushing his hand away.

He followed, grabbing at me. "Are you stupid or what?" Daniel asked.

I whirled around. I punched him. "You made me do it," I said, forgetting I'd wanted him to touch me, wanted the feel of his downy skin, his wheat scent pummeling me. I wanted it, God help me.

So I punched him again.

He doubled over. It was as if I could feel his pain, my gut clenching, my throat all hard and raw. Then I ran into the woods, past the No Trespassing signs. Into the dank. The desperate. The silence.

Daniel followed.

As soon as I stepped over the boundary, from sunlight into shade, I could see that everything was wrong. The trees really were angled and dark. The air crackled, electric. Ferns had molded the ground in lacy, obscene designs, and strange weeds and plants grew about, black with blight. The smell was awful, like garbage kept too long in the kitchen, but I kept running.

Daniel stayed behind me. I could hear him.

I can hear him now, my friend. Oh, God. Calling for me to stop. And only because he loved me. Only for that reason. He didn't care about himself.

Have you ever had someone love you that much? Have you ever loved that much?

I have. My father. Boys and fathers. It's strange. Why did I love someone who didn't return any affection? Why are we so contradictory? Why are our feelings always for the wrong person?

All I could think was, if I wanted to finally win my father's love, then Daniel had to stop. To go away. I turned to face him.

The air was like ice in the sinister woods. Like cold fingers forcing their way down my throat, into my ears, up my anus. My skin puckered with goose bumps.

"Jack . . . ?"

"No!" I stood, letting the shadow and the chill enter me. It was almost sexual, that energy. It teased me. I felt big with it. Bloated. Sick.

I knew I had to give up all that was good and warm and passionate with Daniel to remain my father's son.

He is fey. Weak.

The words blistered inside me. Burst. I stung with them. I saw yellow pus and bile spattering around the bases of black sagging trees as if the bark were oozing. What was inside me was being further infected by this forest. *Come into this land,* the place seemed to say. *Let us take you into our arms forever.* The slimy tendrils of my shame, my self that my father hated became my essence as the forest sucked out everything else.

The ground bubbled with blood, all the blood Daniel and I had shared and mixed. I could feel my palm dripping with it, letting go of anything good Daniel and I had shared.

I thought I saw shapes move beyond the shadows. I felt my father's eyes on us. I was sure of this. Then I heard a distant moaning, like a wind through narrow hollows. The energy here was negative. It took from me. It pulsed for me. It was full of me. And I was filled by it.

"Jack, my God, we have to get out of here," Daniel said, fingers splayed, glancing around like a frightened animal in someone's line of fire. And I saw, from the way he looked, that it wasn't my imagination. That he too was seeing the blood on the ground and the pus on the trees and the misty shapes behind the dark trunks, the leaves beginning to quiver with an anti-electricity that was as unnatural as it was terrifying.

Daniel's pale eyes were wide open to me as if

seeking confirmation. Daniel, who wasn't easily scared of anything, looking to me for guidance. His pale skin, almost translucent, seemed to flicker weakly, as if he were being sapped of his light, his special goodness like a flame about to be suffocated until there was nothing left.

It was all wrong. Everything. Daniel was wrong. There was nothing of him for me to hate, and yet I felt hurt by that. Daniel, perfect Daniel, should be punished for what he had done to me. I should not have to hurt this way. I shouldn't.

"Jack?" he said again.

"You did this," I said accusingly.

He frowned, confused, shook his head. The innocence. The light. I couldn't stand it anymore. The woods made me see clearly how it was destroying me. Daniel would pull me in. He would take me away from my father, throw us into a world that would never accept us.

A tear-polished black branch lay next to my foot. I picked it up. I held it high over my head. It had sharp thorns on it, like a club with spikes.

Yes, the trees whispered. *Yes,* the air hissed.

I've tried not to remember for many years now. It's hard to lose your other half. To survive an action that blots another out of your life, even though it had to be done.

What I did . . . what I tell you . . .

There are sinister woods everywhere. And more and more fathers who come from those places, and who knowingly pass their role on to their innocent sons. Humanity is disappearing. Vanishing. The body remains, but winking out are our souls, our real humanity, our closure with infinity. That's why we sometimes do things we don't know are very wrong until afterward, and that's why we're haunted forever after.

I got that knowledge only after I struck Daniel. And struck him again even as he reached for me, even as he clutched at my waist, bloody face pressed to my chest. And somewhere, in parallel time, in a separate world where no sinister woods exist, I hear him. Pleading. Asking always, "Why?"

I hear his footsteps always behind me. My other half. Still holding on to me for dear life.

Holding my soul in his cupped, scarred palms.

I left his body in the sinister woods, and no one ever found it. But a part of that place came with me—the dark, and the constant feeling of my father's spying eyes. It's only Daniel who keeps me from repeating my mistakes.

So now can you understand, my friend, why this can't be? Why you deserve better, more? For you see, I can never love another again. What you see, or think you see, isn't so. You may sense Daniel, for his hold over me is unbreakable. You may be taken in by my polite remarks. But know the darkness is also in me, and it is there to stay.

And now, my newest friend, it must be over.

You will leave and love someone else. Someone who is free to be like you, as I am not. And I shouldn't stay out much longer on this porch.

I hear my father coming. And he wouldn't approve.

LOVE LETTERS FROM THE RAIN FOREST

Jack Ketchum and Edward Lee

Dearest Clara,

This field excursion has really turned out to be wonderful. You'd be astonished—my God, how I wish you could be here with me! This place is so different, so unimaginable! The rain forest is a world of its own, teeming with life and filled with the strangest beauty. The team and I have already made several noteworthy finds, and I've personally isolated a half dozen species of *Thallophyta* that have never been cataloged. I couldn't be more excited, but . . .

You haven't written, Clara.

Surely you're not still angry with me over our spat. I won't believe that. What I said to you I said out of love—you know I did—the purest love. I know I was jealous, childish. Even harsh. But a love like ours is rooted in truth. We must be truthful, Clara, and what in this world can be more important than truth? I know that you still love me. And I also know that once I return, our love will bloom again like the beautiful night flowers here, opening gently to each other in the dark.

Until then, never forget: you own my heart.

All my love,
Howard

"Ready for a gander?"

Straker turned out of the station and cruised past the administration buildings. The campus shimmered in the high summer sun, a blinding green haze.

Bilks felt bored. Straker bored him, and the campus work bored him, and he damn near bored himself.

White . . . string . . . bikini was all he could think.

Yeah, he was ready.

He knew he shouldn't complain. That was why he'd quit the city in the first place—he couldn't hack the rough stuff. He'd walked into a project laundry room one day and found two of his crack stools strung upside down and gutted like deer. The ME had noted that their genitals had been burned off first with a blowtorch. Another time Bilks and his partner had answered a routine domestic just in time to see some PCP cowboy pull a tire iron out of his wife's head. The guy's little girl was in the bedroom, sliced up like cold cuts. The baby was in the tub.

Fuck that shit, man.

Whereas here, on the campus department, your real tough call was breaking up a frat party or running smoochers off the quad at night. And this time of year was even slower. The campus was in between summer sessions. No students—though most of the profs and TAs stayed on. That's what this babe was—Clara Holmes—a grad student working for the botany department.

And an eyeful.

How many times I jacked myself thinking of that rock-hard bod? he articulately asked himself. How many times I jumped Barbara's tired bones pretending she was Clara Holmes?

"You're a pretty quiet fella today," Straker remarked behind the cruiser's wheel. "What, the wife wear out your tongue last night?"

"I'm bored," said Bilks. "As in shitless. And you ain't helping any."

Straker laughed. When he laughed he cackled like the witch in *The Wizard of Oz.* It was a skinny laugh, and Straker was a skinny person. Bilks hated Straker's laugh.

"Well, you won't be bored long. I got that new pair of binocs I was telling you about. Bushnells, man, with a zoom. We'll be able to count her eyelashes. Zoom right up her crack when she's lying on that tight killer belly of hers."

It sounded good to Bilks. While scoping female grad students with binoculars did not exactly equate to conduct becoming of an officer, he saw little harm. He figured God made women beautiful for a reason; therefore, peeping on Clara Holmes was, in some esoteric sense, accommodating the will of the Creator. Besides, a job like this had damn few perks, and she sure as shit was one of them. A jam-packed, bodacious hunka-hunka red-hot woman.

Every day at noon she'd lie out on the grassy campus quadrangle, working on her tan. Bilks considered the sexist-cop image: the tight tan skin shining with oil, the zero body fat, the 36Cs with nipples as big as the end of a thumb, all wrapped up in that white string bikini.

Jesus wept, thought Bilks.

"I saw her coming out of North Administration the other day," Straker said. "No bra. Just this tight orange halter and cutoffs creepin' so high up her ass her cheeks were showing. I swear it's hard to believe a dish like that was dating Moley. Bet his dick was one happy camper in that pie."

"Hold on. Back up a minute," said Bilks. "Who?"

"Moley. Howard Moley. Assistant prof in the botany department. You know. The guy who died."

Howard Moley. Oh, yeah. He remembered the item in the campus paper. Some kind of mushroom scientist or something. Or fungus maybe. The guy got sent down to the rain forest on a Smithsonian grant. And died. But . . .

"Howard Moley dated *Clara Holmes?"*

" 'Swhat I heard. For a couple months at least."

"But Moley was a fucking *creamcake!"*

"You got that right. Egghead wimp to the max. Word is she was only after him for his family's money, but in the end she couldn't keep her hands off other guys, so she dumped him."

Bilks sighed. Some things just didn't make a whole lot of sense in this life. Moley dating Clara Holmes was like Sharon Stone dating Mr. Rogers.

"Jesus. Clara Holmes could be in *Penthouse.* Moley must have had the Loch Ness Monster in his pants."

"Like I said, he came from money," Straker reminded him.

"Still . . ."

"Funniest part is she dumped him a month before he croaked."

Straker parked in the back lot of the undergrad library, which overlooked the vast quadrangle. He reached for the Bushnell binoculars.

"Hey, don't look so sad, good buddy. The lady is the biggest, toughest cock tease on campus. *Everybody* knows that. She was cheating on Moley right and left. Probably goes through box springs like you go through cigarettes."

That meant something to Bilks. He was a three-pack-a-day man and counting. Still . . .

"How do you like that shit?" Straker griped. He was combing the quadrangle with the Bushnells. "First day she's missed all freakin' summer. Figures, don't it? We're all set to viddy that hot sweet tush with my brand-new glasses and she ain't even here. *Piss!*"

Piss was right. Bilks felt disheartened. "Let's wait a while," he said, trying to be optimistic. "Maybe she'll show. What've we got to do anyway? Fight crime?" He stuck another Marlboro in his mouth, lit the match, and then paused over the flame. "By the way," he said, "how did Moley die?"

The first letter came about a week after he'd left. She remembered it clearly even now, a week after he was dead.

Her memory was about a half step from photographic. In matters regarding Howard there was reason to wish it were poorer.

Dearest Clara,

I feel awful about our spat. I want to forget it ever happened. Can we? You know how much I love you, don't you? And that I always will? Write and tell me you do know. And that you love me too. Make me the happiest man alive.

I miss you terribly, darling.

All my love,
Howard

And she'd thought at the time that the man couldn't take a hint.

Okay, so she'd been involved with him for a couple of months. The guy's parents had millions! What girl in her right mind wouldn't take a crack at it? Maybe the two of them could get along for a while, she thought, long enough for her to get her hands on a little of that green for her old age. Marriages could be short. *Real* short.

She'd tried it out, tested the water, so to speak.

And decided it wasn't worth the swim.

The guy was pathologically dull. Didn't dance. Didn't like movies. Never even wanted to go to any of the campus parties. Too busy reading about goddamn shelf fungus and mushrooms. Clara was interested in botany, sure—it was the easiest master's the college offered—but she wasn't *obsessed* with it, for God's sake. Howard pored over botany journals the way most men pored over skin mags. And that was another thing about Howard: he was equipped with neither the zeal nor the architecture to, uh, satisfy a woman's, uh, needs.

And a woman like Clara had many needs. But of course she'd filled *that* gap—no pun intended—with all the other guys, unbeknownst to poor little Howard.

No problem.

But he took too damn much attention. Smothering her with flowers and sticky displays of affection. She got sick of it.

So they'd had their little spat. That was what Howard called it, anyway.

She'd stood him up for dinner, then ducked his calls for a week, hoping he'd catch the drift.

No dice.

Howard was not only dull, he was often perfectly dense. He'd appeared at her dorm, actually curious at first, concerned, thinking that maybe something was wrong with her. And then, understanding, ludicrous in his ninety-pound-weakling rage.

"What the hell's going on?" he demanded.

She was cleaning up the room, faking a kind of nervous energy combined with a forlorn expression and, well, maybe a little cocaine. Double whammy. It pretty much worked every time.

She picked up a stocking, worried it in her hands a little—though not enough to run the damn thing—and turned to him, sighing. "Oh, Howard," she said, "I don't know *what* I want."

"After six months? You don't know?"

"Has it been that long?"

"Yes. It has."

"It's just that the things I like to do you seem to hate."

"What things? I *love* being with you."

"I know you do—if it's dinner and long walks or sitting by the fire over sherry or playing chess. But you know, I like to go places. I like the clubs. I like to go dancing."

"Dancing!"

She did not appreciate being yelled at. She yelled

back: "Yes! Dancing! And you can't dance! You don't even try! You won't dance and you won't even go to a movie unless it's got subtitles and twenty old Frenchmen sitting around drinking wine. Do you even know who the hell Arnold Schwarzenegger *is* for chrissake?"

Of course it wasn't the dancing. Howard Moley was just a card-carrying nerd. Polyester slacks. Button-down shirts with a pocketful of pens, an academic scarecrow. Plus, he had long stringy hair, which Clara hated on men. And he fucked the way he danced—like a puppet on strings.

Howard was incredulous. "You want to break up with me because of dancing? Isn't love more important than *dancing?*"

"Howard, I never said I loved you."

"Of course you did!"

Clara remembered. "That was different. I was . . . drunk."

"Drunk, great. That's just great!"

He stomped back and forth across her room, waving his skinny arms. A plucked chicken reciting his litany of grievances.

"You lead me on, you sleep with me, you say you'll marry me, you tell me you love me . . ."

"Oh, Howard, I did *not.*"

"And now all of a sudden you don't know what you want. You think you'd rather go dancing. That's just great. That's very mature. You'll go really far in life with ideals like that."

To hell with this, she thought. Enough's enough.

"Howard."

He stopped at her tone and looked at her. The tone

was a very cold one. It was very, very easy for her to make it that way.

"Just leave, Howard," she said. "Just go away."

She watched the color drain out of his face and the thin lower lip start to tremble. And then he was jerking past her toward the door.

"Fine! I will. Have fun on the dance floor, Clara."

She opened the door for him as he babbled his way out into the hall.

"I know you'll find lots of genuine fulfillment there. Absolutely. You'd rather dance than be in an honest, mature relationship with someone who really loves you. That's great. That's—"

She slammed the door.

"Wonderful!" she heard him say through the door. "Go ahead. Dance your life away. See if I care!"

Jesus, Howard, she thought, you can't even make a decent exit.

And now, musing as she douched out the sperm Johnny had left in her last night, she wondered how decent an exit Howard had made out there in the rain forest.

She wondered why she was even thinking about him when she could be thinking about Johnny. Johnny with the great tan and the runner's body. Whose IQ was probably close to his penis size—about a twelve.

But who was counting?

She appraised her nude body in the mirror—high breasts and plucked nipples, the dark blond pubic plot—but still her thoughts drifted.

She refused to feel guilty about Howard. He'd been dead for over a week now, and their relationship had been dead for over a month. She was sorry, naturally, but his death really had nothing to do with her.

Sometimes a girl's gotta do what a girl's gotta do, she thought.

How dumb could a guy be? All those silly drippy love letters he'd sent her from Brazil. As though she hadn't made herself perfectly clear that night.

The schmuck had gone to his grave thinking they were still in love.

I love you so much. The words drifted back. They were the last words he'd spoken to her. He'd called from the airport, just before his flight to Brazil. She'd said nothing. Hung up.

The rain forest was burning, its systematic destruction exposing new botanical phyla every day. The government had issued grants to get as many experts down there as possible. Every bio-nerd's dream, she thought. Howard was a mycologist, an expert on fungi of every category.

She also considered what else he was, or had been: kind, considerate, generous.

Shit. There I go. Feeling guilty again.

Okay, maybe she *had* led him on a little, said she loved him once or twice when the subject of marriage happened to come up, maybe even indicated a kind of *enthusiasm* for the idea.

Hey, there was a lot of money involved. A lot to consider.

And she'd been pretty damn good to him, all told, hadn't she? For a while?

She stepped naked into the bedroom. Her eyes went to the little box of letters on the bureau. Like a miniature coffin.

Howard had been cremated. The letters were all

that remained of him now. They made her feel suddenly sad.

To hell with that, she thought.

I sure hope Johnny calls.

He was a drunk, but he was gorgeous, and at least he liked to dance.

The more she tried to focus away from Howard, though, the more precisely she envisioned the skinny, knob-kneed little nerd.

That was happening to her a lot lately. She'd be lying in bed masturbating, for God's sake, a kaleidoscope of sweat-sheened studs writhing and panting through her brain, plugging all three orifices at once . . . when in would walk Howard.

Jesus!

She guessed she did feel a little guilty. Poor guy. All alone in the rain forest with his mushrooms and his fungi, his sample bags and his mosquito nets. He'd died loving her. . . .

My God. She was about to start crying.

Over Howard!

The phone rang. She lunged for it.

"Johnny!"

The voice on the other end was loaded to the gills, but she was still perfectly glad to hear it.

"Go for a ride, babe? A little dancing maybe, then maybe a little . . ."

"Get your gorgeous ass over here right now," she cooed.

Approximately one month earlier, Howard Moley, mycologist, botanical scholar, and jilted lover, looked down in dismay at the dead ocelot. Creek scum filmed the animal's fine spotted fur. It had crossed the river just east, which struck Howard as odd. Why? he wondered. Why did you cross the river?

Ocelots were known to avoid water in all but life-threatening situations. This seemed strange. Stranger still were the dozens of bright and nearly blood-red bracki that studded the animal's hide. Most bracket, or shelf, fungi were saprophytic—they grew on stumps or dead trees. But this one clearly demonstrated a mammalian-capable mycelium, meaning that its food support could be absorbed from dead animal tissue. This was very rare among stemless mushroom phyla.

In fact Howard had never seen a shelf fungus like this. The bright scarlet color, the white gill-like sporaphores, the razor-sharp ridges.

This was another new genus, he realized.

He'd already discovered several dozen unindexed thallophytes—bodied fungi. Zoned polyphores, clitopili, tricholomas, rough-stemmed paneoli. The grid-by-grid burning of the forests was creating passages to areas that were virtually unexplored. The collection teams were all going nuts—new insects, new reptiles, new birds, new plants. Everywhere. And lots of new fungi.

Howard unslung his pack, removed a specimen container, and knelt beside the ocelot carcass. A cellulose gel lined each container to keep the specimen fed. Fungi didn't need sunlight. No chloroplasts. Instead they procured carbohydrates from dead plant matter. And sometimes dead animal matter. *Vermilius moleyus,* Howard dubbed this fungus. With forceps he withdrew one of the bright red bracket scales from the ocelot's hide. But then—

Clara, he thought quite suddenly.

These days not even the distraction of discovery lasted. Even here, where stepping on the tiniest snake could mean death, where a wrong turn could leave you skinned alive by a Urueu-Wau-Wau tribe, all he could think of was Clara. Why hadn't she answered his letters?

He sat on a stump and stared, his knobby knees sticking out. Sweat drenched his khakis. All around him the vegetation teemed—hopping, dripping, crawling with life.

The enormity of the thought astonished him: I'm sitting in the middle of the Rondonian rain forest, walking where no human being has ever walked, seeing things no human being has seen, discovering fungi we didn't even know existed a week ago, and all I can think of is Clara.

Oh, my God, I love her so much.

Surely by now she'd forgiven him for what he'd said in haste and anger that night. How could she not, knowing how much he loved her? Everybody had arguments. Everybody made up again.

Why hadn't she written?

He removed his jungle hat, wiped his brow.

Even this far west of the Guaporé Reserve he could smell the smoke. It seemed sheer madness to destroy all this for grazing and tin mining. The only wood they took out of the forest was the cherry and mahogany. The rest they burned. It was easier. The World Bank teams were long gone, and the FUNAI officials had all been paid off.

No one cared.

They're going to destroy all this, he thought, this treasure trove of life, because it's the easiest way to decongest the cities. Just that.

Insane.

Howard was a mycologist, not an activist. All he could do was what he knew best—isolate and identify any new thallophyte, acquire as many specimens as he could before it was all gone. It was a pity, but . . .

What the . . . ?

He was staring down at the dead ocelot. It occurred to him now that the bright red brackets seemed to *surround* the animal.

He flipped it over. The big red scales covered the other side too. Which meant . . .

The implication couldn't be denied.

The ocelot had been *carrying* the fungus.

These things were growing on the ocelot while it was still alive.

There were many types of fungi that lived parasitically on live animals, but they were only the lower orders of fungi—the mildews, yeasts, and molds.

An advanced shelf fungus like this had *never* been known to grow on a live mammal.

Until now.

Oh, my God, he thought. Oh, my God.

Wait till I tell Clara!

Clara rolled her eyes. After all of these letters dripping with lovelorn drivel now this one arrives, full of botanical revelry.

The boy she'd met at the bar last night was gone. The bed still smelled of his sweat. The young ones never lasted, she theorized, but at least this one had lasted four times.

She lay back naked against the pillows and read.

* * *

Dearest Clara,

I've made an unbelievable find! I've discovered a new thallophyte classification that is absolutely remarkable.

At first it appeared to be a typical deuteromycetic shelf fungus, unusual enough, though—and you will appreciate this—in that it possessed a mammalian-parasitic propensity. I found it on the carcass of a dead ocelot that had crossed one of the tributaries of the Cautario River, which cuts out of the nearly impenetrable Guaporé Botanical Reserve. What, you may be thinking, could cause an ocelot to cross water through such a treacherous perimeter? I pondered the same, and fast realized the obvious. Of course! The animal was fleeing the northeast fires and had no doubt picked up free spores during its trek.

This fungus grows at an incredible rate, Clara, with a strangely fibrous and unusually active mycelic network. And the evidence is clear—the fungus body was growing while the animal was still alive! Absolutely unheard of for a deuteromycetes! It's beautiful, too. Large blood-red ridge bodies and bright white sporaphores. Gorgeous!

I'm calling it *Vermilius moleyus.* The journals will be bending over backward for the story. I'll be famous!

More later. The team leader and I are about to autopsy the ocelot. Argh! Please write.

I love you,
Howard

She tossed the letter aside, rolled her eyes again.

He discovers some new shelf fungus and acts like it's the Holy Grail.

Why did he even write at all? She'd deliberately answered none of his letters. When was he going to see the light? She was having too much fun now even to *think* about Howard. Too much fun and too much . . .

God, I'm insatiable! she thought.

She reached for the phone. Just about anyone would do now, she realized, flipping through her address book.

Anyone but Howard.

"*Exemplary* find, Mr. Moley," remarked the leader of Team Grid BR-429 SW. The weathered, white-haired zoologist from MIT had been doing fieldwork for forty years. "And a most unique classification, I should think. With this discovery, you've just entered the most respected circles of mycology. Congratulations."

Exactly what I wrote to Clara, Howard thought. I wish I could see her face when she reads it. She's going to be incredibly proud of me.

He was bothered that she hadn't written. But possibly his own letters hadn't arrived yet. The courier only came once a week, and there were dozens of stops along the long stretch of pocked mud that was Brazilian Road 429. A delivery to the States could take weeks.

"Conclusions?" asked the Team Leader as he prepared the Stryker orbital saw. "We haven't seen an incident like this anywhere. Why here, and why now?"

Howard shrugged. Wasn't it obvious? "Seventy percent of the rain forest is uncharted. Unexplored. And the Guaporé Reserve? No humans have ever crossed it. It's impassable. There must be innumerable thallophyte phyla in there that have remained undisturbed in the same grids for hundreds, even thousands, of years. But the fires are driving wildlife into areas they wouldn't normally dream of traversing—this ocelot, for example. It fled through the wrong grid, a grid exclusive to this genus. If it weren't for the fires the animal would never have picked up the spores on its pelt and this never would've happened. *Vermilius moleyus* would have remained in its grid, undisturbed, unknown to us—perhaps forever."

The old Team Leader nodded. "My thinking exactly," he said. "The fires are playing incredible hell with the ecosystem. You have to wonder how many similar incidents of displaced flora and fauna—and how many other first-time encounters between them—are taking place even as we speak."

Howard winced as the TL revved up the autopsy saw and calmly slit open the animal. Hair and coagulated blood flew out of the saw's groove. The sound was atrocious.

He was aware of the still, humid air inside the tent and wished he were over at the field-showers tent or even over at the supply depot where you could get something somewhat cold to drink. Howard didn't mind looking at cut-up mushrooms, but cut-up ocelots were another story. . . .

They inspected the open carcass under magnifiers. The ocelot stunk to heaven. Then: "Hmmm . . ."

The TL was examining a lung.

"Extraordinary," he said. "It's infested, as if with a virus. See? Some of the fungi bodies are nearly microscopic."

This was true, and . . . strange, Howard admitted. The bronchi, the sinitic conchae, even the alveoli themselves looked shiny with the bright red scales, while the larger ridges had clearly erupted *from,* not grown on, the ocelot's hide.

The TL stated the obvious. "It's spread . . . from the inside out."

"Yes," Howard said. But his mind felt far away. The image had come to him abruptly and without any apparent cause: Clara naked. Her tight, high breasts, her sleek thighs. That wanton glimmer in her eyes as her arms reached out for him . . .

The TL looked puzzled, even irritated. "You're the expert here," he said. "Just how rare a phenomenon is this?"

"It's not rare. It's unheard of."

"Then how do you account for it?"

"A unique transfection of spore proliferation. Generally thallophytes replicate in a confined propinquity. Sporaphoric dispersion occurs via the wind, insect mobility, animal movement, that kind of thing. This particular spore, though, seems to exhibit the ability to be *inhaled* by passing animal life. It then replicates within the host's respiratory tract. Further sporaphoric production is then dispersed through the bloodstream. Hence the inside-out effect of the shelf growth you see here."

The Team Leader stared, then dropped the magnifier into the animal's glistening innards. "Mr. Moley," he said, "do I understand you correctly?"

For a moment Howard didn't hear him. He was

picturing a wedding, and how lovely Clara would look in her long white gown. Then the honeymoon. Where to? The Bahamas? Cancún?

He dragged himself back. "I'm sorry, sir. What was that?"

The TL's eyes were wide and staring. His words sounded honed, like a blade running along a whetstone.

"An air-dispersible thallophyte spore that remains intact *after* mammalian inhalation? And can replicate in the *bloodstream?*"

"That's right."

The old professor thrust his face forward. *"Do you know what you're saying?"*

All at once, then, Howard did.

If it feels good, do it, thought Clara. And this felt *incredible.*

She'd picked up Barney and David at Kaggie's, one of the more raucous off-campus dance clubs—and now they were playing a delightful game called Sandwich.

Clara was the cheese.

She felt squeezed in a vise of lust. The bed shimmied; she thought of a truck driving over railroad ties. This definitely scratched her itch, relentless alternating thrusts drawing in and out of her lower places. Yes, Clara was the cheese, all right. . . .

Her next orgasm went off like subsurface demolition.

They lay there three abreast in bed, lolling on one another as their sweat cooled. Clara's perfect tanned skin felt shellacked. And these two guys? Meat-rack jocks. Typical 1.9-average campus boneheads whose only genuine endeavor seemed to revolve around the perpetual emptying of their seminal vesicles. It was too bad the university didn't offer a B.A. in intercourse; they'd each put the proverbial blocks to her three times already, and it wasn't even midnight yet. They were, in other words, perfect male specimens as far as Clara was concerned.

"Well," Barney said, "now that we've played Sandwich, how about we play another game?"

"We could play Doctor," Clara suggested, unabashed in her gleaming nakedness.

"Sounds good to me," David offered, stroking his elephantine penis just as unabashedly. "And it just so happens that Dr. David has a first-class proctoscope."

"Let's play Ball Game instead," Barney countered.

"Ball Game?"

"Yeah, and tonight's a doubleheader. Get it?"

Barney began to stroke himself too. "Or how about just a good old all-American game of Hide the Salami?"

"Maybe I'm a vegetarian," Clara slyly remarked.

"In that case, honey, I've got a summer squash that'll make your day!"

Jock laughter erupted forth. Both their penises, hard yet again, bounced like springboards. But then Barney interjected:

"Say, I wanted to ask you something. Is it true you date Howard Moley?"

Jesus! Howard again! "Don't be ridiculous. We went out a few times, that's all. It was . . . an aberration."

"*I* heard you were gonna marry him," David added.

"Howard *Moley?*" Clara lied. "Are you kidding?"

"No, huh? So then what's this?"

He reached over to the nightstand. Howard's latest love letter lay open there.

Shit!

"I noticed all the pretty postage on the envelope. Noticed it right away."

She tried to grab the letter. Her breasts bobbed in his face. He kissed the still-moist surface of one of them and held the letter out of reach, laughing, turning to read it.

"Come on! Give me that!"

"Hmmm. Sounds to me like things are still on."

"Give me a *break!* He's nuts. It's not my fault. The guy . . . imagines things. He keeps writing me these crazy love letters! Like he's supposed to *mean* something to me. I haven't answered one of them. Doesn't matter. He just keeps on writing."

David laughed. "So you want him to get the message and he won't. That it?"

"Exactly."

"Got a Polaroid?"

Clara's brow creased. "Yeah. In the closet."

David got up and went to the closet. She admired his muscled backside and then admired the rest of him when he turned around holding the camera.

"Is this thing loaded?"

"I think so."

"So let's send Howard some pix!"

"Hey. Terrific idea!" said Barney.

The smile blossomed on Clara's face. "You guys are geniuses," she said. The mere idea, in fact, filled her more than plenteous bosom with wanton heat. More heat trickled elsewhere.

She took on Barney first while David played close-up lensman. "Say hello to Peter," Barney said. "Peter likes to be talked to." The flash popped as her mouth engulfed his penis.

"I'll bet you always wanted to be in pictures, huh?" David suggested. Another flash pop as Clara climbed over Barney and put it inside her. And then again as she rode him, his hands squeezing her breasts.

David was using a lot of film, but that didn't matter.

There was another pack around here somewhere.

The forest teemed with vibrant color. Insects buzzed the mosquito net. Strange birds whooped and cawed.

The forest didn't care.

Three of them were dead.

Three of the team's five members. Howard and the elderly team leader lay in a field medical station in a grubby thatch-and-mud village called Alta Lidia, consuming I.V. ampicillin. Tomorrow they'd be helicoptered to the hospital in Vilhena.

"They're treating us like lepers!" the TL complained, noting that the sullen medics had roped their cots off at the far edge of the station and that they wouldn't come near them without rubber gloves and masks.

The TL looked like death already in his netted cot. Nevertheless he managed the energy to rail at Howard.

"You goddamn idiot! We were breathing those spores for over a day! You and your rare fucking thallophyte. We're going to die, you asshole! Do you realize that?"

Howard ignored him. It was a whole lot better and

perhaps, even more profitable, to lie there thinking about Clara, to let her memory caress him like a sweet breeze from home. He remembered all of the sweet things she'd said to him, the times she'd said she loved him, her promises of fidelity, their affectionate way of making love. In Clara he had something to live for, something real and strong. Providence would not allow him to die.

It only remained to try to reassure the white-haired TL, who was obviously suffering.

"Try to relax," Howard said. "Most spore infections are no different from any foreign bacterial invasion. Simple antibiotics will knock them out. We'll be fit as fiddles and back in the States in no time. Guaranteed."

"God damn you, you asshole," the TL sputtered.

And gurgled and died coughing up a gossamer mist of fine white spores.

Clara felt kinda bad.

Howard was a dufus, but she didn't suppose he deserved this.

Dearest Clara,

The entire Team is dead, save for yours truly. *Vermilius moleyus,* it seems, possesses a highly activated replication mechanism, air-dispersible. We all inhaled the spores. I'm at the main hospital now in Alta Lidia, on an impressive array of antibiotics. Thank God the med unit arrived in time. Please don't worry, I'm going to be okay.

Soon I'll be home—and in your arms again, Clara.

My love for you is stronger than ever. I can

actually feel it growing every day. I close my eyes and see us walking hand in hand. I see us growing old together. There's just no room in me for depression or worry over this. I'm so full of you.

My love always,
Howard

She sighed. The poor blind sap. Sick, lonely, holed up in some awful South American hospital—and still thinking she loved him.

Well, her own letter would finally cure that.

It made her feel a bit shitty, knowing he'd receive it bedridden, sick, a thousand miles away. All those pictures. All those positions.

Her most recent pickup stirred beside her on the bed. Young, muscular, and very enduring. Nickname "Cucumber," and for a reason that was more than understandable. His eyes were half open, his face half buried in the pillows. The monumental turgidity against Clara's thigh reassured her.

"A little more cream for your kitty?" Cucumber inquired.

Clara brazenly spread her legs.

"Meow," she replied.

The doctor's voice sounded muffled behind the baby-blue surgical mask. He was American, one of the last U.N. Assessment Group members, so at least he spoke English. At least Howard could understand the words, however grim.

"I regret to say, Mr. Moley, that the blood tests don't look promising. The spores—"

Howard coughed white dust, his throat aching like

a strep infection even as he interrupted: "I don't get it. The spores are a simple unicellular gamete! Even the weakest antiobiotics will kill them."

The doctor's eyes were small and hard above the blue mask. "The blood-borne mechanism of these *particular* spores, Mr. Moley, seems to be functioning identically to that of a lipid-aggregating virus. Once in the bloodstream they encloak themselves with medium- and low-density serum triglycerides, so they're able to protect themselves from all immune-system response and from antibiotic therapy. In other words, Mr. Moley . . ."

Howard waved him off; he didn't need to finish. Already Howard's body had fully broken out in the bright red ridges of the fungal shelf. Some were quite large, the size of saucers cut in half. Because of the tough, fibrous mycelium that had grown through his body like a web of wires, they couldn't be removed. He could feel smaller ones growing in his mouth, in his nostrils, even at the edges of his eyelids.

Yesterday he'd lifted his hospital gown to check his groin. No penis remained visible. Just a sharp red nest of glistening fungal ridges.

"In other words," he finished for the doctor, "I'm going to die."

"We'll do everything we can to keep you comfortable," he said.

Howard nodded.

"Here's a letter for you, by the way. If you like, I'll open it and read it to you. If that's easier."

A letter!

"No!" Howard reached out a fungus-chipped hand. "Please. Leave."

The lovely florid script was Clara's. His pulse rose. Suddenly, in spite of the terminal prognosis, he felt that he was blazing with light.

The light of love, he realized.

And Clara had at last written back to him, to verify her own love.

I can die now, he thought, even before opening the perfumed pink envelope. He did not fear death now. He wouldn't die alone and forgotten.

She's written. She still loves me.

His scaled fingers fumbled. His ridged face drew up in the brightest smile.

Out dropped a stack of Polaroids.

He looked at the letter. It contained one line: "Here's how much I love you."

His eyes felt held open by fishhooks. His heart slugged in his chest as his blood reverted to sludge.

His scale-encrusted fingers flipped through the deck of photos one by one. Each picture, once its image registered, felt like a shovel of grave-dirt dropped into his face.

It was a bright, wickedly hot Saturday afternoon when Clara learned of Howard's death. She'd been walking back to her dorm from the quadrangle where she sunned herself every day in a white Bill Blass string bikini. A good tan was top priority. She was surprised how few women strove to be appreciated; Clara's most personal goal was to turn every male head she passed, and it was a goal she'd long since achieved. It particularly tickled her to know that the two campus day-shift cops went out of their way to scope her on the quad with binoculars every day. She always gave them a show, to tease them up. Yeah, it was nice to be appreciated. Her body, and the extent she went to keep it looking good, she regarded as an aspect of her womanhood that deserved to be celebrated. And, well . . . it's was also a great way to reel in cock, she thought, and a woman like Clara needed to reel in a lot of that.

But—

She'd stopped at the student union for a campus paper. And there it was in boldface: "Assistant Botany Professor Dies in Rain Forest."

Poor Howard. The genus of shelf fungus that was going to make him famous had also killed him. A "blood-borne spore infection," the article reported. "Antibiotic-resistant."

A heavy grief settled over Clara like a weighted net.

It lasted for all of two minutes.

Because suddenly Barney and David were coming through the lobby, smiling. David in his tight jeans, Barney in his more fashionable khaki baggies. Muscles straining their tank tops, and something else straining at their groins.

"*Sandwich* anyone?" asked Barney.

And Clara was hungry.

It was weeks later that she received his final letter, delayed by overseas mail.

She read it over, thankful that he'd obviously died before getting those awful Polaroids she'd sent. They'd been weighing on her conscience lately.

"Dearest Clara," the letter said. "I still love you—Howard."

It was shorter than usual, thank God.

"Rest in peace," she muttered, and tossed the letter into the garbage.

I'm a monster, he thought, giggling as he plodded toward the nurses' station. Walking didn't come easy when your body sprouted hundreds of fungal shelf bodies. But he plodded on, inspired to the very end by love.

At 4:00 A.M. the floor was quiet, the skeleton crew of nurses all busy with bed checks.

Howard crunched across the floor.

Writing had been harder even than walking, yet his scarlet scale–encrusted hand had eventually penned his final love letter to Clara Holmes.

Before sealing the envelope, he had coughed up onto the letter several million white spores, invisible against the paper. By now the tendrillike mycelium of *Vermilius moleyus* had wormed its way into his brain. He could think only in snatches: *Air-dispersible . . . blood-borne . . . via inhalation . . .*

He shuffled down the hall to the desk, then shuffled back to his bed, where he died moments later, his ridge-studded face set in the faintest of smiles. Love had prevailed. No one had seen him place his letter in the out-box on the counter of the nurses' station.

"Just our luck, huh," Straker was still complaining. "I look forward to a gander at that dish every day. I mean, she might as well be wearing dental floss."

Bilks frowned. No gander today. Where the hell was she?

Just as the car backed out of the undergrad library lot, their radio started squawking. "Campus Unit two-oh-eight: eighty-two with guard at Morril Hall, room three-oh-four. Investigate possible signal twenty-two."

Bilks frowned. He frowned a lot. "Ten-four," he answered.

"What the fuck's a signal twenty-two?"

"Unknown trouble," Bilks recited off the code sheet.

"Some call. Shit." Straker pulled onto Campus Drive. "What was that loke again?"

"Morril Hall, three-oh-four." He checked the student directory. And stared.

"Anybody we know?"

"Morril Hall, room three-oh-four: Clara M. Holmes."

"What's this twenty-two shit?" Bilks asked.

The security guard, a criminal-justice major part-timing, seemed fidgety. "Complaints about a smell."

"You don't say. Stinks worse than a Georgia hoghouse."

"No answer when I knocked. And her car's in the lot."

Bilks nodded. A moment later the floor RA appeared, a chubby blonde in flip-flops and an avocado sundress. "What *is* that smell?" she asked, her nose crinkling.

"We won't know till you open up," said Bilks.

The girl unlocked the door with her master. Took one glance into the room and fainted.

The stench hit them like a runaway truck. The security guard turned away and threw up in the hallway. Bilks and Straker gagged as they entered the cramped room.

Time to go back to the city, thought Bilks.

At first he wasn't even sure the thing on the bed was human. But it had to be. A mass of queer flat glistening red ridges, like slimy chips of stone, covered the body so completely you couldn't see an inch of flesh between them, but the figure had to be human because it had a head—topped by short butter-blond hair, neatly coiffed.

That, and a white string bikini.

ORIFICE

John F. D. Taff

She told me on the way home, "When you make a hole in something—anything—something else will want to get in through it—or out."

She had flounced away after that—flounced, with her sparkling brown hair bouncing and shimmering in the sunlight, dancing across the freckles on her bare shoulders. I remember how her hair had smelled, sunny and clean and vitally alive. I can inhale even now and draw in the ghost of its presence, haunting in its intoxication.

And she had smiled. I caught a glance at that smile before she turned to walk away, bright and sharp enough to cut and cauterize in one swipe.

"Or out," she had said.

Christ . . .

As she turned, her midriff top hiked up a bit—just a bit—to expose her taut, early summer belly, the smooth curve of her abdomen as it swept up to her breasts, and . . .

Her tattoo.

It was supposed to be a rose, red and black with touches of green here and there. Its stem began at her diaphragm, with the petals of the flower unfolding within the valley of her breasts.

A flower. That's what she had wanted.

To me, it never looked like a flower.

But this is now, and that was . . . before. . . .

"You want a what?" I asked as we sat shoulder to shoulder at the coffee bar in one of the bohemian parts of town she preferred.

"A tattoo," she responded as if it were the most natural of desires. "Don't tell me you of all people have a problem with that?"

She giggled over her double latte, and that sound irritated something deep inside me, something of whose existence, up to that point, I had been unaware.

I *was* open-minded, damm it.

Jesse moved in a strange circle, filled with slackers and hackers, New Agers and X-ers, post-hippies and post-yuppies, head-bangers and rappers, white supremacists and Black Muslims, and I moved with her—albeit mostly in her wake.

Her friends were into wild music, strong liquor, stronger drugs, wilder sex, everything. As Jesse succumbed to the varying gravitational influences of these friends, I tried all of it with her, without prejudging the experiences, without carrying away a lot of baggage afterward.

Most of the things we did with her friends I had never even considered before meeting her, and I would never again do some of those things. But Jesse seemed to enjoy our relationship, and I happened to, also, so what the hell, you know?

In fact, I think that's what angered me most—my own response to her wanting a tattoo.

I tried not to screw my face up too much as I formulated my answer. "A tattoo," I repeated thoughtfully, really just giving myself time to think of something more meaningful to say. "That's . . . umm . . . interesting."

I hid my ambiguous face behind the steaming mug of herbal tea that sat mainly untouched before me. I hated the stuff, but Jesse thought I looked pale and said it would help.

"You're serious. You really don't want me to get a tattoo," she said, setting her own cup down and peering intently at me.

"It's—it's not that," I stammered, trying desperately to think of what it was. "It's just that I don't . . . Okay, I don't want you to get a tattoo."

"Why not?" she pressed, her look turning to one of baffled wonderment.

"I don't know. It's just that I think they look . . . cheap." I whispered the last word, turned my eyes away.

"Mikey!" she giggled again, touching my arm. "You're so sweet. Dopey, but sweet."

She kissed me, and it was strawberries and cherry licorice, sweet and sticky, and I remember it so vividly that it hurts me even now.

"Of course they're cheap. That's why I want one," she said, flashing me a wicked leer and raising her eyebrows.

"Where?"

"You're not jealous, are you? Of Mutt?" And her voice rose an octave, as it did whenever she thought some miraculous insight had been visited upon her.

Mutt.

I hadn't even thought of him. He worked in a tattoo shop down on Seventy-second. He was one of the crazy satellites Jesse still held in an erratic orbit; he was a past lover of hers who came to more of our parties than I might have preferred and who still, I thought then and know now, had some sort of hold on her.

Jealous? Yes, sir. Guilty as charged. Sign me up. Book 'em, Dano.

"No," I responded evenly. "And I meant where on your body, not where in the city."

"Oh," she said dismissively, as if destroying that particular insight meant little to her. "I was thinking of my chest or stomach."

I grimaced. "I like your chest the way it is."

"I know you do, silly. You didn't mind me getting my nipple pierced, though."

"You can take that out. Tattoos are just . . . I don't know, Jesse. I've gone along with nearly everything you've wanted. Christ, I even wore that male skirt you bought me—for an entire weekend. But this . . . it's so permanent," I argued.

When I turned back to her, I saw a face I didn't see often. It was not cross so much as crossed—full of silent measuring and analysis.

"Mikey, *you* decided to wear the skirt, which, by the way, I still think you looked really hot in. But this is *my* body, *my* decision."

She was right. This was the first time I had ever tried to impose my feelings on something she wanted to do to herself. I never told her how to dress or how to wear her hair, never even thought about it.

"You're right," I admitted sheepishly. "But you asked me, and I told you."

"Fair enough," she said, her mood shifting back to playful. "You'll come with me and hold my hand, won't you? At least to make sure that Mutt doesn't make a pass at me."

"I'll come," I growled.

The needle touched skin, vibrated with the small hum of a person in deep concentration. A smell—electrical, full of ozone with metallic undertones—crackled from everything in the cramped little back room of the tattoo parlor.

There was a brief moment of contact, full of excitement and anticipation.

Jesse grasped my hand, squeezed it tightly.

Then the needle broke the skin, punched through.

A dot of color, a bright iridescent green, lay side by side with a perfectly circular dot of blood that had been coaxed to the surface by the tattooist's instrument.

Jesse's skin flinched, relaxed.

The needle approached again, penetrated.

With casual impatience, Mutt wiped a cloth across Jesse's quivering belly, brushed his long, braided white-boy Rastafarian hair out of his eyes and over his shoulders with a great clacking of wooden beads and a smell not too dissimilar to that of a wet dog.

Mutt was just that—a shaggy, brooding dog of a man. He leaned over Jesse, shirtless, his skin a dirty, greasy olive in color, with numerous piercings and tattoos covering his well-muscled yet slight form.

I didn't really find him repugnant, merely mildly disgusting. Yet I could see it was these very same qualities that had attracted Jesse to him originally. I could see, despite myself, how they had been together, how his careless hygiene and rumpled demeanor might have appealed to her.

As I thought these things, Jesse was stretched out topless upon a battered barber's chair of dubious lineage. Mutt straddled her, bracing himself as his hands moved on her, roving here and there over her, stretching her skin, wiping at it.

It was impersonal enough, but she writhed under his touch, seemingly as excited by him and the constant pricking of his needle as pained by it. Her compact rose-colored nipples were stiff and achingly erect, her breasts a mass of goose bumps. Light shone from the single gold ring that looped through the aerola of her left nipple.

I began to feel distinctly uncomfortable, voyeuristic in a jealous, envious way that I had not experienced before with Jesse.

This is what they looked like together, I realized self-consciously, when they made love long ago.

This touching, as professional as it appeared, grabbed a part of me—the part that had shambled into the light earlier when she first mentioned the tattoo—and shook it fiercely, like a dog worrying an old shoe.

And that part of me was becoming angry.

A rapier-thin moan hissed from between her lips, drawing me back. When I looked again, a bright green line snaked from just above and to the right of her navel all the way up to the midpoint between her breasts.

One of Mutt's hands, large and flat like the blade of a shovel, clutched Jesse's right breast, held it away from the area he was working on. A single, dirty-nailed finger rested casually, familiarly atop her nipple.

"Hey," I muttered, almost at a breaking point, "watch it!"

Mutt looked up at me through the veil of his hair and smiled the smile of a cur, toothy and nervously courageous.

He slowly, conspicuously removed his finger from Jesse's nipple, moved his hand so that only the heel of his palm held the pendulous breast aside.

Jesse failed to notice—or chose to ignore—this exchange, and Mutt, too, quickly forgot it and me.

It took nearly another two hours to complete this particular piece of body art, as Mutt called it. Jesse lay exhausted when he finished, but I still held her limp hand, patted it.

Mutt told us in diffident tones that the area around the tattoo would hurt a little for a while. Maybe a couple of days. Then he shrugged and helped me put Jesse's shirt back on. I wadded up her bra and crammed it into my pocket.

I paid Mutt myself, with my own money.

It was, I thought, as good a way to make my earlier disapproval up to Jesse as any I might be likely to come up with later.

As I forked over a rather large amount of money to Mutt, I asked what it was he had permanently affixed to Jesse's chest.

Mutt folded the cash into a thick, dirty bundle and pushed it into the front pocket of his long, baggy shorts.

"It's a flower, man." This time his smile was disarming in its brutal, blunt dislike of me. "A fuckin' flower."

He shook his head, laughed roughly, then disappeared into the recesses of the filthy little tattoo parlor.

He took my question as an insult.

But I truly couldn't tell what it was.

We stumbled home after it was done, she and I.

Jesse seemed overly tired and sluggish for so simple a procedure, but who was I to know? I had no tattoos; certainly no other friends or lovers of mine sported them.

Like so many things that Jesse dragged me into, I was not experienced in this.

So I half walked, half carried her back to our apartment, a cheap industrial space on the north side of town. We talked a little on the way until she became so tired that I had to carry her.

"When you make a hole in something—anything—something else will want to get in through it—or out," she said, describing her personal philosophy of tattoos.

I laughed, too. She could make you feel giddy even when you were mad at her.

Two buses, seven blocks of walking, and countless wondering stares later, I got her home and closed the door behind us. My arm was numb from holding her up, but I gathered her to me nonetheless and carried her through our open, minimalist living space to bed.

Jesse didn't stir much as I removed her Doc Martens, unsnapped, then slid her jeans down and off. She wore no panties, and her bra was still a ball in my pocket.

I hesitated at removing her shirt when I saw that virulent green line oozing up her belly in the darkness underneath. I thought of her rolling over in the night, pressing her naked body to mine, pressing that thing to me . . . and I shivered.

I left her shirt on, stripped myself, and crawled into bed with her.

She smelled like the tattoo shop, like Mutt, like blood.

I fell asleep facing away from her.

Late that night, I awoke.

The wind stirred the sheer curtains covering the huge open windows that ran along one entire side of our apartment.

I heard the ghostly huff and rumble of a train in the distance, near the river.

Industrial dusk-to-dawns spilled pools of orange sherbet–colored light onto the floor.

Something moved next to me, rubbed against me with urgency.

"Mikey?" I heard her breathe into my ear. "Are you awake?"

Suddenly I was. Very.

"Umm," she purred delightedly, her hand reaching around me, grasping me. "You are."

I turned over and found her face, kissed it.

Her lips were as cool as the night air, moist.

Her skin, though, was hot and sticky. For a moment I thought she might be delirious, feverish from an infection due to her damned tattoo.

But her hands and lips left me little time to think.

So I didn't.

As we embraced, I noticed that, at some time during the night, she had removed her shirt.

Jesse seemed frantic in her lovemaking, nipping and rubbing and pulling me to her until the sheets and pillows were kicked away, leaving just us, tangled, sweating and breathing heavily.

She lay back, relatively docile, as I trailed kisses across her breasts, down her belly.

As my head pushed lower, my hand reached up for purchase in the darkness, slid across flesh.

Something wet and accommodating engulfed my index finger, drew it in, sucked it.

My excitement neared crescendo. I became more frantic, my kisses more fervent, lingering as I descended.

Her mouth scoured my finger, released it, drew in the next one.

I can't begin to describe how intense this experience was, how it overwhelmed my senses.

Until she spoke.

"Come up here."

Aside from panting, her voice was certainly ungarbled by any of my fingers.

I instantly broke the surface of my drowning desire and, with chilling clarity, moved the hand that was being sucked upon.

It swept up the curve of a breast.

In one motion, I uncorked my finger from whatever held it and lifted myself to see what it was.

My finger came free with a sound not unlike that of pulling a wet sneaker from a puddle of thick mud.

"Here," Jesse pleaded enigmatically, still writhing beneath me as I hovered over her on unsteady arms.

I looked down, and my arms nearly gave out.

The ridiculous orange light oozed across Jesse's body, falling full on the tattoo that lay between her breasts.

Where the bud of the supposed rose should have been, though, there was a dark hole in her flesh. It gaped like a glistening wound, and its edges opened and closed wetly, making little slurpy, kissy sounds.

I closed my eyes. Opened them.

My fingers had been there—*in* there.

With force that was more spasm than coherent movement, I pushed myself away from her, tumbled over the edge of the bed, and thwacked my head on the cold concrete floor.

Not too hard, but it stunned me for a moment.

It took some time for Jesse to realize I was not there anymore.

"Mikey?" I heard her voice above me. It sounded normal now.

"Here," I grunted, pulling myself up and rubbing the back of my head.

"Where did you go?" she asked, moving across the bed toward me.

I saw a slim white hand, hesitated, took it.

"What happened?" she asked again, helping me to a sitting position next to her on the bed.

"I don't know . . ." I hesitated, hoping she would think it was the blow to my head, and not the terrified beating of my heart, that had me rattled. "My arms just gave out, I guess."

From within the orange-tinted darkness, I saw the gleam of her smile.

"Dopey," she whispered. "You're probably still exhausted from carrying me home. Just lie here with me."

Even that was more than I was capable of at that point.

She drew me near, and I stiffened, resisted a bit, put my hand out . . . to ward her off? To see if it was still there?

It wasn't.

My hand encountered smooth, unbroken flesh that arced gently upward in either direction.

No ragged, slurping hole.

"Hey!" She giggled, pulling my groping hands away. "Don't start something you can't finish. Just lie back and relax now. Fall asleep."

Jesse pulled me to her again, and my head fell toward her breast.

But I couldn't relax, couldn't nuzzle my head to her . . . not there, anyway.

"I need a drink," I said, pulling away perhaps a bit too brusquely.

"Sure, okay," she blurted in surprise. "Whatever."

"I'm gonna get a glass of juice. Want some?"

"Nope. I'm going back to sleep. Hurry back." She yawned, gathering the sheets and pillows and nesting them around her.

I padded across the floor to the kitchen area, drew open the refrigerator door. Light exploded from it, and I reached in, dazzled, and grabbed the juice container.

The acidic orange juice, drunk straight from the container, cut through the dust and mucus that filled my mouth, cleared my aching, swirling head.

I didn't hurry back to bed.

Don't know how long I stood there watching her as she fell quickly back into sleep, as if the past fifteen minutes had been no more than a dream.

Must have been a while. The orange juice container slipping from my grasp roused me. Rather than open the fridge again and let the light out, I drained the rest of the juice, left the empty container on the counter.

I fell asleep on the couch near the windows, feeling the breeze and the edges of the curtains tickle my skin.

And watched the pale crescent of Jesse's body wax under the approaching light of dawn.

When I arose late in the morning, she was gone.

It was already becoming hot as the sun climbed the blue hill of the sky. A thin, lazy wind curled into the apartment without disturbing the curtains at all.

The heat also brought with it more of the industrial smells of our neighborhood—tar and asphalt; unknown, probably caustic, and most certainly carcinogenic chemicals; burning diesel fuel and oil from the hundreds of tractor trailers that swarmed around the area, all topped by the rich, rotten miasma of the nearby river.

As my head cleared, I remembered the day, the night, before.

The tattoo.

And Jesse was gone.

Where?

For some unfathomable reason, her absence alarmed me.

Angered me.

Understand, if you don't already, that Jesse and I were what are charitably called free spirits. Or, as my father called us, deadbeats. We had no schedules, no constant source of employment. Nowhere we had to be at any given time.

And it certainly was in keeping for Jesse to leave without telling me where she'd be. I never worried about this, because she always turned up none the worse for wear.

I told myself this as I scrambled into my clothes, laced my boots.

I told myself she was okay.

I told myself she wasn't with Mutt.

That she wasn't at the tattoo parlor.

She was, of course. I knew it immediately, instinctually.

But why?

Was she getting another tattoo?

Was Mutt finishing the flower he had begun yesterday?

Or was it something else?

The word "affair" went through my mind then, derailing my thoughts.

What a dumb, antiquated word! Not a word for the Pepsi-MTV generation—a word suited more for the nine-to-five middle manager screwing his secretary or the bored suburban housewife seducing the paperboy.

Not for me. Not for Jesse.

I mean, Christ, we were living together; we weren't married.

As I considered all this, the dark, hulking thing within me, which had flexed its muscles while Mutt shimmied atop Jesse the day before, was growing stronger.

It had quietly fought my conscience; it had won my heart.

And had I been listening, I could have heard the sound of it coming now for my brain, screaming like an enraged juggernaut.

Maybe I could have gotten out of its way.

Maybe I would have wanted to.

By the time I reached the tattoo parlor, it was late afternoon. The waning sun already threw down shadows into the canyons between the buildings, and everything looked uniformly gray.

Of course there was a Closed sign in the yellowed, barred window of the shop. But lights were on, and I could hear music from within, vibrating the glass; Green Day or Hole, something.

Of course the door was locked.

I was prepared for these eventualities.

Slipping around the corner, I made my way down a narrow, littered alley to the back of the building.

A battered metal door was embedded in the building here, rusting like a raw sore. Blocking it was a municipal trash Dumpster filled with garbage.

It was on wheels, and a few hard pushes got it moving easily.

Mutt must have been depending on the Dumpster to block access to the building, because the door was unlocked.

The knob turned easily, quietly, and I found myself in a storeroom filled with darkness, stacks of boxes, and garbage from lunches past. But mostly, darkness.

Another door, half open, led into the back room where, yesterday, Mutt had made holes in Jesse's skin.

Something will want to get in . . .

I closed the outside door behind me. It creaked loudly on its ancient hinges, but the music was so loud in there I didn't worry.

I stepped cautiously into the wedge of light that pushed through the open door.

Even as I peered around the doorjamb, some part of me—some part that had not been thoroughly cowed by my anger—did not expect to see Jesse there.

That part of me understood that I was about to make a fool of myself.

It was pretty damned surprised, then, when I saw Mutt and Jesse locked naked together on the battered and spotted reclining chair.

His mouth and hands were all over her body, and her response was much the same as it had been with me the night before—feral and unthinking. Her hips pumped, grinding into his lean body as he worked her into a frenzy.

One of his spatulate hands stroked the area between her breasts . . .

The tattoo.

As I watched in anger and anticipatory horror, the tattoo rippled, as if his hand had passed across the surface of a pool of water.

Suddenly it took on depth, became three-dimensional.

It was a hole again—the hole that had sucked at my fingers last night.

It was oozy-shiny, raw and wet, coral pink at the edges.

As Mutt's fingers toyed with this orifice, he pushed

himself up along Jesse's body, positioned himself above her.

I saw his erection bob into view, and I was horribly sure where he meant to put it.

Something will want to get in . . .

With a flash of insight Jesse would have been proud of, I realized what he was doing.

He loved her; that much was evident. He had not broken up with her a year ago; she had broken up with him. Or, as was more likely, she had simply drifted away from him, like an errant moon breaking orbit.

Some time after that, Mutt must have come to realize why he had lost her. It was for the same reason I knew, standing there watching this, that I, too, would eventually lose her.

I will put it to you bluntly: you could fuck Jesse, but you could never touch her heart.

Mutt had tried, and she had ended up stealing away from him, as a prisoner escapes from jail.

And me . . . ?

She had stayed with me for so long because I had never tried.

Never cared enough to bother.

Mutt, though, had waited, waited until he had finally seen his chance.

He had tattooed a hole, an entrance over Jesse's heart, not a flower.

Mutt wanted Jesse back. He loved her.

Something will want to get in . . .

Now he was going to touch her heart in the only way he knew how . . . in the only way she knew how to let him.

His back arched, his buttocks tensed.

Somewhere at the back of my mind, I heard a small,

deeply annoying voice tell me, " 'I shot an arrow into the air, it fell to earth, I . . . knew not . . . where.' "

Where?

The curve of Mutt's back, so pronounced now that his knobby spine threatened to pop through the taut, shiny skin, flattened, drove down.

The tattoo above Jesse's heart accepted him.

He pressed down to her chest, shuddered deeply, like a dog shaking off water.

I could not watch any longer . . .

Nearly falling into the room, I caught myself, stopped beside the chair as the two heaved and groaned near me.

When I looked down, tears squeezed from Jesse's closed eyes.

Mutt turned his head sideways, grinned ravenously at me through his lank braids, grunted.

In anger, I reached out, closed my hand around the first thing it touched.

It glistened in the light, cold in my hand.

With another move from me, it began vibrating in my hand, oddly comforting.

Arcing it over my head, I brought it down hard onto that straining, undulating wall of muscle.

Mutt screamed.

The instrument skipped over his skin like the needle of a kid's cheap phonograph, leaving a meandering trail of red that looked like . . .

Like I had drawn a ragged cut, a wound, onto the unbroken flesh of his back.

And it became one.

"Noooo!" wailed Mutt, his arms flailing out behind him in an attempt to yank the needle from my hand.

But it was too late.

Blood—or was it red dye?—gurgled from the wound, pooled across the ridges and scarps of his back, ran down Jesse's sides and over the cracked autumn-gold vinyl of the reclining chair.

Jesse screamed then, I think.

At least I hear her scream when I have my nightmare. . . .

I remember raising the needle again.

The music was very loud.

Mutt's body flopped to the floor, didn't move.

Red dye, red tattoo dye was everywhere. . . .

I brought the needle down to Jesse.

"I love you."

I said it. Or she said it.

It doesn't matter now.

I remember her eyes then, wide and vacant, trying to stare up at the red blotch I had made on her forehead.

Right before the blood started. . . .

Now . . .

That was a year ago and many states away.

I don't even know the name of the city I'm staying in now . . . one of those California names, "San" something.

I'm in a one-room apartment in a part of the city that's so seedy it's nearly fashionable.

Nearly.

Jesse would have liked it.

I often stand naked here at night, as I'm doing right now, with the lights of the bars and tattoo parlors winking at me, reflecting off my body.

I look in the mirror that hangs on the door in my room.

And I remember what Jesse told me.

When you make a hole in something—anything—something else will want to get in through it. Or out.

I roll the last two words over and over in my mind, like a mantra.

Oroutoroutoroutorout.

I have tried, you see, to let it out . . .

But so far, nothing.

I am afraid that I am empty, devoid of love.

Every square inch of my body is tattooed.

I have shaved all of my hair, replaced it with tattoos.

I have forgotten what color I was—black, white, yellow?

It doesn't matter.

It didn't work.

I have pierced every limb and appendage my body has to offer—my ears and nipples first but then my eyebrows, nose, cheeks, navel, penis, scrotum, the webbing between my fingers.

Nothing.

Last week I had my tongue pierced and could not talk for three days.

They did it by hammering a nail through it.

Still nothing.

And then I realized . . .

It was so simple, really, when it came to me.

Jesse would be proud.

The holes, of course, were too *small.*

Too small for my love to get out.

Of course.

It took me a little while to save up the money to buy it.

The tired, disinterested clerk at the gun and liquor

store told me that bullets—dum-dums, he called them, I think—made the biggest holes.

"That"—I smiled—"is what I need, then."

When I saw myself smiling in the two-way mirror behind the man, I saw Mutt.

I think this will work.

I'm ready.

I just hope that I will see Jesse when my love finally gets out.

Because I will tell her that I love her. . . .

SOLE MAN

Lois Gresh

Chuck slammed Tanya onto the hard bench of the steam room. A loud splat, and she slid giggling to the floor. Chuck grasped the slippery handle, then swung the heavy door shut. To one side, steam billowed from a wall vent. One hundred ten degrees, the building locked for the night. Alone. Just Chuck and Tanya.

She'd been flirting with him for months. She knew he was married; she'd teased him about it. Now she crouched at his feet in the filmy tank suit that concealed nothing. Pale hair dripping down her dark face like icing down the side of a cake. Sleek legs of steel on a Jaguar body. Tanya: hot, sweet, and sticky. Melting in the steam room's swelter.

Through misty swirls, Tanya was every man's dream: ephemeral, faceless, hot for it. The Y's youngest aerobics teacher. Any other man would have thought he'd died and gone to heaven.

But Chuck was no ordinary man. He had to take it slowly. Couldn't jeopardize his marriage to Monica for *ordinary* sex, even with a goddess like Tanya. And she wanted only him, no doubt about it.

Tanya dug her heels into his calves, and he felt a jolt of excitement. He reached back and grabbed her heel in his fist. She giggled again, slapped him, feigned a struggle.

He squeezed the heel, a firm, gently sloping mound.

Her toes brushed his thigh. A shiver bolted through him. Careful, careful, he told himself. Don't lose it.

Tanya smiled coyly and slid the straps off her shoulders.

Chuck drew back and slid his trunks down. Tanya's smile faded to an animal glow. Must have been admiring his firm body, honed from twenty years of service to the Y. Chuck: Aqua God, Lord of the Pool.

Tanya made a sound somewhere between a growl and a purr. Breasts, perfect behind, sleek stomach. She was indeed something to behold. But there was only one part of Tanya that really excited Chuck, only one part that made the risk worth it.

Her feet.

He wanted to suckle the toes and tickle the soles. He wanted to splay the tender little toelets and lick, to run his tongue along the tight arch until she screamed.

And if she went for it, if she was that one in a million . . .

He could barely move, thinking of the possibilities:

Tanya in stiletto heels.

Tanya in leather sandals.

Tanya's wet feet flip-flopping in thongs to the pool's edge.

Tanya's sole bared.

Chuck lunged and ripped at her suit. She squealed and clasped his head, ran her fingers through his hair.

Her breath was wetter, hotter than the steam pouring from the vents.

He wrenched off her suit, threw it to the bench.

Thrust. Tanya gasping.

Toe pads slathered in oil.

Thrust. Tanya panting.

His hand slid down her leg, lower, lower.

His fingers slipped past the ankle. Farther, down further, and now, yes, her feet. While he worked her, steady, like an engine, his hand caressed the soft curve of the arch, the nub of her heel bone where the skin was tightest.

How long it went on, he didn't know. He felt himself losing control—Not yet, he told himself, don't go all the way yet, you'll scare her, *this is too good to ruin*—and finally he decided that he had to end it.

A few more sullen thrusts and he was done. He pulled away, gasping the superheated air. He looked down at her. She was staring back—admiration? The aftershocks of orgasm?

Good, she didn't suspect. Next time, maybe, or the time after. Soon he would move Tanya to the next phase.

"Again, baby, just once more?" Tanya cooed.

Her toes curled at him, beckoned. It took everything in him not to grab them and stuff them into his mouth and eat them right up to the sockets where the bone joints held them fast to the feet.

His palm shivered, his fingers stretched. "Let's get outta here, Tanya, before it's too late and we're caught."

They snaked back into the damp swimsuits. They didn't say much; conversation wasn't Tanya's strength. Chuck steered her through the steam room and into the iceberg of the men's locker room. Stole a glance at her heels; they were wrinkled and pink.

By the showers was a rusty trophy cabinet. Chuck pointed. "See? I wasn't kidding. All-county in free style. Second place in the statewide." His trophy was tall and slightly warped at the top. The gold plate was tarnished.

Tanya arched her feet and stood on tiptoe. "What does it say, Chuck?"

"'Charles Malley, Second Place.' I would have taken first, if I hadn't blown the flip turn."

Tanya's nose wrinkled with confusion. "How about tomorrow?" She rubbed against him. Their wet skin stuck.

He shook his head. "No, Monica will have a fit as it is. I'm half an hour late already, and she'll give me hell."

"All right. Wednesday, then." She turned at the doorway to the women's locker room. Another sly look, a mock pout. "I'll just have to control myself until Wednesday." Then she was gone. The last Chuck saw of her was her right foot as it disappeared through the doorway. God, it was beautiful, so small, but powerful, exactly the right proportion. A little jewel made of flesh.

He let Tanya leave first, just in case anyone was hanging around the parking lot. The year before, Monica had actually parked around the side of the Y, hoping to catch Chuck with his latest girlfriend.

He twisted the key in the lock of the main door, then shuffled across the lot where, under one flickering bulb, his old blue Escort waited. Lord of the Pool, driving home in a scaly blue junker.

Before he started the engine, he unlatched the glove box and riffled through the magazines. *In Step,* for the lover of feet. *Sole Survivor. Footloose Fancier.* All his favorites. Heels, toes, arches. He opened to the personal ads in the back. Photos of feet, fake sexy smiles. Phone numbers and addresses. He'd never had the nerve.

He stopped at the centerfold: a woman's legs from the knees down. High heels, feet so tiny and pearled and toe-tipped in red. If only. God, if only they were real.

He used a wad of napkins from Burger King to clean up.

He took his time getting home, knowing what was waiting for him.

"Where the hell you been, Chuck Malley? It's almost ten." No surprises from Monica. The same accusations, the same venom. From her slippers poked the feet he had married. Once smooth and mouth-stuffingly plump, now all callused.

She shoved him against the metal trophy case by the TV. "So what's your excuse this time, Chuckie? 'I had to adjust the chlorine level, Monnie'? Or 'I had to redo the lifeguard time sheets'?"

"Come on, Monnie, you'll wake the kids."

"So what if I wake the kids? Sally and Louie know their Daddy's a loser. They know you're just an overgrown lifeguard."

Her nose was an inch from his eyes. The nose that jutted from her face like a big hairy toe. Twenty years ago, when they first met, she hadn't been half bad looking, and her feet had been the finest.

She slammed him into the wall. One of his plaques rattled and fell and bounced off his shoulder to the floor. "I work all day, earning the money that keeps you in that idiot pool job. If not for me, why . . ." and on and on she ranted, and Chuck just tuned out the grating whine, same as he tuned out bad songs on the radio.

He left her fuming and headed for the basement steps. Down in the cellar he'd have some peace. She rarely followed him down there. It was dank and cold. Knotty pine. In the corner was his bed: the plaid couch vomiting tufts of stained stuffing.

He twisted the caps off the chlorine bottles. His nose burned from the essence.

He pulled the string, and the light died.

He was back in the steam room. Aqua God nibbling on Tanya's toes . . .

A squeak. Light jetted down the stairs. He looked up. Monica in a spotlight. She said, "So you're just gonna hide down there, is that it? You fooling around again, Chuck?"

His eyes shot to their honeymoon picture. Monica in a turquoise bikini on a deck chair. Her feet close to the camera. Huge feet. Splayed toes. "I'm not doing anything, Monnie. I had a hell of a day."

"Yeah, right." The spotlight snapped off. Monica's slippers scuffed across the kitchen floor and faded into the carpet.

His fist banged into the knotty pine. It wasn't fair. They'd never overtly discussed it, never admitted that he was a foot fetishist, but still, Monica had always known that he'd married her for her feet.

Chuck knew he'd better watch it, had better dump Tanya. Monica was capable of just about anything. She'd brained him last year with an ashtray. They'd had to lie to the emergency room doctor as he put in the eight stitches.

This time Monica would probably kill him or take away the children.

When Chuck left for the Y the next morning, he knew he had to steer clear of Tanya. He had to forget about Tanya's feet.

He hid behind his desk for a few hours, pretending to do paperwork, hoping Tanya would have the good sense to stay away.

His office was a concrete cubicle: four cinder-block walls painted with pea-green enamel and covered with crayon drawings, CPR dummy slumped in the corner, the smell of chlorine permeating everything. Chlorine: the smell of success, the sting in your eyes when you win the big trophy.

"Oh, Chuckie, I don't think I can wait another day."

She was wearing short shorts, a tight tank top. Her feet were trapped in running shoes. She perched her behind on the one clear corner of his desk and crossed her legs.

Chuck stared across the room at one of Louie's drawings. "Daddy" was scrawled on the bottom in red crayon.

"Close the door," Chuck said, and regretted it before the words had left his mouth.

Tanya smirked and eased the hollow metal door shut. "Right here?" she whispered.

The air immediately became heavy, close as a sodden blanket. "No, we can't do it in my office. Everybody in the place will hear us."

"So you fixed it up with the wife? You can stay late again tonight?"

"I don't think we should. . . . I don't think I can. . . ."

She unlaced a shoe and let it drop. She ran her bare foot up and down his leg. Jesus, did she know? Did she understand? Was this some kind of sign?

She said, "You know, I like you better when you're not talking." The other shoe was off now, too.

He grabbed her foot, stroked the sleek curve of the instep across his whiskered cheek. The soft plush at the roots of the toes grazed his lips. Desperately he wanted his tongue to flick out and lick, but . . . but . . . Monica and the kids . . .

Tanya fell back and grabbed the sides of the desk. There was a strange look on her face. Not fear exactly, not even revulsion. Just some sort of understanding, a flicker that told him she found his obsession exciting.

Now she was sweet by his ear. "Tonight. Take them tonight."

Take *them?* Fireworks shot up his back and into his brain. For the first time in his life Chuck would pump his stuff against real feet, he would feel the thrill of feet massaging and pulling, yanking at him until he just couldn't stand it anymore and he exploded in a . . .

Tanya coiled herself around him from behind, tickled his calf with her toes. His leg hairs tingled. "I checked the schedules, Chuck. You've got the last shift in the pool tonight. Everybody else will be gone. I can hang around, go over applications for next month's classes. Nobody will suspect a thing."

Her toes played at the back of his thigh. This was

the closest he'd ever gotten to the real thing. How could he give up this one chance?

A paper fluttered from the wall. It was the "Daddy" picture. "Not tonight, Tanya. Can't do it tonight. But . . . tomorrow maybe." He could think of another solution by then. "Tomorrow, or maybe the next day."

"But I can't *wait* another day, Chuckie." She shoved him forward against the desk and the metal edge hit his gut, and he gasped. She lifted one long leg, placed her foot on his back.

He'd never known Tanya to be so aggressive. Tanya the she-beast. He must tame her, control her.

"Oh, Chuckie, I can't wait any longer. Come on, let's do it now, Chuckie, come on." She pressed herself against him, a low growl coming from the back of her throat, the rumble of raw animal desire.

He wanted to, he had to, he needed to . . .

"Nobody will know." Tanya's voice was a harsh whisper.

But Monica would find out. Monica always found out. And this time there'd be no way for Chuck to weasel out of trouble. She'd take the kids, the house, the money. He'd be an old man in a cheap boarding-house. Alone with his magazines, all alone.

Or she'd kill him.

He couldn't tell Tanya the truth, so instead he said, "Who do you think you are, telling *me* what to do? Be a good girl, Tanya, and put your shoes on. Come back tomorrow."

She wasn't happy, but she left; and all day, Chuck thought about Tanya's feet. To feel that sharp heel in his crotch, pushing on him, forcing him to the limit . . .

He pulled into the driveway exactly on time. Monica gave him the once-over as if inspecting him for incriminating evidence. She sniffed him, cold and distant; but she didn't argue with him.

Louie and Sally were bickering in the bathroom. Sally ran down the hall, blubbering about her brother. She had golden curls and long limbs, an angel of a six-year-old. Her brother trailed behind her; he was dark and brooding, a nine-year-old miniature of Chuck.

Chuck peeked over his shoulder. Monica was glaring at him. She shuffled the kids down the hall, then said, "I have news, Chuck. Got top marks today on my performance review. Mortman's going for the lateral move. I'm to take his spot."

"Good news, Mon . . . really good." In a few years she would be a vice president of the company. He would still be teaching five-year-olds the doggy paddle and helping fat old arthritics up and down the pool steps.

She stared at him. She, the prosecutor, the witnesses, the jurors, and the judge.

Chuck slid from the stool, inched toward the cellar stairs.

Monica swiveled and shot him the look. "Just don't you start it again, Chuck. Don't even make me suspect something's wrong."

"I got some things to take care of in the basement, that's all. I'll be done at nine, I promise."

"Nine is *Cosby,*" she said.

"Right. Don't want to miss *Cosby,*" he said.

He went downstairs, listened to the idiot sound track filtering from above. He stood there in the dim basement light, feeling like an animal listening to a predator's sounds. Finally he tiptoed to the place behind the furnace where he kept his magazines. Under the box that housed the AeroGym, wrapped in a garbage bag and crammed against the damp wall. He peeled off the masking tape and pulled out his precious bundle.

Feet, feet, and more feet. Beautiful feet. Bold and naked feet. Coy and hidden feet. In spike heels, ankle-strap wedgies, tattered running shoes, clunky oxfords, penny loafers. He stared. He sat transfixed on a packing crate.

"Daddy?"

"Oh, Jesus." He jerked back to consciousness and saw little Sally at the base of the steps.

"Daddy, Ma says to come up now and see *Cosby.*"

"*Cosby,* okay, *Cosby.* Go back to bed. I'll be up." He waited for her to go back upstairs, then carefully repackaged the magazines. He would have to find a new hiding place. Sally might tell her mother by accident. And if Monica found out about his treasure trove, it would be all over.

He crammed the magazines into the exposed stuffing of the sofa, then went upstairs. While his family giggled over *Cosby,* he dreamed of Tanya's feet.

She showed up early the next morning, clad in a crocheted string bikini. Around her ankle was a silver chain. Her feet were nude.

She rotated a few times so he could get a good look at her. Nails glossed in pink, delicate creases on the toe joints, freckles speckled across the top of her left foot, ankle bracelet binding the foot with S&M allure: bind me, strap me, put me in chains, and ravage me.

"You look obscene," Chuck said.

"Glad you like it," she said, and headed for his office.

He eased the door shut. Tanya was fondling the CPR dummy. She cradled its feet in one palm. "Don't hold back on me, Chuck. What was last night, a little necking?" She twisted her ankle bracelet between two fingers.

He took a step forward, dug his toes into the drain hole. "Tanya, don't—not now, not during the day, not with all the kiddies and the grandmas in the pool."

Her toes were bent, the soles perfectly vertical.

A bang on the door. Outside, somebody hooting: "Hey, Tanya and Mr. Malley, there's trouble in the pool. Big fight between two kids."

Chuck said, "For God's sake, you have to get out of here."

"Tonight?" she whispered.

"Tonight," he said.

He couldn't keep his mind off her all day. Between aerobics classes, she was everywhere, plunging from the diving board, slicking back wet hair, sloshing across the tiles. By the time the Y closed at nine, Chuck's nerves were screaming.

He slipped down the long tiled hallway leading to the men's room. He glanced at his mile-high trophy. First place, free style. He kicked open the steam room door.

She was inside, waiting for him on the hard bench by the steam vent. Her fingers scraped the floor tiles. He hardly noticed the crocheted bikini or what was under it, for her feet were bound in pink satin high heels with silken bows around the ankles.

"My God, you know . . . you know," he whispered.

He couldn't believe it. At long last, after all these years, a woman willing to give him what he wanted, what he needed, what he had to have.

She swiveled to a sitting position, stretched out the long legs, displayed the feet. Five-inch heels, by God, with sharp points.

He started to shake. The vent belched, and a feverish blast of steam enveloped them both. He knelt on the floor, took the pink spikes in his hands.

Tanya shook him loose. "I want more than that, Chuck. I want it all." Her hands rustled through a brown bag, which she had shoved under the bench. Through heavy steam he saw her pull out several objects. "Is the door locked?" she asked.

"Door doesn't lock from the inside. Only from the outside. What'd you bring, Tanya?"

She arranged several items on the bench. He craned his neck, then scooted closer for a good look.

His heart leaped into his throat.

She pulled more articles from the bag and placed them on the bench far away where he couldn't see. But he didn't need to see any more, for on the bench before him was everything he'd ever dreamed about: leather thongs with flesh-biting straps; silken stockings with snake patterns up the back; clunky old-fashioned schoolmarm shoes that laced up the front; toe rings in all sizes.

He gasped, thrust his nose into one of the schoolmarm shoes.

Tanya eased back his head and said, "Not yet, baby, not until you give me what I want."

His head was lost in steam and chlorine. He was in a neon cyclone, caught in the swirls. He was light and energy; he was Aqua God. He grabbed Tanya's arms and pushed her to the tiles. She squealed, kicked her heels into the air. He pinned her down, peeled off a shoe, spread her toes.

She was laughing now. "No, no, Chuck, I don't want that. I want the real thing first. *Then* we'll get down and dirty."

He had the toes in his fist and couldn't resist; and he licked the bottom of her foot and slicked the little toe tunnels with saliva.

Tanya jerked her foot out of his grasp. She slid away from him across the wet tile. "I said no, Chuck, I said not that, yet."

The schoolmarm shoe called to him. Chalk dust. The clacking of a ruler on his desk. The sweat of the schoolmarm's foot as she whacked him one across the wrists.

He grabbed Tanya's foot again and rammed her big toe into his mouth to suck its salt, to flick his tongue under the nail.

She wrenched her foot back. "Wait. Wait a second."

He pulled away, and she slipped out of the steam room. In an instant she was back, carrying a bucket of water, filled, he assumed, in the shower. She sloshed the water on the steam element, and immediately the room was engulfed in even thicker steam. Hard to breathe now, hard to see, like being trapped inside a boiler.

He moved toward her, and an eddy of steam curled around her head. The cloud cleared just long enough for Chuck to see her lacing on the schoolmarm shoes. "Okay, okay, Chuckie, you want it, you really want it."

He grabbed her, and they clung to each other for a moment. Then he looked down at the schoolmarm shoes. Black, hard, forbidding. He felt himself growing hard and melting at the same time.

"Is Chuckie happy now?"

Mrs. Decentia, fifth grade. Math. A real witch, all the boys hot for her.

He pulled her to the floor. "I deserved a B, you bitch, not a D."

Mrs. Decentia was shrieking now, giggling and rubbing herself against him. She pulled away and lay on her back. Chuck whipped her legs asides, cradled a schoolmarm in each hand, drank in the smell of old leather.

"Give the teacher what she wants."

Before he could descend on her, though, she'd wriggled out of his grasp and grabbed the bag. Her hand shot inside and emerged holding something metal and shiny. Two hooked blades, a spring mechanism, and rubber handles. She closed her grasp and the blades bit against each other. A pair of brand-new garden shears.

"Come here, you bad, bad boy."

Chuck stared, transfixed.

"I said come here!" Mrs. Decentia in her worst mood.

"I said . . ."

He did as he was told.

"Put your foot up here."

Again he obeyed.

He thought at first that she just wanted to trim his nails, but when she grasped his ankle and fit the steel blades against the last joint of his baby toe, he knew that something worse, something better, was in store. "You've got to pay for what you've done, Chuckie. You've got to give me something in exchange."

She squeezed and the blades pressed against the skin of his toe.

Terrified, completely under her spell, he stared at his foot.

Was it just luck? Were they somehow fated to meet? Or had they been attracted to each other, coming closer and closer for years? She was just like him, one in a million, a woman with the same devotion to feet. But what did she want?

"We need to really prove ourselves, Chuckie. I want a little souvenir. Just one little snip and then you can do me." She quickly fit a piece of nylon cord around the toe, cinched it in tightly to make a tourniquet. Then the shears returned, two thin cold lines of pain. Maybe a half inch from the tip of his toe. How much could it hurt? Wouldn't it be worth it?

"It'll be a sign, just you and me, just us. We'll do each other and exchange them. It'll be a little secret marriage."

Just then Chuck heard a noise from outside the steam room. Footsteps? A door closing? He looked toward the foggy window. A face appeared, or what seemed to be a face. Blurred and distorted by the shifting mist. Just a flash, a female face? No, it was just his guilty conscience. Feeling the shears biting into his flesh, gentle but insistent, he said, "Wait. Wait!"

"You only get one chance, Chuckie. I'm it. And if you really want me, you've got to prove it."

He closed his eyes, clenched his fists. Then he thought of those schoolmarm shoes. Tanya naked in shoes hard and black and cruel. Tanya, his forever.

"Okay."

"You're sure?"

"Do it."

She tightened the tourniquet. "You won't regret this, I promise."

A shriek, loud and crazed. At first, Chuck thought it had come from his throat. But looking down, he saw that Tanya wasn't at his feet any longer. He spun, and another blast of sound hit him, from outside the room. Behind the misty glass was a female face. He saw Monica coalesce suddenly, her mouth wide open, screaming.

Her face pressed hard against the glass, smeared into a putty mask of hatred. Chuck stared, then heard a loud crash from the other side of the door. Chuck's mind was a blurred welter of panic. Again the noise came, louder now. A stab of dread hit him, and he lunged for the door. It didn't budge. A third clunk. Chuck hammered on the door, crying, "Monnie, Monnie, don't do this! Let us out of here!"

Tanya shoved him aside and hurled herself against the door. "Jesus! What the hell did she do?" The door was barricaded with something very heavy. "What the hell does she think . . ."

Chuck reared back, cocked his leg, and let fly. But the door didn't move. "God, I can't believe it, I can't believe it."

They were going to die, cooked like fish. They'd be found the next day, naked, dead, with the boots and shoes and sandals scattered around them.

Chuck slammed his fist against the window. Plexiglas, for safety's sake. He picked up one of the high-heeled pumps and, using it like a hammer, battered at the window while Tanya braced herself against the bench and put all her weight against the door. "What're we going to do?" she cried.

There was a vent hole in the ceiling. Chuck climbed onto the bench, jammed his hand against the vent grate, but it was far too small for either of them to get through.

"Why did she do it? Jesus, is she crazy?" Tanya was shrieking at him, as though it was his fault that he'd married a madwoman. "You're going to kill us both!" No playacting now, no Mrs. Decentia. Tanya was furious, on the edge of sanity herself.

Then Chuck saw the shears. He picked them up and held them like a knife. "Shut your mouth."

"It's all your fault. We're both going to die because of you."

"I said shut up!"

He lunged at her with the shears, and she backed into the steamy shadows and said, "You got us into this, now you get us out!"

They would never survive until morning. If the heat didn't reduce them to puddles of skin and hair, they'd end up killing each other.

He stabbed at the window, but the shears bounced back. Then he noticed that the window was seated in rubber molding. He jabbed the shears at the rubber and a piece came loose. Digging now, frantic, he peeled back another strip of molding. Leaning close, he felt a tendril of cool air waft through the hole. He stabbed and ripped at the molding until he had two sides stripped clean. He pounded the butt of the shears on the glass. He went at the other side, then the top. Then, with a sudden thrust of his fist, he knocked the window loose. A blast of cool air flooded past him.

In an instant Tanya had pushed by him and shimmied through the gap. He followed, a much tighter fit. Soon they were both outside the steam room, panting, naked, staring at each other as though they were both aliens.

Tanya burst out laughing, a wild, giddy laugh. "Wow, that was some close call, Chuckie."

He looked around, expecting Monica to pounce from the aqua-blue shadows, screeching accusations and threats. But they were all alone. "Have to clean up the mess, maybe break another window, make it look like kids broke into the place."

But he was talking to himself, for Tanya was not listening. Her laughter died. Her face flushed a deep red. She lifted a leg and kneaded his stomach with her toes. "I was willing, Chuck. Finally I would have gone through with it. And Chuckie, I'm still willing . . . if you are."

He sank back against the trophy cabinet, let his body slide to the floor. He could barely breathe her name, "Tanya . . ."

Her toes tightened. Her nails dug into his flesh. She was growling, eyes shut tight, head thrown back.

He'd never seen her so excited, so passionate, so clearly in control.

"Time to finish what we started, Chuckie. Be a good boy and give me the shears." She swept her toes over his cheek and under his nostrils, and musky sweetness filled his head. She arched her back and hissed, and he knew that he could no longer resist, that he would do anything she asked.

She slipped a toe into his mouth. He trembled and sucked, ready to explode right there and then.

She slipped the shears from his fist.

Deep inside he knew that something was very wrong, that he should run; but then he thought of that toe in his mouth and he just couldn't let go.

He shut his eyes. "Do it, Tanya. Do it *now.*"

But Tanya shrieked.

Chuck bolted up, saw a flash in the air. It was the fake-bronze trophy: it swung like a hammer and crashed down on Tanya's head.

Tanya crumpled to the floor.

Monnie stood there leering at his naked groin.

She wore no shoes. Callused feet, toes knobby with corns. In her gloved fist was the bloody trophy. "Charles Malley, Second Place. Don't you think it's time we faced facts? You are just a born loser, Chuck."

"Come on, Monnie baby, what about the kids?". . .

"Their daddy's a sick, womanizing, toe-sucking piece of shit. I *am* thinking about the kids."

What was she going to do?

He squirmed toward Tanya's body—that beautiful body no longer breathing, those gorgeous toes growing cold.

"Monnie, how could you kill her?"

"How could I *not* kill her?"

"What do you . . . what do you—"

"What do I *mean?"* And now the look on her face was awful: utterly determined, totally enraptured. She pressed a sole to his chest and pinned him to the floor. Before he could open his mouth and scream, before he could pull back his fist and punch her, the trophy came down in a blaze of bronze and blood and bashed his forehead.

Half conscious, he saw her looming above him. Her foot hovered over his face. Monnie's foot: the face of God.

"It's my turn to have fun, Chuck, *my turn.*" She

took the shears from Tanya's hand and popped them open. She dragged the twin blades along his groin, down the inside of his leg, past his knee, straight down until the blood welled by his little toe. Cold blade on either side of his toe. Cold blade pressing, cutting . . .

She was sweating and gyrating, at the brink now, moaning his name over and over. Her fingers tightened around the shears, and as she squeezed and gasped, the pain in his toe shot like a flame to his head.

Monnie shuddered and threw the shears onto Tanya's body. "That was good, Chuck, deliciously good. And now, after all these years, you'll finally know what it's like to screw *my* feet."

Two toes: she slammed them up his nose. Intense *pain,* intense *arousal.* She slammed them again and then again, and finally she crammed her smooth, cool heel into his mouth.

Suffocating, he thrashed, tried to beat her foot off his face. No longer aroused. Just wanting to live.

But he was too weak and dazed to fight. She tied the black schoomarm laces around his ankles and wrists; then she dragged him down the cold tiled corridor. He was heavy, and it took her a while to get him down to the pool. Tug, drag him a few paces, let go and taunt him, then grab the laces and pull some more. Past the doorway to the steam room, past the office, down the sweaty ramp to the pool.

His mouth engaged enough to mutter, "Monnie, please . . ."

Her bare toes clamped on his lips, curled to shut him up. "You had your fun, Chuckie. Now it's my turn."

Farther down the hall, through the double doors, and they were in the pool room. The acoustics changed: echoes, the subtle slap of waves, the contra-bass hum of the filter. Everything was blue: the air, the ceiling, the tiled floor, the water.

"Monnie, listen to me. I swear I won't cheat on you again, I swear it."

"You bet you won't." She dragged him to the side of the pool. "This is perfect. Nobody even knows I'm here. And now, lover boy, at long last, your big moment has come." She heaved him sideways to the lip of the pool.

One last time: her foot hovering, now sinking to his face. Nose thrusts, heel in his mouth; Monnie's back arched, face flushed, eyes squeezed shut, moaning and trembling and peaking to climax.

And the stink of her feet overwhelmed him, and after all these years he finally knew the thrill of feet massaging and pulling, yanking at him until he just couldn't stand any more. For one glorious moment, *Chuck was happy.*

She braced herself and gave him a shove. He rolled over and began to sink. He fought for a little while, trying to swim his way back to the surface. But he was exhausted, helpless, and part of him thought it was all for the best.

And then he couldn't fight it anymore. The desperate need for air took over. He hit bottom, opened his mouth, tried to breathe.

The last thing he saw was Monnie's feet: ten fat toes hooked over the edge of the pool.

THE PORTRAIT

Jeff Gelb

Jay Amarillo was sitting on a campus park bench, watching the universe melt. His eyes were currently focused on the nearby trees and shrubs, which were vibrating in time, it seemed, to his own heartbeat. He tried to count the variations of green he could see in their leaves and lost track quickly, his attention diverted by the sky, which appeared to be composed of a series of constantly shifting geometric patterns.

"Great acid," he muttered to the universe.

Just then an angel floated into view. Jay held his breath for fear he would lose his focus and she would disappear. To his delight, she continued toward him. As she came closer, he studied her long, tanned, miniskirted legs, and he immediately sprung an erection.

He stood up too quickly and flopped back onto the bench as the oxygen rushed from his dick to his drug-addled brain. He tried it again as she walked by, and he warily took some steps to make sure he could still walk at all, and then, confident he would not fall flat on his face, he ran after her, nearly dropping his sketch pad. As he approached her, he studied the way the late-afternoon sun was shining through her light cotton blouse; obviously she was braless. Braless babes—the latest and greatest trend of the hippie movement! I *love* hippie chicks, Jay thought as he caught up to her, catching his breath, trying to calm his heartbeat, hoping he could even speak.

"Excuse me?" So far so good. His tongue felt like rubber, but somehow the words came out correctly.

At first she kept walking. He cleared his throat. Maybe he hadn't spoken at all; maybe he just thought he'd spoken. LSD was a pretty confusing drug sometimes.

"Hello?" he tried again. This time she turned around and his heart backflipped as he saw her face. My God, she was beautiful, he thought, as he studied her high cheekbones framing cupid's-bow lips and eyes as large as those of the kids in the popular, cheap Mexican paintings on velvet.

She blinked her gorgeous blue eyes, and he felt his knees begin to melt. "Yes?" Her voice was liquid honey. He could almost taste it.

He offered her a shaking hand, and she studied it for a moment as if it belonged to an alien life-form. "I—I'm Jay. I'm an art student here. And I was wondering if maybe you'd allow me to draw your portrait?"

Her lips parted in a smile, showing perfect white teeth that glistened in the early spring Ohio sun. Her eyes met his as she studied his face, probably trying to figure out whether he was serious or just coming on to her.

Reading her thoughts, he shoved his sketchbook in her face, flipping open its pages. "See?"

She took it from him, her lips now curled in bemusement as she glanced at one page, then several others. Jay watched for any reaction and was thrilled when he saw her nod at the last portrait in the book. "This is good," she said. Jay noticed how her hair bounced as she nodded. She was a goddess, he decided, come to earth specifically to seduce him for his first time ever.

He was nineteen and still a virgin, a fact he had tried desperately to alter all during his freshman year at Kent State, with no luck to date. The portrait angle was his latest idea to meet pretty girls, hopefully impressing them enough to sleep with him. It hadn't worked yet. He'd made a bet with his roommate that he would get laid by June 1970, and he was just two months shy of having to pay out. It was maddening.

She interrupted his thoughts, pointing to a detailed pencil sketch of a brunette Jay had met last month. Since nothing had come following the portrait session, he'd already forgotten her name.

"These are great. Did you really do them?" she asked.

"Well, yeah, of course." Jay laughed. "I'm studying to be a cartoonist."

"You mean like Charles Schulz? I just think Snoopy is so cute!"

"Oh, me too," he lied. Inwardly he winced; he hated the *Peanuts* strip. He actually wanted to become a comic book artist like the guys who drew the superhero comics he collected. But artistically, Jay had to admit, he had a long way to go. And he wasn't getting there very quickly, especially since he'd discovered LSD.

"So what do you say?" he asked as he swayed in time with the rhythm of the earth's orbit, which he could feel under his heels like waves lapping at his feet. *Cosmic.*

She eyed him suspiciously. "Are you all right?"

He realized what he was doing and forced his body to stand still. It took some effort. "Sorry. Just excited, I guess."

"Well . . ." She looked around her at the nearby dormitory buildings. "I guess it would be okay. What do I have to do?"

He couldn't believe his good fortune. He was so high he had to physically will his head back into his body. "Well, uh, I work from photos. My camera's back in my dorm room."

She laughed. "Uh-huh. Right."

"Oh, hey, l-listen," he stuttered, watching the words tripping out of his mouth like comic-book sound effects. Good acid! he thought. "You'll be safe. I have a roommate. Nothing'll happen."

She shook her head. "Sorry, but I don't know you or your roommate."

Finally they settled on meeting in one of the art rooms after her last class that day. Jay watched as she clutched her books to her chest, crushing her breasts against their hardness. If only those books were his body he thought, as Captain Billy—his pet name for his dick—reawakened from its drug-induced slumber. She giggled, looked around again, checked her watch. "You're not going to ask me to pose nude, are you? I could never do that."

He shook his head. "No, no, I'd never . . ." Nevertheless, a mental image of her nude, in the nastiest *Playboy* pose he could imagine, sprang up, as did Captain Billy. When he refocused on the real girl in front of him, she was chatting about herself. Her name was Nan, she was from Cuyahoga Falls, and she was studying to become a grade school teacher.

He gave her directions to the art room, and she left him with a smile and a dainty wave of her hand. He stared at her till she rounded a corner and was out of sight. Then he started back toward his dorm room, thinking about her. Of all the girls he'd tempted with portraits, she was by far the most beautiful. If he hadn't been high, chances are he wouldn't have approached her at all. Silently thanking his heroes, Owsley and Leary, he wavered in the general direction of his dorm.

"Not again!" complained Dan Coleman, as he ran a hand through his already-thinning long blond hair. "Like Rocky J. Squirrel says, 'That trick never works!' "

Jay waggled a finger at Coleman. "Trust me, roomie, I feel it in my bones—she's gonna go for Captain Billy in a big way. I mean, she's the perfect combination: dense and gorgeous."

Jay's roommate rubbed his beard in time to Jimi Hendrix's "Up from the Sky," which was playing on the stereo. "Gorgeous, huh? I'll be the judge of that."

Jay smiled. "So you'll do it? Just this one more time?"

Dan sighed but nodded. "Just this one more time." He lowered his gaze to his own drawing board, where he was working on a sketch of a horse. Jay looked over his shoulder.

"Wow, Dan, that's fuckin' great. Give it some wings, man, make it a unicorn."

"Jay, you're high again."

"Fuckin'-A, man!"

"That LSD stuff is gonna fry your brain, take my word for it."

"Hey, not to worry. You know what they say on the TV commercials: 'Acid—one little tab'll do ya!' " he sang in a parody of a hair cream commercial.

Dan shook his head and turned his attention back to his work.

Jay was coming down from his trip by the time Nan arrived at the art classroom, so he could appraise her from almost-human eyes. He was delighted to find she was just as appealing to him from a more normal perspective as she had been when his brain was super-stimulated by LSD.

"What's the matter?" she asked as she walked in the room, setting down her books on a desk. "You were shaking your head."

He blushed, realizing he'd subconsciously shaken his head because he couldn't believe how beautiful she was, nor could he believe his luck in finding her. "Oh, nothing," he lied. "Come over here and let's get started."

He had obtained his professor's permission to use the classroom for his photography, so the teacher had left some lights set up around a model's chair in the back of the room. Jay led Nan to the chair, and she sat down, arranging her hair. "Do I look okay? I've never done this before. How's my lipstick?"

He brought his attention to her lips, which she was moistening with a small pink tongue, and he felt

Captain Billy nod in approval. "Uh, fine, just fine." He fiddled with the light meter on his Pentax and framed her face in its lens, focusing on her eyes. Acid or no, she was breathtaking.

"Well, let's get started." He took a shot, then walked around her, taking several more from many angles. He was straight enough by now that he could actually concentrate on his task, but he was constantly distracted by her sensual beauty and the subsequent prodding of Captain Billy at his pants. At one point he looked down and was horrified to see a tiny spot of precoital fluid staining his crotch. He immediately lowered the camera to cover it.

"Uh, I think that'll do."

She giggled. "That was easy. So when will I see the finished version?"

He shrugged. "This could take a while. How about we have dinner this weekend and I'll let you see how I'm doing with it?"

Her face clouded over for a moment. Was she going to fall for the bait? *Please God, please Owsley, please Leary, let her say yes!*

"Well, I don't know. I have so much homework this weekend." Jay groaned audibly. She pursed her lips. "Tell you what—here's my number. Call me tomorrow and I'll let you know." She took out a notepad and scribbled some numbers.

"Great!" Jay said, pocketing the paper. It was a very good sign.

"So what do you think?" Jay asked the next day, as he showed Dan the proof sheets of the photos he'd developed.

Dan whistled. "Wow. For once you weren't exaggerating. This one is the ultimate flower-child poster girl!"

"Yeah, but did I take good enough pictures? Can you do her justice?"

Dan studied the proofs more closely, tapping his finger to Pink Floyd's "Atom Heart Mother." He finally responded. "Well, I don't know. I'll get started and let you know." He turned to his roommate. "Man, I'm sorry I ever agreed to do these for you. It's dishonest, and besides, I have my own homework to do."

"Hey, it keeps you in practice, Dan. And you know what would happen if I drew the girls—they'd all look like Jack Kirby monsters or something."

Dan sighed. "Okay. But remember, this is the last time I do this for you, understand?"

"Yeah, yeah, I promise." He clapped Dan on the back. "Thanks, man, I owe you."

"Oh, you'll pay, sooner or later." Dan laughed.

"It's not coming together," Dan complained the next night, Traffic's "40,000 Headmen" playing in the background. "I can't get her eyes right. I need to see her in person. See if she'll meet you for dinner and I'll sit nearby. She doesn't know what I look like, so she'll never know."

Jay studied Dan's work. For all he could tell, Dan had done a stunning job of re-creating Nan's beauty on the sheet of drawing paper. But Dan was a perfectionist; it was what made his work special.

Jay retrieved Nan's number and called her. To his astonishment, she agreed to meet him at the student union after her last class for an early dinner, so long as he brought along the sketch for her approval.

The day dragged for Jay, who couldn't stop thinking of Nan, finally admitting to himself that he was already falling in love with her. They met as planned early that evening, and her eyes lit up when she saw the portrait. "It's magnificent!" she exclaimed, touching Jay's hand. "Oh, Jay, you really are talented!"

Jay smiled and turned his gaze momentarily to where Dan was sitting, one table away. The two exchanged winks.

Jay was so high from the electricity of her touch that he didn't even feel like dropping acid. Instead, after leaving Nan at the student union, he went downtown and caught some live blues at one of the local bars. When he came back to the dorm later that night, Dan was hard at work on the portrait, while Al Kooper and Mike Bloomfield traded "Super Session" licks in the musical background.

"Hey, roomie," Jay greeted him.

Dan looked up and smiled. "My God, Jay, she really is an angel."

Jay bristled. "Yeah, but she's *my* angel."

Dan ignored the remark. "C'mere, look at this. Tell me what you think."

Jay approached the portrait and gasped. "You did it! It's her, buddy, it's her!" He was appreciative and jealous at the same time; as an artist, Dan was a hundred times better than Jay would ever be. Besides which, despite his prematurely thinning hair, Dan was a much more attractive guy than he, easily scoring girls. Sometimes life just didn't play fair. Jay sighed, deciding that maybe he would drop some acid tonight after all.

* * *

The next night, Jay fumbled on his dresser for her handwritten note. "Shit," he muttered.

"What's wrong?" Dan asked from his drawing table.

"Can't find Nan's number."

Dan rose, stretched, and walked over to the dresser. "Here," he said, unearthing the handwritten note from under a pile of Jay's things.

"Thanks, man." Jay dialed the number. "Nan? It's Jay. It's done. You gotta see it! Can we get together this weekend?"

Jay listened to static on the line for a few seconds before she answered. "Gee, Jay, I have this paper to write by Monday, and I haven't even started it. Maybe Monday?"

"But, Nan, you don't understand. I think this is my masterpiece."

She laughed, the sound echoing eerily down the phone line. "I'm sure it is, Jay. But it'll really have to wait till Monday."

He hung up a minute or two later, after she agreed to meet him at the student union again the following Monday. In exasperation he turned to Dan, who was putting the finishing touches on the portrait.

"Well, you were right," Dan said. "I think this *is* a masterpiece. *My* masterpiece."

"Don't remind me," Jay hissed, thinking, Rub it in now, asshole, but after I fuck her, I'll tear that fucking portrait up in front of your eyes—all the while knowing she would never sleep with him. Something had changed, and Jay knew somehow that, no matter how great the portrait, Nan would never be his. He reached for his stash of acid tabs, this time breaking his own rule and downing two. He headed for the door and then came back for a third.

The next time he was able to focus his eyes enough to read his watch, it was ten-thirty Saturday night. Jesus, he thought, I've lost an entire day.

He looked around and found he was seated in wet grass behind his dorm in a familiar stretch of woods he liked to call Mystery Land. It was a frequent tripping destination for him; he could be as silly as he wanted and no one would see him. He stood up on wobbly legs, stretched, and looked at the stars, which he was astonished to find were spelling out N-a-n. He blinked, but there it was. *Great acid!*

He started walking back toward his dorm and was struck by the thought that it was lucky Nan had turned him down for dinner tonight; otherwise, he'd have stiffed her. Maybe Dan was right: maybe it was time to start cutting back on the constant trips.

He reached his dorm room at eleven o'clock and was about to turn the key to open the door when he heard groaning from inside the room. He grinned; Dan had scored again, the lucky bastard. Jay had just decided to wander around the campus for another hour to give Dan time to finish up when suddenly he heard his roommate's groan, "Nan!"

Instantly—all of his senses heightened by the acid still pumping through his veins, his entire body tingling as if hooked up to ten thousand volts—Jay pressed his ear to the door. He clearly heard a female's whispers and moans, and then Dan's breathless voice again: "Nan, oh, my God, Jay was right, you're an angel."

Jay unlocked the door and stumbled into the dorm

room. Through geometric color bursts, his eyes barely made out two dark forms locked in a naked embrace on Dan's bed. Jay fumbled for the light switch, and the room was flooded with fluorescent light.

Nan screamed, covering her small, pert breasts with a sheet.

Dan groaned. "Great timing, roomie!"

"You fuck!" Jay screamed. "You stole her from me, you piece of shit!"

Dan shrugged. "I couldn't help myself, man. Like you say, she is gorgeous. And I figured you owed me, after all those portraits I did for you. And anyway, Nan made the choice. It was easy, once she knew who'd drawn the portrait."

Jay stepped back. The acid was making it next to impossible to concentrate. "Wh-what?"

"The portrait," Nan said, her body now completely hidden behind the rumpled sheet. "Dan introduced himself to me that night at the student union after you left, and told me the whole disgusting story of how you try to lure girls to bed by having him draw portraits of them based on your photos." She shook her head. "You're sick, Jay."

"But—but he draws them."

"And damned well, I must say!" Dan chimed in. "Now get lost, Jay. We're busy."

Jay felt his stomach turn inside out, dangerously close to a complete upheaval of its contents. "Oh, my God," he said through gritted teeth. "Dan, I could kill you for this!" He stepped toward them and tripped over her clothing on the floor, falling while throwing up into her bra.

They both laughed at him, the sound echoing in his ears until it sounded like Hendrix's guitar feedback gone crazy. Jay looked up and saw Nan's face change shape to that of another portrait girl, then another, and a third. Her face was changing as fast as he could blink. The effect was dizzying. He threw up again, acutely aware of every tortured muscle in his body that was disgorging any food he'd eaten in the past twenty-four hours. Apparently, he noted with one clear segment of his fevered brain, at some point during the past twenty-four hours he'd eaten a full Chinese meal.

He rose to shaky feet and spotted Dan starting to rise. Jay stretched out an arm that seemed to elongate like Plastic Man from his piles of old comics, until the arm reached Dan's neck and started squeezing.

As it often did, vomiting had brought the acid symptoms back stronger than ever. Jay was fascinated by the veins in Dan's neck and eyes, which bulged in time to the rhythm of the universe, which coincidentally matched the rhythm of the squeezes of Jay's hands. *Cosmic!*

In the background, Jay heard a distant Siren's song. He threw Dan's body against the wall with strength that felt to Jay like Superman's, and turned to face the Siren herself. It was Nan, for an instant, but then her beautiful face melted, cheeks stretching impossibly until the bones broke through, eyes popping like a cartoon wolf's watching Little Red Riding Hood. Then the eyes were those of a wolf, and Jay screamed, lashing out at them with his own nails, which Jay saw had grown claws. They tore at the wolf's eyes until they stained his hands dark red.

The Siren's song ended abruptly as Jay stared at his hands, which now appeared to him to be large brushes, already dipped in red paint. Inspired, he trampled over two fleshy sacks on the floor to stare at the portrait of Nan, his vision clearing momentarily so that he was stunned once again by her beauty. But something was missing. He stared at the portrait, then at his paintbrush fingers, and realized the pencil sketch needed color.

Smiling, he began to apply red highlights to the portrait's hair, to her cheekbones, to her cupid's-bow lips. Occasionally a teardrop fell on the portrait, but he used his paintbrush fingers to daub at it, using the moisture to soften the hue of the color he'd so cleverly chosen.

Faintly, in the distance, he could hear a siren's song again, but this one came from somewhere outside his little universe. He turned back to the portrait and was satisfied. It was *his* work now. Even Dan hadn't thought to add color. And color made all the difference, especially when you were tripping.

Yup, he thought. *Great acid.*

TWO HANDS ARE BETTER THAN ONE

J. N. Williamson

Never before had I met a well-known man and waited for the force of his own personality to tell me just what I should think about him.

That makes me sound as if I always form preconceived impressions of people, but I don't do that with men or women who aren't famous—or infamous, as was the case with Morley Pritchard. You can't tell me you wouldn't already have certain expectations if you were sent to interview, say, George Foreman, Cher, Stephen King, Susan Powter, or James Garner, as I had been.

I just hadn't known what to expect from the man reputed to possess the world's finest collection of pictorial female erotica.

At my age of thirty-five I couldn't understand why a guy would collect it when he was supposedly rich, with access to many women, and when there were new magazines and videotapes coming out regularly with enough young beauties for hundreds of men, if he was too shy to meet them in the flesh. On the other hand, there was Pritchard's fame—or infamy—and the fact that he hadn't granted anybody an interview, according to my editor, in recorded memory. No doubt an in-depth look at the bird would sell copies of *Greedy,* the men's magazine I worked for, especially since Pritchard had agreed to let me choose three of his finest pieces for a photographic spread.

On the other hand I wasn't sure I wanted to shake *his.* Till I met the guy, I hoped he'd turn out to be left-handed.

Then I didn't know what to think all over again.

He had two floors in an apartment building I'd dream of occupying only if I wanted to get depressed. I was admitted downstairs by identifying myself in a speaker and he made me cool my heels, plus the camera I wasn't accustomed to carrying, for six or seven minutes. Of course the editor had wanted to send a photographer with me, but Pritchard wouldn't hear of it. Apparently he ordinarily never allowed anyone but friends to see his gallery; adjusting to *two* intruders on the same day was unthinkable.

So I poked around the ground floor area without touching anything, wondering what ol' Tom Russell had gotten himself into this time. But there was no art in view and what little furniture stood in the front room was antique, incredibly expensive, and so tasteful it was hard for me to imagine it belonged to—

"Mr. Russell," a rolling baritone voice welcomed me, "sorry to keep you waiting." Long arms clad in a suit I also wouldn't bother dreaming about reached out. I stood there feeling vaguely manipulated. He proved to be one of those men who shook while supporting the heel of one's hand, just in case it came off at the wrist. So much for whether or not he was a left—but if this courtly man had any diseases, they were surely the best that money could buy. "I've enjoyed your articles. That's why I returned the call from your editor and requested *you.*"

It could be pretty difficult not to form a decent first impression of a man who said nice things about you, but I felt it wasn't impossible. "Do you want to give me the grand tour first," I said, "or would you prefer we begin with the interview?"

Everything in his face, eyes, and body said—because he let them, I believed—he'd met tough-minded men before and was happy to play a little hardball. Waving me into a tight-squeeze antique, he laughed dryly. "You would find it physiologically impossible to remember your questions or follow anything I said if we began with the tour you mentioned." He lowered himself into a chair that might have been designed for an Andromedan with a penchant for expensive earth artifacts, but he somehow looked comfortable in it. "And I'd like to be accurately quoted, yet you know absolutely nothing about me. I've made certain my life was private."

While I switched on my tape recorder and placed it on a delicate little billion-dollar table, I took a close look at Morely Pritchard, every literately horny schoolboy's idol. Six-three, I estimated, wiry with broad shoulders. Far from old, but over fifty, probably fifty-five. Horsy face, ferret eyes behind glasses with colorless frames, hairline with a widow's peak, possibly a natural dark. Nothing about him said what he collected, and the realization of that reminded me I hadn't answered his remark.

"I know you're supposed to own the world's best collection of pictorial female erotica," I said.

He smiled. "At which point I'm meant to register a protest along the lines of 'I scarcely think that's my public reputation.' Correct? But you see, Mr. Russell, I'm perfectly content with that image. Most men I've known have had no public reputation of any sort."

He wasn't wrong. What I liked about the comment was that Pritchard was smart enough to know it shouldn't exactly endear him to me. "What I'd like to know first is why the word 'pictorial' is always stressed. Surely you have some marginal interest in *written* erotica, a complementary prose collection?"

"Not a single book." He brushed the idea aside with an expression that fell just short of a rude sneer. "I never read the stuff."

"Why not?" I pressed. Earlier in my work I would've added, "Just a question of preference?" At this stage I knew enough not to offer my subjects easy outs. It was also a case of wanting them to say precisely what they thought, felt, and believed.

Morley Pritchard crossed his legs, being careful of the crease in his trousers. "Written erotica is created either for fast money or as wish fulfillment by men or women without the courage to go after what they wish. Some of the men are unimaginatively working out their rape fantasies. I suspect the same is true with many of the women but from a different perspective. My objection is aesthetic, not moral, but the product of the stuff is direct between-the-eyes titillation, then a measure of relief, closely followed by juvenile guilt. All that is decades behind me."

I peered closely at him. "You're saying your masturbatory relief is qualitatively superior to that derived by men who just read dirty books and get off with them?"

I wasn't sure if Pritchard frowned because I'd used such plain talk or because I was forcing him to admit he was an elitist at jacking off. "There are so many incorrect assumptions in what you've asked," he said—and I had thought I wasn't drawing any!—"that I scarcely know where to begin. Please rewind your recorder so I can answer the elements of your question one at a time."

That was clever! I didn't for an instant believe he was stumped, but this gave him a chance to see if I really *was* taping the interview and to shift the pressure to me. I didn't oblige him, however; I simply repeated the question, pausing every couple of seconds for him to answer.

"First," he said when I'd repeated six words, "I've never waited long enough between my periods of pleasure for 'relief' to become a primary concern—except, certainly, at the inevitable, delicious denouement." Pritchard let me glide straight through my use of the term "qualitatively superior," nodding without denying it. "Please wait," he said at the "dirty books" part, pressing his fingertips together while he chose the words he wanted to record on the tape. "I don't doubt the sexual imperative makes demands of countless people to seek 'relief' despite their personally queasy conviction that all sexual activity is somehow dirty." His stare was very nearly challenging, daring me to dispute what he was going to say. "In all honesty, none of the incomparable delight bestowed upon me by my collection has been 'dirty' in any sense."

I didn't take his bait. I completed my sentence, saying, "'and get off with them'? Surely you aren't going to claim you don't, in fact, get off with your collection?"

The elder man's darkly bright eyes gleamed, and he chuckled heartily. "No, no—except to add that the term 'get off' isn't quite appropriate in my case. Because I've gotten *on,* not off. On with the feast of life, thanks largely to the inexhaustible supply of beauteous women that continues, decade after decade, to display its generosity as well as its infinite variety!"

Morley Pritchard was wholly charming in that instant, his honesty and his clear admiration of the opposite sex disarming to the point that his preoccupation seemed less obsessive or kinky, more boyish and man-among-men. I added, smiling, "Have you had many women, Mr. Pritchard?"

"Had?" he repeated. "In the sense of direct, intimate sexual relations, do you mean?" He took my surprised, blank expression accurately for an affirmative. "No," he answered. "I came to the conclusion some years ago that, with my collection thriving, I could not fairly take a wife. I was also uncertain I desired one who understood my overriding interest."

I struggled to retain my impression. "In your youth, then," I said, thinking that perhaps the start of his collection had changed his habits. "How often, or with how many women, would you estimate you've enjoyed sexual intercourse?"

Pritchard hesitated. "Never," he said, *"and* none,

to answer the second half of your query." Then his rather heavy brows rose as memory stirred. "That is, not since 1974. I believe that was the year." Flash of a fast-fading, oddly embarrassed smile. "I'd forgotten."

I was too astonished to follow up. I had slept with a few women whose names I didn't recall, and although I was living with a sweet girl named Beth, I could supply the names of another seven or eight women with whom I had done the dirty deed, I thought in a surge of newfound self-disapproval). One, Jody Turnbull, had been an overnighter since I met Beth.

Yet here I sat interviewing the infamous man with the world's finest gallery of depicted beauties who'd turned out to be a sort-of full-time virgin since 1974 and who hadn't even *remembered* the last woman he screwed! All I could think to ask, then, was the uninventive but time-tested "Why?"

He took his time. He might have been nuts, but he saw my surprise, my initial disgust. "This may prove to be exceedingly hard for you and your readers to understand. But I'm delighted to explain. I'd hoped the lady I mentioned—"

"Seventy-four?" I interjected.

"Yes. That she might challenge a theory of mine. But she didn't."

"What's the theory?"

"Please quote me accurately." He turned his head to face the tape machine. "No woman who is one hundred percent *thinking* of the presence of a man is able to maintain the composure and confidence she finds for photographic sessions with discreet photographers. Nor will she be psychologically free enough to enjoy her own anatomy so much, save for rare encounters, as she does when she is alone before the cameras and an appreciative but remote photographer."

I'd like to say that my first reaction to Morley Pritchard's theory was a feminist-level outrage. Next best would be the realization of hilarity building within me. Truth is, I was intrigued by what he said so unevasively, with such conviction that it sent my mind spinning back to a chat with a onetime best pal, who said, "We've talked over every aspect of the romps in the hay we've wanted, gotten, lost, or gotten again, and neither of us has had the guts to admit the basic thing we've learned from women." I'd asked what he meant. "They've gotten our rocks off every time, whether it was wonderful or just average. And we strut around like cocks of the walk if we do that *once* for one babe out of five!"

"I have found," my host continued, "some women who perform intercourse for commercial films—similarly exhibiting themselves in a self-aware manner—who maintain *some* of the quality men of rarefied perceptions seek. What they, too, are doing fundamentally excludes all concerns but their own." He shrugged the shoulders of his expensive suit coat. "The partners of those women, male or female, are essentially used for decoration, clarification, or audience identification, of course."

It took me a second to get his meaning and to prevent myself from nodding. No interview subject was going to turn Tom Russell into an audience, I swore—and neither would his goddamn collection if we ever got around to examining it, because Morley Pritchard, rich or not, dropped his jock and grabbed his cock when he got horny! "From what you've said, Mr. Pritchard, I take it it's the safety of distance—

yours and that which you theorize the photographed lady also enjoys—that makes you prefer your collection to in-person relationships with women?"

A momentary facial expression made me feel sure I wouldn't want Pritchard as an ongoing foe. "You are quite close to the heart of it, Mr. Russell," he said, "but not close enough to be able to grasp without considerable guidance." He gave me the chilliest smile I had ever seen. "You think of me as little more than a man who's afraid of women, one who plays with himself like a twelve-year old boy. Don't deny it."

I couldn't resist smiling from ear to ear. "All right, I wouldn't want to displease my subject." There goes the picture collection, I thought, and here comes the ass-chewing by assorted editors at *Greedy* magazine.

"You fucker," Morley Pritchard said levelly, distinctly.

"You jack-off," I said the same way and put the pencil I used as a note-pointer into a jacket pocket, ready to book.

Pritchard chuckled warmly. "Now we have established a definition of one passionate interest each," he said, beaming at me. "Tom, permit me to explain my position." I let him use my first name in preference to his patting me on the knee or something. Besides, he was fiercely intense, and this interview would definitely grab the mag's readers. "Most human activities," he went on, "can be performed by *most* people—at some rudimentary level. A three-year-old can work with clay, come up with a shape of one sort or another. Few of us would proclaim him the next Rodin. Basketball fans my age felt they'd seen everything marvelous that players could do with a ball; then Michael Jordan burst upon the scene."

I saw where he was heading but scarcely believed my own ears.

"Some human activities," he said, "can be taken to heights of performance previously unparalleled on earth." Pritchard rolled his eyes skyward.

"You," I said, "are the—the master masturbator?"

He ignored my sarcasm. "I'm the perfect artist. I read long ago all of the available stats and other facts related to my interest, learned what standards existed. Then I set out to please myself while continually demanding more, seeking greater duration, better . . . product." He gestured with his index finger. "Laugh—I don't care. I require no acclaim, and I'm immune to negative criticism. To the extent that it exists, my sole competition has been myself, and"—he paused, perhaps changed his thought—"the woman or women of the moment."

In my mind was an absurd image of an Olympic jacking-off competition. But except for distance, how could it be judged? "Could you clarify all that?"

"I would love to," he said eagerly. "It's why I chose at last to sit for an interview—and to share my collection. As I said earlier, the autoerotic experience causes guilt in most men. Those who resist certain drugs and hypnosis are afraid they'll inadvertently reveal their practice. Men who are subject to neurotic tendencies can become victims of anxiety disorder; they may harbor deep resentment toward others." He sat straight with pride. "I elected to bypass such traps, to rise above the feelings of shame . . . and see what awaited me beyond the commonplace reactions, the surreptitious ten-minute trip to the bathroom. I insisted on *more* from myself, *better!*"

"And what awaited you?" I asked on cue.

"A world of potential, Tom! Vistas of new sensation, thrilling fulfillment—even *completion.*" His long face was a mask of remembered ecstasy. "With no guilt, no concern either for commitment or for illness, I discovered as well realms of unexpected . . . *possibility* . . . spread before me like acres of bare and lovely female limbs." He broke off, got to his feet. "But come, I'm depriving you of that guided tour. A few glimpses of what I've collected will surely prove enlightening enough that the slant of our interview will be rather more sympathetic toward me than you can presently imagine."

"One second," I said, sitting forward, prepared to stand. I'd heard his protracted use of the word "possibility" and thought he might say more strange, possibly crazy things before I turned off the recorder. "What was it precisely that challenged you to delve deep into autoeroticism after you'd beaten back the feelings of guilt?"

Towering above me while I remained seated, he was a talking phallus—a narrow, tubular form rising to a certain width at the shoulders and a head that was big and tapering but not, of course, as broad as the shoulders. "Tom, it's quite simple. The dedicated and skilled lady's man of sophistication maintains his standing and self-respect by striving to become an ever more proficient sex partner. I could not do less myself."

I rose, wondering how a man alone could be anybody's partner, and followed Pritchard. We exited the front room the way he'd come; then he led me onto a narrow staircase lit by an ornate chandelier on the landing above us. "You mentioned allowing me just a few glimpses, sir," I said, struggling with the camera I'd brought. "Did you forget granting me permission to select three pieces to shoot for the magazine?"

He dawdled on the steps. I thought he chuckled. "Neither of us has the time for you to view all I have. Believe me, you'll see enough to make the selection process difficult. Tom . . . are you a virgin? Have you enjoyed coition lately?"

"Of course I'm not," I bristled, "and I have. I live with a beautiful young woman named Beth."

"Your health is good, then." We reached the landing, and he faced me. "I'm not prying, sir. It is my moral duty to warn you to prepare yourself. What you will see might otherwise be too much for your heart, and perhaps for your brain as well." He startled me by giving my shoulder a solicitous pat! "When it starts to be too much for your . . . unrelieved sensibilities, I suggest we go downstairs again without speaking. Or you may use any of the fully equipped cubicles you'll find to your right. Your privacy has my strongest personal guarantee."

I really doubted I'd have any emergency situations and said so. For God's sake, I'd peered closely at the finer details of female anatomy presented to me several times, with *living* women! I worked for a mag some said made men more pent-up than *Penthouse* and offered more play than *Playboy!* We began to walk, and I wondered if this ferret-eyed old dick of a man was running some kind of con.

Just one glance at what came into view with another few steps told me he hadn't lied. But I was a writer on assignment, and I observed certain aids to

Morley's lifelong preoccupation, which were displayed discreetly on open shelves on either side of the gradually widening gallery: gloves made of a variety of materials—silk, chamois, velvet, and the thinnest, most pliable rubber—and exquisite pastel-hued cloths almost the size of scarves, some shaped and outfitted with cords to be knotted around the waist or buttocks—Look, Ma, no hands! There were cubicles, as advertised. And reaching deep into the walls on both sides were, well, receptacles—bottles, presumably made of rubber or plastic—of a uniform length I estimated at between six and eight inches. All were molded into an identical shape that, in the context of where I was, could have only one conceivable use. I assumed they were disposable, *were* disposed of.

The photo portrait that was the centerpiece of the first wall panel we reached was in black-and-white, approximately one-half life-size. Its subject was a woman whose fame as a beauty may be second to none in the past fifty years, and no such photograph of her existed—or was known to. Oh, I'd seen a few adroitly shadowed tits-and-buns-only seminudes, hundreds of shots of her in swimsuits. But here she was facing the camera naked, all the right places highlighted and mouth-watering. My heartbeat became audible to me, partly because the appearance of *this* photo in *Greedy* would make that issue our all-time best-seller.

"I'm forbidden to let this picture be reproduced," Pritchard said from beside me. "I should have warned you." He must've seen my shoulders slump because he added, "Please, don't worry. I have many more who are lovelier, more stimulating. She *begins* the collection, after all. A bit of a novelty."

On either side of Ms. Famous were three smaller portraits, also in black-and-white, and a sweeping glance excited me. Though I didn't recognize her, they were all of the same woman, and I'd have loved knowing her intimately. Dark-haired, in her early twenties, she appeared at the far left side of the gallery in a gown loose at the shoulders, skirt pulled high enough to show she wore nothing beneath it. Perfect legs etcetera. The next photo was taken from above her, and she lay bare on a bed. She reached up hungrily, naturally. In photo three her head was thrown back into a pillow, her exquisite face grimacing as an orgasm sparked her. I hurried past the photo of the lost star to number four, in which the camera had caught her seconds later, blissfully satisfied. Here her whole relaxing body again appeared, shining, and I felt like an envious and aroused intruder. Photo five depicted the girl from behind, skipping on her toes, toward a bathroom. The sixth shot, evocative, heart-tugging, and very erotic, caught her kneeling at someone's feet with a washcloth and towel, every pore of her lovely face and form glistening with drops of shower water.

"Seventy-four," Pritchard said. "You may choose the first photo, if you wish. But—"

"I know." I stepped around him and the partition. "She's at the start, too." He had given *her* up for his collection, for his *hand*. "Pass."

I stopped, staring. I realized he'd truly arranged his gallery in a methodically improving exhibit of gorgeousness, and for the first time I wondered how many dozen photos—if that many—I'd be able to take. Yes, I was fine then, dandy. But it was apparent the partitions would become ever more enticing; we would progress to full color. What if he has films, special videos? I wondered what's the secret of the magic in these girls that's gotten to me so fast?

Four shots, none displaying all of an individual: breasts, her arms raised over her head; a derriere, subject presumably standing straight; two unrouged lips, parted but slightly; three-quarter pose; female genitalia, not *Hustler* style but soft as silk.

I felt a bit woozy and wondered if I imagined music now playing—classical, rhythmic. I had *kissed* all such parts, seen thousands of reproductions of them. Something about these in the four photos seemed . . . special. The breasts were surprisingly round, the curves of their underside like shiny smiles, the nipples—also unrouged—minimally protuberant. Ass cheeks were similarly globular, tilted, rising to a lovely spinal column. The mouth needed to be kissed, *had* to be; I hoped it had been, and hadn't. Untrimmed chestnut-brown pubic hair allowed virtually no view of the folds beneath but gleamed like a healthy animal pelt. I had no idea how old these girls might be. What's special, I asked myself—*what?* Then I couldn't be sure it wasn't just *me* reacting wildly, that if I snapped a few pix my editor might look at the proofs and demand to know why I hadn't done better!

As Morley Pritchard quietly led me deeper into the second-floor gallery, the room widened, and I hardened. I don't mean my heart. Three poster-size pix were next displayed, the subjects extraordinarily lovely black nudes. The first troubled me for more than one reason because I doubted she'd passed fully through puberty, but the sense of girlish frolic in her expression drew my attention away from the usual points of interest. Then I found a glamorous pose of a thirty-something woman with a marvelous wanton quality, and she returned my gaze to tradition. Fruitless to describe her, but I snapped a picture, knowing my boss could not object. The last photo exhibited a naked woman whose face said she could be sixty but whose voluptuous body seemed to lift and thrust itself to me for approval, which I instantly offered. "You may as well choose all three photographs," said the collector beside me, softly. "It's the same beauty." He sounded nostalgic but ignored my surprise. *"She* cemented my . . . interest."

I was glad to speak, to be sarcastic. "So do you ever take a walk down memory lane?"

Blinking, he turned to proceed. "I did in the past. For the day's . . . first." He sighed. "Michael Jordan also gave up hoops."

I had never understood that either. "Sir," I said, "you said you got on, not off, with the collection. You spoke of 'unexpected possibility.' "

He knew that was an implied question, but he pretended not to hear, just stepped aside for me to see a mural-sized photograph mounted on the next partition. For one brief instant—there was so *much,* and the subjects were so intertwined—I didn't know what I was looking at. When I did, I gasped and stepped nearer.

And even then I couldn't tell how many magnificent females I saw, because they were wound in and between and among one another's arms and legs. Unadorned, they had at first appeared to be a golden tapestry; now they became a mostly horizontal, staggering convention of rounded, prominent, extended or dangling, petite, huge, and upthrust breasts combined with a seemingly endless array of exposed buttocks and vaginas. Narrowing my vision for detail, I perceived they were all blondes, ranging in age from puberty to anyone's guess, and they gave every impression of playfulness, of having *fun.*

Pritchard said, "You're wondering why your senses are reacting as they are. So many men have grown jaded because they've seen too many women posed to the point of pain, airbrushed beyond nature's inclinations. Your first reaction is to true *beauty.* It comes not only from the sweet features of their forms but from their being at liberty to enjoy their own bodies while they are alone or with a nonparticipating photographer."

I nodded but didn't look at him. "And with one another, too, it seems."

"This group, on *this* day," he murmured, "chose to cavort this way—*once.* Who knows why? Peer more closely. You'll find no two women engaged in coition."

He was right. I wondered, shooting just a portion of the mural, if they had decided to tease their photographer. I went on, pondering the words "true beauty,' as I moved with reluctance deeper into the gallery.

But between his presentation of a life-size, almost three-dimensional shot of the most glorious-looking red-haired girl I ever expected to see and the second of two videos utilizing some of the women I'd already admired in still shots, the discomfort in my groin began to make it hard to walk. The young woman I'd seen in segments played with many of them all over her apartment, and I'd have sworn she thought she was alone. I imagined she begged for assistance—until she finished (and *I* hadn't). The other video involved several blondes from the mural with the delightful black woman. They too obviously felt they were alone somehow, and their bodies provided most of the sound. I'm sure you think you've seen it before, but . . . well, I hobbled to the stairs, saying nothing. Determined not to touch myself, I stumbled downstairs, where my host wordlessly handed me an ice pack. If he had said I hadn't gone as far as he'd hoped or that the arousal level of the gallery was still building, I'd have hit him. All I knew when I left there was that I'd taken pictures of three pieces—and my roommate's name was Beth. . . .

"But we just *did* it," she protested. "Why should I walk around nude?"

Be quiet, *please,* I thought. "Pretend I'm not here and you're horny, okay?" I was stroking her breast. It was nice, but I couldn't *eat* it without hurting her and winding up like Jeffrey Dahmer. My erection was a flagstaff. My skin twitched. *"Please,* Beth, *do* something—to *yourself!"*

She bounded out of bed. "I won't! You perv, I'm sleeping on the couch!"

Good! I thought. When she was gone I grabbed myself and sorted through a mental panorama of tits, asses, pussies of great beauty, lust jostling for position.

When I'd gotten off twice without being able to center on just one mental image, I wondered how soon I could see the proofs of pictures I'd taken.

At work the next day I couldn't see any of the remembered women clearly in my mind—like the women in the mural, they washed together—and I knew I wasn't in practice. The risky thought spooked me, so I began writing the Morley Pritchard interview and was mildly surprised to find that I was sardonically slicing the master masturbator to ribbons. I knew why, at once—to label *him* the pervert, not me—but that only reinforced my quasi-trenchant wit, coaxed out the sarcasm in dollops large enough to have made the collector proud. That night with Beth my ejaculation was as premature as 4:00 A.M. sunlight on a vampire's ass. A sane nook in my mind told me, when I took over the couch, that our relationship might best be described just then as "undead." I hated that, right up until I found a flick with nudes on Showtime or Cinemax—who cared?—and began to catch up on my practice.

Until he saw the photo spread that went with my hatchet job on Pritchard, my editor wasn't quite sure he approved. Then he signed off with enthusiasm. He and every other guy in the office loved the pictures.

But not half as much as I did.

It took almost three weeks for me to experience the Jordan-quit-basketball syndrome, and by then my relationship with Beth sucked more than Dracula. She stomped out, frightened for me and so thoroughly convinced I'd changed that she was also frightened for herself. The photos from the gallery were no longer enough, my girl was gone (I even missed her for other reasons), and I wasn't worth a damn till the issue with the Pritchard interview and photos hit the stands.

Then it proceeded to do just what I'd predicted would happen, and suddenly, arriving late to work and looking seedy or not, I was *Greedy*'s fair-haired boy.

And Morley Pritchard himself phoned to ask me politely to "come back and hear the rest" of his story. My mercurial reaction was a stall; then, in his cultured tones, he purred an irresistible message into my ear: "Complete the interview and you can go straight to the parts of my collection that are truly the *pièces de résistance.*"

I want to say I went back because I knew another three photographs—yet more exciting ones—would make *Greedy* number one, or because I could write a book about my experiences that would top every best-seller list for a year and a half.

But you know, if you're a man and can admit it to yourself, why I returned.

Pritchard was at the front door to greet me this time. Of course he wanted to begin with a conversation, and by the time we were seated in his front room I had noticed with shock how drastically he had changed. There are better words to capture his appearance but this will do: he looked old—old enough to be dying. It occurred to me that my unflattering slant on the first interview might be responsible, and I was trying to summon the suitable words of explanation when he spoke again before I did.

"You implied I was a coward for no longer pursuing real women. Your own appearance proclaims *you* a hypocrite, as I knew you were when you left the gallery so precipitately." He held up a wavery palm to stop my comment. "I'm quite old. I'm dying—please, no crocodile tears—and I have chosen to set the record straight. Whether your publisher has the courage to print my revelations or not, I want *you* to know what they are."

"That's why I'm here," I said, starting the tape recorder.

"No, Tom. You're here because, inevitably, you wanted to see the remainder of my collection."

Pritchard drew in a breath so labored that a union negotiator would have demanded a new contract. I wondered if he'd die while I was there. "I shall tell you of the 'unexpected possibility' you were so avid to know about. Nothing I say will mean a thing to you until I've finished, so bear with me, please."

Even though his obsession with masturbation had cost me a girl I might have loved, he looked like death warmed over so I nodded. Besides, I had a job to do.

"I learned that our pupils expand when we see something that interests and excites us. Of course you know we perspire and our heartbeat accelerates when we're aroused, that there's a tremendous, energetic outburst at any climax, autoerotic or not. These facts set me to thinking." Pritchard drummed his fingertips on the arm of his chair. "I perceived that I was not diminishing my intellectual faculties, as the old wives' tales had it, but getting shrewder, making more profitable investments. It was then that I chanced upon a line of Kant, who called the hand the 'visible part of the brain'—and I understood." He smiled despite his illness. "From our earliest years we're encouraged to *exercise* our *intelligence.* In masturbation a person quite healthfully exercises that 'visible part' of his brain. Benjamin Walker suggests, in fact, that we *can't* think 'without the hand becoming involved.'"

I grunted. "The smarter we get, the better we can rationalize what we do."

Morley's ferret eyes reassumed some of their old combative cleverness. "I'm telling you what happened. I'm not rationalizing, not fantasizing. Returning to the topic of eyes, certain contemporary neurophysiologists say our eye movements produce small electrical discharges that may be batterylike. I was reminded of the belief of Platonists and Stoics that we actually transmit from our eyes a stream of energy capable of making contact elsewhere, at great distances." He coughed hard, produced a handkerchief, and used it, not exactingly enough to conceal the blood from me. "I saw," he said hoarsely, "the possibility of . . . *personal* contact. With the women of my collection. One they'd accept happily because it seemed simply to evoke the sexual *best* from them while omitting any direct, purely physical intrusion."

"I've interviewed some dirty old men," I said shortly. "You take the cake." Not that I *believed* him; the "possibility" of what he was saying disgusted me.

"But, Tom," Pritchard said, leaning forward, "it *worked!* The mixture of my sexual imperative, hand, and brain—while my expanded pupils dispatched images over the miles, alerting those on whom I focused—encouraged them to *join* me in delight! I needed only to know they were alive and where they resided, and then dual autoerotic connection—safely, without obligation or commitment—became available to me at any moment!"

Against my conscious will I recalled, from my visit to his gallery, perfect white, black, and Asian women whom any heterosexual man might have adored to contact at will. Of course, what the dying bastard was saying was mere fantasy.

"You can't believe me," Pritchard said with no asperity, "until you've heard all of it." He was flushed, feverish. "I didn't stop there. I wished to be *in the room* with them, to see them *in person.* And I learned in a priceless book that the skilled autoeroticist may evoke, at climax, an extraordinary biomagnetic energy—the kind that produces a temporary *thought form,* akin to the Tibetan tulpa, or perhaps to the astral body!" He tapped my hand with clammy fingers. "It is known as the 'silently waiting spirit.' "

I shuddered with a combination of fear of his insanity and terror of what dark "possibility" might dwell within me. Before I answered him, Pritchard began to cough rackingly, chest heaving, and I wondered what part of this death could be attributed to solitary sexual pursuits conducted on an unoccupied second floor, all alone inside an aging mind—and his desperately pumping gloved hand.

He had fallen back against his chair, and I was loosening his tie and collar when Pritchard peered up at me with piercing eyes that scared the shit out of me. "When I die," he whispered, "you will go up, alone, to see all of my collection." He waggled a hand feebly. "It's all right. I understand! For your sake, remember that sight is the one sense we can immediately cut off. You only close your eyelids." His hands were tangled in my shirtfront, dragging me closer. "Yet there's one thing I don't know, Tom . . . and it's important."

I should have called 911, but all I did was ask gently, "What is it?"

"When human lids fall, our eyes automatically roll *up.* For at least an instant, the brain's internal machinery is . . . *suspended.*" His hands fell into his lap. He didn't have long. "When that occurs at the point of death I don't know how long what I created will . . . will . . ."

Pritchard's eyelids dropped. My face was inches away from that of a dead man.

Of course I checked his pulse before straightening, turning toward the stairwell. If a "silently waiting spirit" was in the building, I thought, it was Tom

Russell. I would finish my tour and call somebody. Weird old Morley Pritchard wasn't going anywhere.

The chandelier illuminated the second-floor landing as I took two slow steps, my blood already dancing in my veins—and just then I saw the most innocent-seeming, lavishly curved, devastatingly exquisite nude girl step under the light. Though her hair and skin tones were in flux as I gaped up at her, she was too real to be a ghost, and, even if she was, that didn't matter for my purposes. I took two more steps, audibly panting with desire, aware that she was what Morley had seen when his eyes closed for the last time. That didn't matter either, I found as I unzipped my bulging fly. This girl was an amalgam of everything physical that Morley, I, or any man could desire, and—unaware that I stood below her—she was feeling herself. I couldn't do less myself. *Some human activity can be taken to heights of performance unparalleled on earth.* Pritchard had experienced that; now I could too.

Suddenly, instead of pink folds, I was staring at an erect penis—then at a horsy face with ferret eyes! I wilted at once, but it took me longer to realize what had gone wrong: several lovely women had also heard about the "visible part of the brain" and had made dual autoerotic connections of their own. The amalgamation above me meant that Morley, seeing them at the instant of his death, had *joined* them "in delight."

I couldn't go up to see the rest of the gallery then, and I never would; I couldn't have walked around—or through—*that.* I was left to wonder if Morley Pritchard had, in a way, experienced intercourse.

And if he'd *liked* it.

UNTAMED SEX

James Crawford

Are you tired of safe sex?
Do want to experience sex as nature intended it?
Do you want to experience animal passion?
Then call 1-800-UNTAMED, right now!

"Honey, they're running that commercial again," Bill called from the living room.

"Did they give any more details yet?" quizzed Sheila, coming from the kitchen where she had thrown out the containers from their microwave dinners.

"How are they gonna give details about some sex service on network television? This isn't cable, you know." He reached for his glass of cola and found it empty. Bill held it up for his wife. She took it and returned to the kitchen.

She's still an attractive woman, he thought as he watched her walk away. Maybe tonight he'd offer to fly her to the moon. Naw, that was just the sugar and caffeine from the cola talking.

He still loved her, and he was pretty sure she still loved him. They still had sex once in a while, when it didn't interfere with what was on television. The years had taken their toll on Bill and Sheila's sex life.

"So are you going to phone?" Sheila handed him the glass.

"Huh?"

"You call me every time that commercial runs, so you must be thinking about calling the number."

"Next you'll be accusing me of having phone sex." Bill shook his head and took a swig of cola.

Sheila knelt down next to his recliner. "If I thought it would help us, I would."

He saw her eyes were moist. "Honey, what's wrong?"

Her head dropped and her shoulders shook. "Oh, Bill, it's been so long since you've touched me."

"What do you mean? I touch you all the time." He knew she needed affection, but he just couldn't provide it.

"You know what I mean." Sheila looked him right in the eye. There were lines on her face that he hadn't noticed before, and he saw a little gray in her brown hair. Bill still found her desirable. Did she feel the same about him? After all, he wasn't getting any younger.

A sense of loss swept over him, and he reached out to touch his wife's hair. "I'm sorry, honey. Work's been a bitch, and I've got a lot on my mind."

Sheila caught his hand and held it to her face. "It's more than that. We've been married so long that there just aren't any surprises left. We know each other so well that we've gotten bored."

"I still love you," he murmured.

"And I still love you," she answered. "But we need something to give us a kick in the pants. Maybe . . . just maybe Untamed Sex is the answer."

Bill's mouth dropped open. "You *want* me to call?"

"Yes, I want to rekindle that spark we used to have."

Sheila jumped up and ran into the kitchen, then hurried back holding the cordless phone.

This was unreal. Sure, he'd thought of calling to find out what the deal was, but he hadn't wanted Sheila to see the number on their phone bill.

The ads had started running a couple of months ago. Short little spots on the tube. The questions spelled out in bold letters as a drum beat out a savage tempo. They didn't give any details, just their number to call for information. A couple of guys at work had talked about it, but so far no one would admit to having called the number.

Now here he was calling, with his wife standing at his shoulder. He could hear her breathing a little quicker, the excitement of doing something wicked bringing a youthful flush to her cheeks. Bill had to wipe his suddenly sweaty palms on his pants.

There was a click and a businesslike voice answered. "Hello. Untamed Sex. How may I help you?"

Bill froze. What was he supposed to say? Sheila slapped him on the back of the head, and the blow jump-started his brain. "Hi, I'm interested in your service."

He listened closely and grunted a few replies into

the phone. Sheila was so nervous she danced from foot to foot. Finally Bill said yes and hung up.

"What did they say?" Sheila grabbed his arm.

"We have an appointment with a counselor this Friday at six." Bill sat staring at the phone.

A couple of days later they were on the road following directions they had received in the mail. Sheila was reading a leaflet from their packet of information. "This brochure says that their compound is secluded and beautifully landscaped to complement the nature around it."

"What the hell do they mean, 'compound'? What are we headed for, Stalag Seventeen?" Bill snarled, tired from the driving and a bad case of nerves.

"It says it's a lovely place where we can experience our Untamed Sex encounter to its maximum benefit," Sheila told him.

For all the photos, maps, directions, and superlatives in the packet, Bill and Sheila still had no idea what sort of "encounter" this was going to be. They had read all of the folders a couple of times, but they still didn't know what to expect. Bill was nervous and skeptical, but Sheila was looking forward to the encounter as part of an adventure.

As the car topped a rise in the road, they saw a massive gate with the name UNTAMED SEX emblazoned across it. From either side of the gate a tall fence stretched off into the distance. Bill pulled up the gate and looked around.

"What the hell is this, Jurassic Park?"

"Can I help you?"

Bill jerked around to face the speaker set into the gate. "We're here for the orientation."

"Name, please?"

"Bill and Sheila Wilmer."

"I have your name on my list." The voice was pleasant, and the speaker had none of the tinny quality that might be expected. "When the gates open, just follow the road to the Main Center. Please keep your windows rolled up and do not leave your vehicle. Someone will meet you at the center."

With that, the gate slid silently back and Bill drove through. The road curved into a wooded area, and they were surrounded by dense forest.

As they continued through the woods, Sheila called out as she spotted various wild creatures moving through the shadows. "Bill, I'm sure I saw a bear . . . and look! Isn't that a lion?"

"You're seeing things," Bill answered tersely. "What do you think this is, Lion Country Safari?"

Sheila didn't have a chance to answer before Bill slammed on his brakes. The road ahead was blocked as a couple of elephants crossed majestically and disappeared into the trees on the other side. He turned to say something to his wife, but cut it short when he saw the smirk on her face. Grumbling under his breath, he started forward again.

The Main Center was a modern chrome-and-glass building. The flower beds around it were reflected in the mirrored windows over and over again so that the building seemed to be painted with flowers. Standing outside the entrance was a young woman dressed in a simple but expensive-looking suit. After what they had just seen, Bill wouldn't have been surprised if she had been wearing jodhpurs and a pith helmet.

"Welcome, Mr. and Mrs. Wilmer." She greeted

them as they got out of the car. "Please leave your keys in the ignition so that one of our staff can park your vehicle for you."

They were shown into a small room with a desk and a couple of chairs. The woman who had led them there asked, "Can I get you something to drink? Coffee, tea, Perrier, soft drink?"

Before they could answer, a young man entered the room. He was in his early twenties and was very well dressed. "Hello, my name is Dr. Henry Offut. You must be the Wilmers."

Bill took the proffered hand. "Yes, I'm Bill, and this is my wife, Sheila. Doc, are we finally going to find out what this is all about and how much it's going to cost us?"

"Bill!" Sheila said with a slight edge to her voice.

"That's all right, Mrs. Wilmer," Offut said with a beneficent smile. "We do tend to be a little secretive about our process. You see, we've made a breakthrough here, and the way we've decided to use it is not well thought of in the scientific community."

"I don't understand," Bill said, puzzled.

"We're in this for the money." Offut sat behind an expensive-looking desk. "We make no claims about laboring for the benefit of mankind or about the lives we might save. Here at Untamed Sex, we're businessmen trying to turn a profit on our discovery."

"Sounds like the American way to me." Bill leaned forward in his chair.

"You came here because of the ads you saw on television. You wondered what we were offering. Your sex life is less than fulfilling, and you're looking for something to spice it up. Am I right so far?"

Bill looked at Sheila and found that she was nodding vigorously. That hurt a little, but he realized it was the truth.

"We have that something." Dr. Offut hit a couple of switches on his desk. A wall panel slid up into the ceiling revealing a large television screen. The lights in the room dimmed and the TV commercial for Untamed Sex played, but this time it continued.

The announcer's voice went on to say that man had forgotten what sex was all about. It was primal, he said, one of nature's strongest drives. Every creature on the planet has sexual needs, but only man tries to rationalize them.

Clips started rolling, and Bill and Sheila were staring at pictures of animals copulating. The variety was amazing, and so was some of the equipment, but they were just animals. The narrator went on to say that sex at its best was savage, unfettered by convention or morals, pure and animalistic. That was what Untamed Sex was all about.

The screen went dark, and the lights in the room came back on. Bill was red-faced and jumped out of his chair, "That's what all this mystery is about—animal porn? That's sick! If I wanted to hump a sheep I'd spend a summer on a farm. Come on, Sheila, we're getting out of here."

"Mr. Wilmer, please sit down." Offut calmly gestured to a chair. "We are not about bestiality. This is all part of our breakthrough." Offut switched on the television screen once again, but this time he narrated what was shown. "A few years ago some scientists, working on mapping the functions of the brain, hit on a revolutionary discovery.

"As you know, information is transferred to the brain as electrical impulses. Everything we see or feel is translated into information that is fed to the brain and then interpreted. The sum of all that electrical input becomes our experience.

"We've found that we could insert tiny microchips into certain portions of an animal's brain and, with the latest computer technology, transfer that data to a receptor that a person could wear. In simplest terms, the person would feel everything the animal was feeling."

The screens showed scientists hustling around the room amid banks of computers. There were a few scenes of surgery, and then of the scientists in protective suits and helmets that looked like something out of a science-fiction movie.

"Have you two heard of virtual reality?" the doctor asked.

"I saw a special on it on PBS," Sheila volunteered. "You put on the goggles and you can see things created by computer, but it looks like you're really there."

"Right. Well, we have taken that process to the next step. The stimuli we offer are generated not by a computer but by the mind of a living creature. With our process you will see, feel, and be whatever animal you choose."

"So what?" Bill started to rise again. "So I can be a sheep instead of humping one? How's that going to help our sex life?"

"Mr. Wilmer, you are missing the point." Dr. Offut leaned over the desk. "You must have noticed that on our preserve we have a wide variety of animal life."

"Yeah, so?"

"What you can't tell is that our stock is raised with just one thing in mind . . . sex."

Sheila asked a little too quickly, "You mean they all just . . . ?"

Offut smiled at her. "I mean that with the aid of electronics and chemicals we can assure you the animal you want to experience will be in heat while you are a part of its life."

"And?" Bill grumbled.

"You will be able to experience sex as you never have before. Sex the way nature intended it, unfettered by taboos, learned response, or social mores. Completely safe, with absolutely no risk. Sex just for the sake of sex."

Bill noticed that Sheila was hanging on every word the doctor said. Bill had seen that look in her eyes before, but not for a long time. It was the look she used to get after a really good bout of lovemaking. It surprised him how the look hurt him. How long had it been since he had put that look on her face?

"Would we be . . . ourselves?" Sheila asked in a quiet little voice.

"For the duration of the session you would be the animal you chose." Dr. Offut directed his comments to just Sheila.

"And this is a good thing?" Bill asked sarcastically.

"A lioness can be in heat for over sixty hours and can have as many as one hundred seventy couplings. Elephants engage in foreplay that can continue for hours." Offut turned and smiled at Bill. "Callicebus monkeys engage in a nonstop orgy during estrus."

Food for thought. Sex just for the sake of sex. No

small talk, no commitments, no guilt afterward. It would be fun and no one could get sore, because it was all just a fancy video game. It was tempting, Bill had to admit.

Dr. Offut sat quietly at his desk while Bill and Sheila thought about the possibilities. When he judged the time was right he asked, "Are you interested?"

Sheila started to answer, but Bill cut her off. "Are there any side effects?"

"There are no chemicals involved. We hook you up to our receivers, and when the encounter is over, we unhook you. While you're hooked up you'll be totally safe and secure, as if you were dreaming. We've even had people fall asleep for part of their session." The doctor paused for a moment. "We have noticed one side effect in some of our clients, but we see it as a positive one."

"Tell us and let us decide." Bill still had some misgivings.

Dr. Offut smiled at them. "Some of the subjects have gone away with some of the animal's characteristics. We say this is positive, because they tell us that their own lovemaking after one of our sessions is the most intense of their lives."

"When can we try it?" Sheila burst out before Bill could interrupt again.

Bill had an almost uncontrollable urge to wipe the smile off Dr. Offut's face.

"We have a special trial offer for our new clients," Offut said. "One fifteen-minute session for both of you for only ninety-nine dollars."

Sheila quickly said, "We'll take it."

The doctor nodded and left the room to prepare the session, leaving the two of them alone for the first time since they had arrived.

The door closed and Bill turned to Sheila, but she spoke first. "Why are you being so negative?"

"Me?" Bill did his trout-gasping-for-air impression. "Why are you so eager to try this? I'm just asking questions any sensible person would."

Sheila leaned over and grabbed his hand. "Bill, I really want to try this. We've gotten into such a rut that I think this might be just the thing to get us back on track."

"Sheila, are you sure?" He put his hand on hers.

"When was the last time we did anything wild and crazy?"

"Just last week I drank some milk after the expiration date on the carton had passed." She gave him a smile and a quick kiss, and Bill acquiesced. "Okay, it's too long a drive just to turn around and go back without trying it out."

With that, Sheila laughed out loud and jumped into his lap. They were locked in a passionate embrace when the doctor entered the room. Offut quietly cleared his throat. Like two kids caught necking on their parents' couch, Sheila and Bill stopped and quickly straightened their clothes.

"Keep that up and you won't need our service." Dr. Offut gestured to the door. "Everything is ready. Mrs. Wilmer, please go with Sally. Mr. Wilmer, you will follow me."

"Can't we go together?" Bill wondered.

"We find that the first experience is more effective if the couples try it on their own. The next time you can try it as a couple, if you like."

For some reason Bill didn't want to let Sheila go. He hung on to her hand until she gave him a sharp look. Freed from his grip she went off with the young woman in the lab coat, smiling and joking. Bill stood and watched her go. Dr. Offut cleared his throat, and Bill followed him down a long hallway.

After it was all over and they were in the car, Sheila and Bill were desperate to get home. They were lucky that there were no traffic cops out to make their quota that day. Pushing the car to its limit, they raced home, dashed into the house, and destroyed each other's clothes as they tore them off. Bill grabbed Sheila and flung her to the floor. With a growl he leaped on her, and the two of them thrashed around, knocking furniture aside and destroying a couple of pieces of bric-a-brac.

It was savage. He grabbed her hard enough to leave bruises. Her nails left bloody furrows down his back. Both of them were grunting and growling as they fought for release. Abruptly Sheila tore away. Bill howled in frustration and reached for her. She batted his hand aside, then got down on all fours, her back to Bill. She lowered her head and raised her ass. Her legs spread wide, she smiled at Bill over her shoulder. The surprise almost broke the mood. In all the years they had been together, Sheila had never liked this position, saying that if she was going to make love to someone she wanted to see his face.

Surprise didn't last long, and the lust that had been controlling Bill rushed back. This was the way sex was supposed to be, savage and frenzied. With a low rumble in his throat he rushed forward and penetrated her. The two of them howled as they climaxed.

When they came to, they were lying crumpled

among the debris that had been their living room. Bill was shocked at the amount of damage they had done. When he started to rise, a sharp stinging made him reach behind himself to touch his back. His hand came away red with blood.

"Jesus!" he exclaimed. Stiffly he got to his feet. "Sheila?"

His wife was lying so still on the floor that he was afraid he had seriously hurt her. Concerned, he turned her over onto her back. Bruises were already forming on her arms and legs. Some of them were obviously from his fingers. He felt sick—what had he done to his wife?

When Sheila opened her eyes, she had the biggest smile on her face that he had ever seen. "That was incredible. What were you?"

"What?" He was stunned with relief.

"What were you in your session? Whatever it was, I think you should try it again."

Bill laughed and embraced Sheila. "Before we try that again, you might want to look at yourself in the mirror. You look as if you were mauled by some wild animal."

"I was, and I love him." She pulled him closer for a kiss. As she slid her arm around his neck, he winced. Sheila stopped and looked over his shoulder. Her face registered surprise, and maybe just a bit of delight. "You didn't come out of it unmarked either."

They went upstairs and fell into bed. He lay on his stomach while she tended to his back. It stung as she rubbed ointment on it. Bill was drifting off to sleep when she asked him once more about his session. He turned to look at her and asked what she had been.

"I thought I'd try something small to start out with."

"So what were you?"

"A mink."

"A mink?"

"Did you read the description of what they do?" Sheila asked. He nodded, and she went on: "I knew I couldn't have the whole courtship ritual. Sally told me that could take as long as eight hours, but it sounded fierce."

"A mink?" he said again.

"Yes, the female mink isn't docile in the slightest. The male comes at her all ready for a quick wham-bang, but she fights him off until she's good and ready. They hooked me into a couple who were right at the end of the process.

"I'm telling you it was amazing. I still had some of my own thoughts, but all I wanted was sex. I was completely hot and ready to go. He kept coming after me and I kept dodging and fighting till I was so crazed I couldn't stand it, and then he was on me.

"It only took a few seconds after that, but it was the most intense feeling I've ever had." She kissed him on the back of neck. "Until we got home, that is."

Bill shook his head. Sheila nudged him in the ribs. He looked up at her, and she gave him a quizzical look.

"Okay," he started. "I tried one of those monkeys he was talking about."

"Why the monkey?"

Bill was embarrassed, but he finally managed to spit it out. "I always wondered about group sex and this seemed like the ideal way to try it."

Sheila laughed and lay down next to him.

"It was wild," he admitted. "Suddenly I was this monkey—not very big, judging from the size of everything around me, but I've never been so horny in my life.

"There was something in the air, and all I could do was grab any nearby female and jump her. I'm not sure how many times I did it, or with how many, but it was a lot. It was the damnedest thing—I never saw anything so desirable in my life as those girl monkeys."

"Women monkeys," Sheila corrected with a giggle.

"It was amazing. One minute I'm me, and the next I'm Tarzan's pal on a wild night in the jungle. Then I was myself again, and all I could think about was getting together with you and doing something hot and sweaty."

"I can see now why they get their money in advance," Sheila joked as she nuzzled closer. "When can we do it again?"

"It'll be a while. I'm exhausted," Bill said, sinking into the bed.

"Not that, you goose." Sheila smacked him on his back, and suddenly he was very attentive. "I mean, when are we going back for another session?"

"We're going to have to wait for a while," Bill said, looking closely at his wife. "The regular sessions are longer and cost about five hundred dollars for the two of us. We just don't have that much money lying around."

"Please." Sheila nipped at his shoulder. She still had a wild look in her eyes.

"We'll see. Now can we get some sleep? If we want

to get more money, I'm going to have to go to work tomorrow."

Sheila smiled a big lazy grin and started to stroke Bill. Eventually they got to sleep, but it wasn't till much later.

The next couple of days were the best that Bill could remember. The two of them were like horny kids again; they could hardly keep their hands off each other. He would walk into the house, and Sheila would tear his clothes off. Then the two of them would crash around the house until they were too exhausted to move. They destroyed a couple of possessions, but they had great sex.

Eventually, though, the ardor began to die down. Sheila urged Bill to go back to the center for another session. He tried to explain to her that it was the end of the month and there were bills to pay, but she just became more insistent. It was almost as if she had become addicted and needed another fix.

He began to dread coming home. Untamed Sex was all she would talk about—how freeing it was, how great the sex was afterward, what an adventure it was. Bill tried to ground her in reality by telling her how expensive the encounters were. Trouble was, Sheila wasn't listening.

He arrived home one evening at the end of a lousy day and eased the door open. If he was lucky he could avoid Sheila and get himself a beer and have a couple of quiet moments to himself. Bill had just opened the fridge when he heard a noise from upstairs—a low moaning, and he could feel the house shuddering slightly. Worried, he called Sheila's name and rushed upstairs.

Their bedroom was a mess, clothes tossed all over the place and furniture knocked over. His first thought was that there had been a robbery. Rushing into the room, he stopped dead in his tracks. Sheila stood facing the closet, and she was humping the door.

She was so wrapped up in what she was doing that she didn't hear him come into the room. Suddenly she stopped. Her eyes opened wide, and with a combination snarl and moan she threw herself on Bill. He tried to talk, but she was too insistent. She shredded his clothes and then climbed on top of him and impaled herself on his cock.

It was so primal that Bill came almost immediately, but Sheila was still unsatisfied. She leaped off him and used her hands and mouth to fire him up again. She still hadn't said a word, but she was so desperate that it scared him. Seeing her like this was also arousing, however, and he soon responded to her frenzied stroking.

She assumed the female position on her hands and knees, as she had done the first time. This time he lasted longer and was rewarded with howls of delight from her. After he finished, he dropped down on the bed only to find Sheila once more trying to revive him.

"Sheila!" He grabbed her shoulders. "Stop it! I want to make love to you again, but you're just going to have to wait for a few minutes."

His wife got a crazed look on her face as she glanced around the room. Bill knew she was searching for something to satisfy her lust with. That scared him, and he wrapped his arms around her and pulled her down next to him. With soothing words and gentle strokes, he held her tight. She fought him at first, but soon calmed down and fell asleep in his arms.

He didn't know how to deal with the situation. Part of him was angry as hell. She had obviously gone to the center without him, after he had repeatedly told her they couldn't afford it. But part of him was worried about her and how wild she'd acted.

Sheila woke up and looked around in a daze. Gradually her eyes focused and she stared at Bill. Her face flamed a deep crimson. She turned away from him and buried her face in a pillow.

"You went back to the center again, didn't you?" She nodded. "I told you we couldn't afford it this month."

Sheila turned to him, her eyes wet with tears. "Bill, I'm so sorry. I just couldn't help myself. I had to have it again."

"I just wish you'd talked to me before you went." Bill pulled her into his arms to show her that he wasn't too mad.

"It happened too fast." Sheila gazed into his eyes. "When I woke up this morning, I just knew I was going to have to go back. The urge to have another session just kept growing. Today I couldn't fight it anymore. As soon as you left for work, I got dressed and drove out there."

"Whatever you were this time made you really crazy," Bill said. "Just what animal did you try?"

Her eyes lit up as she remembered. "I was a lioness."

"A lioness?"

"Yes, queen of the pride. Hunter, provider of food for the young and the males, in heat and desperate for sex. I was there for over an hour, and I can't tell you how many couplings I had. One male kept going till I wore him out, and then another one took his place."

"Queen of the jungle is right," Bill joked. "Being serviced by members of the court, or should I say the court's members."

She punched him lightly on the arm. "Then the session was over, but I was still in heat. I drove home like mad, but then I realized you wouldn't be home till later. I was going crazy; nothing would satisfy me but the real thing. I had to have sex."

"Thank God the mailman didn't knock on the door."

Sheila growled at him.

"Okay, Sheena, take it easy. It was great, but I want you to promise me that you won't do this again without me."

"I promise." She seemed sincere, but looked up at him with a sexy smile. "But promise me you won't keep me waiting too long."

Bill hoped he could make it soon, for her sake; she seemed almost obsessed, like a junkie who needed a fix. The truth was that he felt like going back too, but he fought the feeling. The problem was the economy. Business was in a slump, and the money just wasn't coming in. Sheila reminded him a couple of times about his promise, but there just wasn't any way he could swing it.

He could tell she still felt guilty about the last time, because of all the things she did for him: his favorite meals, back rubs, and long sessions of loving sex that left him floating on a cloud. But nothing lasts forever, and the good times are no exception.

Sheila became more insistent that they go back to

the center. First it was gentle hints. Then she tried to appeal to his sense of adventure, there being so many types of animals to choose from. When that failed, she sulked and ignored him.

There was nothing he could do about it; there wasn't any extra money to spend on needless luxuries. Trouble was, part of him wanted to go back too. But one of them had to be responsible, and unfortunately it seemed to be his turn.

It had been a lousy day at work, and Bill wasn't in the mood for any more discussions about sex. He just wanted to loosen his tie, get a cold beer, melt into his recliner, and watch television until his brain turned to mush. If he could just have a few quiet moments, he'd be all right.

"Bill, I figured out a couple of things we could trim from the budget so we could go back to the compound." Her statement hit him in the face, and he staggered back against the door. So much for a night of peace.

"Goddammit, Sheila," he snarled as he savagely ripped his tie off, "can't I get one moment's peace in this house? Every second it's sex, sex, sex. For Christ's sake, give it a rest!"

Sheila blinked rapidly as her face took on an ugly cast. "I wouldn't have to go on about it if I had someone who could satisfy me!"

"The entire San Diego Zoo couldn't satisfy you, you crazy bitch." His temper was running away with his mouth. "You're not going back to that freak show—not now, not ever!"

"Who the hell do you think you are, ordering me

around?" She got right in his face, and he could see some spittle in the corner of her mouth. "You're not my lord and master. I'll do whatever I damn please."

With an inarticulate roar Bill put one hand on her chest and shoved her away from him. Sheila bumped into the wall and staggered back toward him. Without thinking, he raised his hand to hit her.

Reason crashed through his anger, and the shock left him feeling nauseated. What the hell was he doing? He wanted to say something to his wife, but words failed him. Waving his arms at the air, he turned and rushed out of the house. Bill jumped in the car and, with a squeal of tires, sped away from all the ugliness that had suddenly filled his life.

He went on a bender, the first in many years, hitting one bar after another till he blacked out in the back seat of his car. A raging headache woke him up. Muscles jeered at his effort to straighten up, and for a while he thought he would spend the rest of his life doing an impression of Igor. Promising himself that he would never drink again, he drove slowly and carefully home.

Bill was still fumbling with his keys as he heard the phone ringing inside the house. He listened to see if Sheila would get the phone, but it just kept ringing. The unrelenting noise grated on him. Finally he got the door open and rushed to pick up the offending instrument.

"Hello?" he snapped.

"Mr. Wilmer? Thank God I got hold of you." The voice sounded out of breath.

"Who is this?" Bill asked.

"This is Dr. Offut at the clinic." There was a pause, as if the doctor was trying to think of how to say something. "Mr. Wilmer, we need you to come out to the clinic as soon as possible."

"What the hell is this all about? I'm not spending any more money on your damned sex machine, and that goes for my wife as well."

"Mr. Wilmer, it's about your wife. She's here."

"What?" Bill was instantly furious. "You're not to hook her up to your damned apparatus. Do you understand me?"

"I'm afraid it's too late for that." The line buzzed for a moment. "Please come quickly."

The phone went dead, and Bill looked at the handset as if trying to figure out what it was. Suddenly fear closed around his heart; something had happened to Sheila. Guilt about the things he'd said to her hammered at him. Bill ran out to his car and sped off toward the Untamed Sex compound.

The gate swung open as he approached, and he roared along the drive to the building. Offut was standing outside the main building wringing his hands. His face was damp with sweat, and his tie was askew.

Bill exploded out of the car and grabbed the doctor by his lapels. "Where is my wife, you money-grubbing quack?"

"Mr. Wilmer, please calm down—" That was all he got out before Bill threw him aside and rushed into the building.

"Sheila . . . Sheila, where are you, honey? Come out, sweetheart. I promise I won't be mad." He ran through the halls yelling her name. He saw other people, but they avoided his eyes or looked down at their feet.

Rounding a corner, he saw a group of people in lab

coats talking and pointing. The computer behind them was aglow with flashing lights. The people were pointing at one another and shaking reams of computer printouts in the air. Their conversation ceased when they became aware of Bill's presence.

He charged at them, yelling, "What have you bastards done with my wife?"

Slowly the group parted, and he could see through a window into one of the rooms. There, strapped to a chair, was Sheila, struggling against the restraints. Her mouth twisted open, but Bill couldn't hear a sound. A technician threw a switch behind him, and the hall was filled with a shrieking roar that had nothing human in it.

Bill slumped against the glass as if he had been hit. "What's wrong with her?"

"Mr. Wilmer," Dr. Offut came toward him. He held a handkerchief to his mouth and was careful not to get within Bill's reach. "Something has gone wrong here, and we are at a loss to explain it."

"What's wrong with Sheila?" Bill couldn't take his eyes off her as she tried to claw her way out of the chair.

Offut explained that Sheila had arrived earlier that day and asked to repeat her lioness experience. Everything had gone perfectly normally until it came time to disengage. When they had tried to end the program, it wouldn't reset. Nothing they could do made any difference. Sheila was locked into her lioness persona.

"I assure you this has never happened before." Offut moved closer, fear of a lawsuit apparently making him a little braver. "We're not sure what happened. It's almost as if her personality never reasserted itself, as if a stronger personality had supplanted it."

He went on, but Bill didn't hear a word. He moved away from the glass and had found the door into the room. No one tried to stop him. The door opened, and the awful cacophony pooled out into the hall, making people huddle closer together.

He moved toward his wife as she squirmed in the chair trying to free herself. Saliva drooled from the corner of her mouth; her fingers were bloody from trying to claw her way out of the straps. Bill made soothing noises, and for a moment the creature in the chair stopped struggling.

Not sure what to do, he just kept talking, trying to calm her as he inched forward. As he got to the chair and started to put his hand out, Bill could hear a low growl coming from deep in his wife's throat. It froze him where he stood.

The figure turned slowly toward him, eyeing him without a glimmer of recognition. He started to speak again, but then looked into Sheila's eyes. What he saw was not his wife. Something looked back at him with an ancient intelligence and a quiet power. She smiled, licked her lips, and purred in a deep, throaty rumble. His mind couldn't cope, so it just shut down and Bill shuddered and fainted dead away onto the floor.

The thing in the chair broke through its straps and lunged.

METALICA

Patricia D. Cacek

You wait in the cold white light, naked beneath the thin gown, knees pressed tightly together, hands clasped on your thighs. Waiting. Anticipating his touch and trembling as you remember the last time.

And the time before that.

And the time before that.

And the . . .

He enters, smiling, and the trembling stops. Everything stops except the working of your lungs and heart as you watch him close the door and walk toward you. The white light reflects off his gleaming flesh like diamonds.

His hands are cool as he places them over yours. Strong, capable of crushing you to a powder if he wants to. You begin to tremble again when he tells you to relax, that there's nothing to be afraid of.

He doesn't understand.

You tremble because he is with you again. And it's

been so long since the last time. You can't relax for exactly the same reason.

You have been so long apart.

Lie back, he says, *and spread your legs*

And you do.

The trembling finally stops when he places a hand on your thigh and slides the gown out of the way.

"Ms. Dylan," the doctor said, nodding as he took her chart from its holder on the outside of the examination room door. "How do you do?"

He didn't know her from Adam . . . or, more correctly, from Eve. Not that he should, he'd never seen her before, didn't know anything about her except for those things she'd written down on the New Patient form. That was the way Kate liked it. Doctors weren't supposed to know you—not like the real people you had to deal with every day of your life. They existed only when you needed them and faded away when you didn't.

Kate smiled and returned his nod.

"Just fine, Doctor."

"Good." He studied the form, his head doing little bobbing jerks. It reminded Kate of the way a pigeon's head moved when it walked. "So . . . you must be new to this area."

It was amazing how they always asked the same questions.

Accepted the same lies as answers.

"No. No, I've lived here almost all my life, but my regular doctor's office is becoming an HMO and . . ."

The doctor nodded, accepting the plausible lie. Shrugging, Kate made a great show of keeping the front of the disposable gown closed while at the same time smoothing down the thin paper sheet that covered her lower half. Her palms were already sweating.

And the doctor noticed.

"There's nothing to be nervous about," he said gently, fatherly, although Kate guessed he couldn't have been more than five years older than her own twenty-six years. "Finding a new doctor is probably one of the hardest things a person can do . . . and I should think it would be even more difficult for a woman. Sorry, I didn't mean to come off sounding like a politically incorrect poker just then."

Kate shrugged again and accidentally let the front of the gown gape open momentarily. It wasn't her job to tell him he was full of shit, even though he was. And not in it alone. Every new doctor she'd ever gone to voiced the same sentiment, as if lying naked with your legs spread while a strange man fiddled around was the worst thing a woman could suffer.

Jesus, it wasn't like they were *dating* or anything.

Kate noticed him chuckling and echoed it.

"But I can assure you I have never seriously injured anyone during a routine Pap smear," he went on. "Unless you consider that night watchman who happened to be bending over and . . . well, never mind. Besides that was before I got my astigmatism corrected."

This time Kate chuckled in earnest. He was funny! It was a shame she would never see him again.

"Thanks," she said. "I needed that."

Which was a lie. She didn't need that; she didn't need anything except the item he had just joked about . . . one of which was lying beneath the sterile drape on a tray directly across from her. A young nurse had brought it when she came to take Kate's temperature and blood pressure. Kate had convinced the woman the elevated readings were due to nerves.

"Okay, then," the doctor said, walking back to the door and opening it. "Let me just get a nurse in here and we can start. Now, why don't you lie back and relax?"

Kate swung her legs onto the table and lay back, but relaxing was out of the question. Her heart was pounding so hard she was surprised the doctor hadn't noticed. Keeping her eyes trained on the moronic poster of a smiling tabby kitten someone had taped to the ceiling at waist level so that it would be directly overhead during the pelvic exam, Kate heard the nurse's rubber-soled shoes squeak into the room at the same time a tap was turned on somewhere to her left.

The nurse who had taken her temperature appeared in Kate's periphery—as moral support and subpoenable witness should the matter of sexual misconduct be raised.

Kate took a deep breath and held it as the doctor threw back the gown's lapels to squeeze, poke, prod, and manipulate her breasts. His hands were warm and doughy.

"Fine," he muttered, first to one breast then the other. "Good. Any tenderness?"

"Only during my period," she answered automatically, realizing he would hear her only if she mentioned something negative.

"Fine. Good. Okay, this part's done."

He folded the gown back together, being very careful not to touch the same flesh he had, only a moment before, kneaded like clay, and accepted a white paper packet from the nurse. The words

"Gloves, surgical—one pair" were printed along the side the doctor tore open.

". . . ease."

"Excuse me?" Blinking, Kate glanced at the nurse and saw the reverse-color image of the kitten superimposed across her face. "I'm sorry, I didn't hear you."

"Scoot to the end of the table, please," she repeated—efficiently, effectively, and professionally detached as she extended the gynecological stirrups and positioned Kate's stocking feet in them. "There are hand grips on both sides of the table if you'd like something to hold on to."

Kate mumbled her thanks. At least she thought she did. She wasn't sure and didn't really care if she had or not. The doctor was smiling at her over the paper sheet covering her raised knees; one gloved hand already moving toward the hem.

"Okay, then. Spread your knees a little wider and try to relax. This won't hurt."

Kate caught her breath as the sheet fell back.

You gasp without thinking, raising your hips to meet him as he parts the tender folds of flesh and plunges into you. He is hard and cold as if he's been racing naked through freezing rain.

But that doesn't matter because at last you're together again.

The days and weeks of separation fade like a bad dream when you feel him grow . . . filling the emptiness inside you.

i'm here now . . . relax

You close your eyes and feel him begin to move—gentle, furtive strokes that you're not even sure you feel, not at first. Moaning, you wrap your legs around him and pull him closer until you're sure . . . until you can feel the hard knob of his cock against your cervix.

But now he knows what you're doing. He punishes you by stopping.

God, he can be so cruel.

It's the thing you love most about him.

are you all right? he asks, laughter in his voice.

You don't answer . . . wouldn't even if you had breath enough to form the words.

He teases you with his stillness until you open your eyes, until you succumb to the game he's playing. He smiles at the same time he thrusts forward . . . laughs when you whimper.

that's what happens to bad little girls, katie
and you're such a bad, bad girl
what am I going to do with you, katie
tell me

"Tell me if there's any discomfort," the doctor said, his voice muffled by the paper barrier between them. "But I have to say I don't think I've ever had a more relaxed patient. Just a couple more swabs and we should be all done. Nurse, may I have a slide, please?"

The woman left her position at the table long enough to get the sterile wafer of glass the doctor had asked for.

"Okay, Ms. Dylan, you may feel a little prick. . . ."

your prick's not that *little,* you gasp, afraid for a moment until you hear him laugh . . . feel the vibrations of that laugh through his cock.

He's not little at all.

Unwrapping your legs from his waist, he grips them just below the knees and holds them apart. You reach out to him, caress his face, and he takes your finger into his mouth, sucks greedily as he begins again to move.

Slowly.

Steadily.

The bones of his hips pummeling the backs of your thighs as he begins to move faster . . . faster . . . his hard flesh melting with yours . . . faster . . . harder . . . slamming himself against the closed door of your womb. . . .

Closed and sealed forever, you told him. No babies to tear the door off the hinges and make the tight flesh he loves go loose.

No babies to take his place.

He bites down on your finger as if he can feel the orgasm building inside you. Head tipping back against the clean white sheet, you suck air into your already bursting lungs and taste salt on your lips.

i'm almost there don't stop don't

"Almost finished," the doctor said. Kate's eyes popped open. "But I think we can make you a little more comfortable in the meantime."

The doctor released the speculum's lock, and the pressure in Kate's vagina instantly vanished.

No!

"Better?" he asked and, without waiting for an answer, handed the closed speculum, its chrome dulled by Kate's cooling juices, to the nurse as he stood up between his patient's parted legs. "Now, compared to the last bit, this should be a snap. Just relax."

Kate closed her eyes before the nurse dropped the speculum into the sterilizing bath.

don't worry, he tells you as he pulls back . . . pulls out, gently lowers your legs to the bed. *I won't leave you like this*

His fingers slip easily into the place just vacated by his cock, but it isn't the same . . . never the same and never as good.

why do you always do *this to me?*

you know why, katie, he answers, fingers caressing you from the inside.

they won't let me stay long enough to finish you the right way.

and i want to, katie

i really want to

i hate them, you tell him, closing your eyes when you see your own pain reflected in the polished metal of his face.

i know, katie

i know

but maybe someday

maybe

And you shush him, not wanting to hear the promises of a future that can never come true and focus all your attention on the slippery, silken touch of his fingers. He's good. A knuckle brushes against your clitoris and you jump.

oops, he teases, *sorry*

just try to—

* * *

". . . relax, Ms. Dylan, are you okay? You jumped. Did I hurt you?"

"N-no, doctor," Kate said from behind her closed eyelids. "Sorry. I-I just had a toe cramp."

"Oh, okay, I just wanted to make sure *I* didn't hurt you. Hang in there for a few more seconds. . . . We're . . . almost . . . finished. O . . . kay, now if you'll take a deep breath and . . ."

let it come, katie

let it come.

Your body jerks uncontrollably, plunging into the icy waves that sweep up over your legs . . . your belly . . . your breasts . . .

Gasping for breath you arch your back, pivoting your back off the thin mattress with only your shoulders, thrusting your hips against his questing fingers.

Hot and cold—fire and ice—you feel him growing warmer, incandescent as the orgasm builds.

Peaks.

Crashes down over you.

You shriek.

Exhaling slowly, Kate opened her eyes and smiled. She could hear the sound of her scream still vibrating off the room's disinfected walls and postpartum decor.

The giggle burst from her before she had a chance to stop it. The doctor was just standing there with his mouth hanging open and his fingers still crammed into her snatch, looking much less tanned than she remembered.

"You can let go now," she said, pointing between

her legs. He looked down and faded another degree. Kate shivered when he finally pulled out.

"Sorry."

She didn't look at him until she'd scooted her rump fully back onto the table and pulled her feet out of the stirrups. No man liked to be laughed at after the fact. Sitting up slowly, Kate tucked one side of the gown over the other and made sure that nothing was showing from the waist down either.

The show of modesty seemed to help the doctor recover some, if not all, of his composure. By the time she looked up, he'd disposed of the gloves and washed his hands, and his tan was back to full color.

"That's all right. Nothing to be embarrassed about." He spoke so quickly it took a minute for Kate to separate the words from the supposed sentiment. "Um, okay. All finished, ah . . . we'll have the results of your Pap smear back from the lab in three days, so you can call the office then and get the results. Okay."

He didn't move, and Kate didn't answer.

"Okay. Get dressed and, um, if you won't mind stopping by my office before you leave? Ah, I always, um, like to, ah, talk with my new patients. Just getting acquainted. . . . You don't mind, do you?"

Kate looked long and hard at her wristwatch, making a point. In truth, the office didn't expect her back for another forty-five minutes, but she didn't want *him* to think she was easy.

"Uh, no. But I—"

"Great, no more than fifteen minutes. Tops," the doctor promised quickly. "Okay, then, uh, my office is straight down the corridor, last door on the right. I'll be waiting."

He didn't so much leave the examination room as flee. This time Kate was able to catch the giggle before it got away.

"Must be a busy man," she said to the nurse.

The woman didn't look amused.

You sigh and feel it quiver all the way down to your groin. Sighing again, you pull your clothes around you, suddenly cold, and stare at the closed door.

When you close your eyes you can hear the echoes of the promise he made . . . always makes even though you both know it can never be kept.

one day, he promised, *one day i won't have to go and we'll be together always*

One day.

i love you, the echoes say, even though neither of you has ever said that to the other.

The blank door mocks you, but you lift your chin and touch the moist flesh between your legs. The warm softness of your finger feels almost strange after his cool hardness, but you adapt.

Closing your eyes and spreading your legs, you pretend it's his hand stroking you . . . making you tremble.

Your clothes fall away as ice and fire sweep through your body, and in the fading echoes you hear him call out to you.

"Ah, Ms. Dylan, please come in. Take a seat." Back to normal and smiling, the doctor gestured to the pair of low-back chairs in front of his desk, then swept the air in a wide arch. "My inner sanctum, so to speak."

Kate looked around the cracker-box-sized office and nodded. The overall effect, with its white painted walls, acoustical-tile ceiling, framed kitten prints, and dark furnishings, was similar to that of the examination room. Only less comfortable.

"It's very nice," she said and took the chair closest to the door. If the nurse hadn't been standing in the hall when she finally came out of the examining room (panting shallowly), Kate would have paid her bill and been halfway to work already. "I like the cat pictures."

"Thank you. Yes, most of my patients like them." He nodded and followed the visual path Kate had just taken. When his gaze finally came back to her, his eyes were cold. "But then, you're not really my patient, are you, Ms. Dylan?"

Kate crossed one leg over the other. The post-orgasmic tingle was almost gone. She sighed before answering.

"Well, I filled out all that paperwork when I came in, and the physician's referral service I talked to gave you an excellent recommenda—"

"You should have checked the service's fine print, Ms. Dylan. Then you would have found out that they also produce a list *for* physicians. Its main purpose originally was to prevent one doctor from accidentally infringing on another doctor's patient. However, with the growing problem of substance abuse, especially in prescribed medicines, all a doctor has to do, if he or she suspects that a patient is obtaining multiple prescriptions . . ."

Leaning back, the doctor picked up a thick sheaf of fanfold computer printouts and flapped it at her. "I hadn't intended to pry into this particular . . . area of your private life, Ms. Dylan, you have to believe me."

"Then what *were* you trying to pry into, Doctor?"

His tan took on a rosy glow. "Your . . . reaction in the examination room startled me, and I swear I was only curious to see if you were under another doctor's care. There have been cases where some women who, after experiencing an orgasm during a pelvic exam, make appointments with new doctors to reassure themselves that what they . . . that their arousal was not caused by an unconscious desire for their primary gynecologist.

"But you, Ms. Dylan . . . Jesus, I don't know whether to applaud your energy or your stamina. If the printout is accurate, you're seeing twelve gynecologists on a monthly basis, and you've had non-repeat visits with fifty-three others."

He dropped the printout on the desk and laid one hand over it. The gesture gave Kate the impression of a cleric about to offer a blessing.

"Ms. Dylan, a pelvic exam once a year is all a healthy woman needs. Unless there's a problem or, for example, during pregnancy when more frequent exams are required, then . . ."

Kate derailed his train of thought by gasping out the litany that had served her many times before when one of her many gynecological studs began sticking his professionalism in places where it didn't belong. Terms like "cervical polyps, "pre-cancerous conditions," "fibroid tumors," "hysterectomies," and "familial traits" fell from her lips like the names of the blessed saints.

Amen.

When she stopped, her mouth was drier than her panties.

Praise the Lord.

The doctor didn't look any more convinced than when she started.

"I can understand your concern, Ms. Dylan, and I have to warn you that I noticed scarring along the vaginal wall and a pronounced thickening of the cervix. Until I get the results back from the lab, I can't rule out the possibility that these may be indications of some specific pathology, but now that I'm aware of the number of exams you subject your body to, I can only assume . . ."

Yaddah, yaddah, yaddah. Kate glanced down at her watch and really checked the time. Unless he shut up within the next five minutes she wouldn't be able to get in a quick once-over rub in the ladies' room before having to turn back into a worker bee.

". . . thought about seeking professional help for your problem?"

Kate stood up so slowly she could hear the bones realign themselves along her spine.

"Just what are you implying, Doctor?" she asked, letting the tone of her voice allude to the fact that if he answered she'd make sure the only beavers he'd see from that point on would be in the zoo.

He took the hint. "Nothing! I'm only suggesting that you might want to talk to . . . someone about . . . this."

"I don't think so," Kate said as she walked to the door. Hand on knob, she turned and gave him a look she generally saved for gropers on the bus. "Besides, I don't see anything wrong with a woman trying to stay healthy. Do you?"

Steepling his fingers, the doctor placed them over his lips and frowned.

"Of course not, Ms. Dylan, but tell me, have you ever had a *normal* sexual experience?"

Kate smiled, twisting the knob but keeping the door momentarily closed. He had more balls than her usual stable of metal-wielding studs.

"By that I take it you mean with a man?"

"Yes," he answered, "with a man."

You watch the patterns in the ceiling change shape, trying to make out shapes the way you used to see images in the clouds when you were a child—trying because it's easier than thinking about what he's doing.

If he'd just let you turn off the lights it might be all right, but he wants to *see* you and that means you can see him.

But you don't want to, so you look for shapes in the ceiling while he grunts and sweats and pushes back and forth, in and out of you.

God, you wish it was over.

Making love—it sounded so wonderful, and the touching was nice. You liked that. The feel of his hands and lips on your naked flesh as you both undressed sent shivers into places you were never supposed to touch or even think about.

Yes, you tell yourself, *that* was nice.

And you really didn't even mind the pain when he parted your legs and crammed himself inside you. You still don't mind . . . not really . . . but you wish he would hurry up and finish.

So you watch the patterns in the ceiling and pretend you see a man riding a unicorn.

* * *

Kate opened the door and stepped into the hallway.

"Of course I have, Doctor," she said.

Kate cocked her head to one side and smiled at her own lopsided, elongated reflection in the curved metal. It was lying still and cool in her hands but part of her couldn't believe she'd taken it. An even bigger part didn't know *why* she'd taken it. Impulse? Maybe. Or maybe it was the doctor's final, insulting remark . . . as if she were some sort of sexual psycho or something.

Or maybe she'd finally decided to take matters into her own hands.

So to speak.

Kate laughed and hugged the cool metal to her breasts. It'd been so easy. A quick "Oops, I think I left something in the examination room"—and it was hers.

All hers.

She'd been lucky, just managing to get it into her purse before the next patient—a young woman with baby-swollen belly and milk-swollen breasts—waddled in.

Sorrys were exchanged, the payment for her visit made in cash, and Kate fled into the waning afternoon light.

"All mine," she whispered to it softly. Then a darker thought occurred. "At least I hope you're mine."

There'd been a total of three specula drowning in the purple sterilizing bath when she lifted the lid and they all looked alike—stainless-steel peas in a sanitized pod. Kate had played "eenie-meenie-mynie" then picked the topmost one, figuring it was most probably hers.

"Not that it really matters," she cooed to it. "I think we both could do with a nice hot bath. Then when we're all dry we can . . ."

Kate watched the blush spread across her flattened reflection and blew it a kiss. She'd phoned the office from the lobby of the Medical Arts Building, complaining about cramps and minor bleeding caused by a misguided vaginal swab and noting the lateness of the hour. "I thought I'd be done by now, but he poked me a little too hard, and . . ."

Sympathy poured through the phone line, that and a promise from the office gossip to tell "everyone" about "the bastard."

The perfect end to a perfect day. Well . . . not quite the end. Not yet.

Kate ran a thumb along the speculum's side until she came to the dilation wheel at the end. The size of a quarter, its edge had been scored for better traction, and just touching it made Kate's blood run hot and cold.

Fire and ice.

A drop of fluid that had somehow avoided capture by the discarded tissues and gum wrappers in her purse fell onto Kate's thumb like an amethyst tear.

Shivering, Kate wiped the drop into her skin.

"Definitely a bath first," she whispered.

Once at home, Kate laid the speculum back across her palms and carried it to the kitchen. She'd filled and set the spaghetti cooker on to boil a moment after she closed and locked her apartment door. The water was boiling—white, steam-filled bubbles churning the surface.

She'd decided against adding salt or vinegar. She preferred her lovers natural.

Taking a pair of rubber-handled tongs from the utensil drawer, Kate gently gripped the speculum just below its calibrated hinge, being careful not to scratch the mirror-smooth surface, and lowered it slowly into the steaming bath.

Thirty minutes, she decided, would be enough to kill anything that might have contaminated it. Besides, it had been soaking in a sterile solution when she liberated it. Boiling it now was just an added precaution, mostly to remove the lint and germs it might have picked up in her purse . . . and whatever trace remained of the other women who might have used it.

Kate watched the roiling water for another minute before heading for the bathroom. A quick shower and shampoo—maybe a little hand job to get the ball rolling—and she'd feel like a new woman.

A very horny new woman.

Fifteen minutes later she was beyond even that. Not even her usual method of tension release—for those times when she wasn't able to get to a doctor—brought any relief. Back pressed against the shower wall and standing on tiptoe, Kate had pulled the outer lips of her vagina apart until they throbbed and taken the full force of the shower's "massage" pulse right on the clit without getting so much as a warm glow.

The only chill she got was when the water went cold.

"Dammit to hell!"

It was as if her body had suddenly turned against her. Either that or it knew what it wanted and wouldn't settle for anything else.

Turning off the water, Kate patted the damp ringlets between her legs and stepped from the shower. She didn't bother drying off or throwing on a robe before hurrying to the kitchen. There was no need, her lover had already seen her naked . . . and wet . . . hundreds of times before.

He was waiting for her, a smile on his dolphinlike lips, as she reached over him to turn off the stove.

Using a dish towel as a makeshift pot holder, Kate carried the steaming pot to the sink and turned on the cold water tap. The exposed metal sizzled for only a few seconds.

While she waited for her lover to finish soaking, Kate rinsed off a wooden chopstick she'd gotten with a take-out order of kung-pau chicken and began wrapping one end in Saran Wrap. The chopstick was longer than the cotton swabs the doctors used. Sturdier, too. He would like that.

Her fingers shook as she worked the plastic into a knob the size of a golf ball.

He'd like *that* most of all.

You close your eyes and spread your legs, clutching him as he enters you.

He's warm, almost hot, and that startles you because your body remembers all the other times when he was so cold . . . so very cold.

Fire and ice.

because i'm yours now, he whispers, lying still, warm and hard between your legs.

only yours

And you answer, *yes*

only mine

You curl forward slightly and feel him grow, swell

until he squeezes all the emptiness from you. Your internal flesh bruises and you whimper, but you don't ask him to stop because this is what you've longed for.

i love you, one of you whispers.

Smiling, knees spread so wide they tremble from strain instead of passion, toes curling into the bed's silken throw, you take a deep breath and nod.

please

you're ready? he asks.

And you answer without words, push his massive shaft farther in and bite your lips to keep from crying out as your lovemaking begins in earnest.

i love you

This time there are to be no timid strokes. No teasing. No stopping. Red-tinted ecstasy dribbles from between your legs as he finally breaks down the door you've held closed for so long.

there'll be no babies, he promises you.

nothing to come between you and me

i love you

Pain-and-joy. Fire-and-ice.

You cry out, urging him on . . . driving him deeper and deeper until you miscalculate and he slips from your fingers . . . disappears into the cave of your flesh . . . his flesh becoming your flesh . . . your flesh swallowing him whole.

painandjoy fireandice

Ice-hot he comes before you, the sticky wash gushing from between your legs and spraying red hearts across the bed.

fireandice pain and joy

Groaning, your body heaves in agony, in ecstasy, as you come and come again, each orgasm building on the last until . . . until . . .

He comes again, you know he does, and your mixed juices flow from you in a crimson tide.

You curve your mouth into a dolphinlike smile and thumb the wheel on your jaw, opening your mouth so the sound of your love can fly free.

You're not surprised that it sounds like ice striking metal.

Shuddering, suddenly cold, you watch the bright white light darken and wait for the echoes to fade.

i

lov

. . .

CALL IT

Tom Piccirilli

Phone clamped to his ear, eyes dry and burning instead of filled with tears welling up from the depth of nausea, Cord thinks to himself now, You must make a choice.

You either chew through your tongue and throw up half your weight in bile and learn to live with your soul flayed, or you free yourself from rage and bitterness, take the knife in hand and kill a man you've never seen.

He continues to listen to them: he's been sitting in darkness for an hour, gripping the phone so tightly that the seams of the plastic casing are cracking in protest, holding the handset with a more human attachment than he's perhaps ever had yet with a woman. If he pushes his sanity aside another inch he can linger in the belief that he no longer exists; in the night, he can free himself from the betrayal of the body and the confines of the skull.

He listens to them making love, damning Diane for leaving the phone off the hook; he'd been sneaking in a brief conversation with her, planning the time and place of their next meeting, laughing as he shut off the light so he could pretend they were in the same room. She was nearly cooing at the comfortable intimacy they always found themselves in whenever their voices met.

And then, in a frightened, wheeling moment, she'd heard the front door opening, the amiable voice calling her name—her husband, Bennet, entering. Frantic and paranoid, the way she often got, she'd whispered in a husky, guttural manner, "He's home!" and shoved the portable phone down against the nightstand, failing to fully press the Off button.

So, Cord thinks, you have been huddled near the edge for a long time now. It is not entirely your own fault, this repression that has forced you away from the women who would have you and into the arms of those who can't give the love you need. There are other factors involved: you are a creature of designs created long before you were born, made by grandparents and parents, the death of siblings, events from your childhood, the nightmare of puberty, these scars on your neck. Still, it's time to take matters into your own hands. You are not completely a man, no, not yet. You are merely the lover, and that's not enough.

Cord curses his own perfectly honed imagination, his nearly photographic memory. He's viewing the scene from forty miles away. He knows every nuance. Dropping the phone, Di had turned to Bennet and said, "Hi, dear!" in a loud, hideously happy voice. The poor fool had answered with words of greeting, and laughter, so ignorantly blissful without the damning knowledge of who his wife actually was, and of what lurked in his bed.

Bennet doesn't possess imagination—Diane has

described him in great detail. He comes home every day at the same time, in the same manner, with the same hangdog look, too tired to think of anything besides dinner and a shower. But today, after her compressed dirty dialogues on the phone, she was inviting and excited, and so Bennet chuckled almost shyly, believing he was the reason.

Of course. Cord saw them clearly, as Di led her husband to the bed: she had quivered in the man's hands, and the bedsprings had snapped and twanged beneath them as they fell tumbling over each other, her laughter rising higher and higher, until she was keening like a madwoman. Bennet prefers missionary position, she's said, and he usually accepts her constraints of time and place for their lovemaking. But today was different.

Cord's hands are numb. The cheap plastic of the phone has splintered in his grip, driving a wedge-shaped shard through the meaty flesh between his thumb and forefinger. Blood is dripping along his arm; he smells the acrid odor in the dark without realizing where it's coming from.

You never realized you left her in this state, he thinks. You should have understood that she'd become as horny as you, and how she would use that urge—the urge *you* gave her—to satisfy a husband she does not love, whom she does not wish to touch. You finally see that you have helped their marriage immeasurably, and doomed yourself in the process.

The knife may be an answer. It wasn't a present from his father given to a boy while hunting through the woods, searching for animals to kill; his father was a pacifist who believed in the sanctity of life, but who was, oddly enough, always distanced from it. His father is another reason why Cord is on the phone. His dad's lack of affection was apparent in every movement, as if the man did not like being covered with his skin, did not have his fingers connected to his hands, his hands to the wrists. He walked as if he were actually much shorter than he was, like a child hidden inside a mass of malignant tissues; strange to learn that this was actually the case, with the cancer ripping through him from prostate to voice box.

The knife. It is just a steak knife. It will do the job as well as any other.

Diane and Bennet are rolling and smacking the headboard with rhythmic *ka-thunks*. His wet lips will leave silvery tracks down her breasts, his spit pooling with her sweat between them. His kisses are loud and obscene. Di doesn't kiss as much as she rends flesh, leaving blood-crusted marks behind. She begins to grunt, their rhythm speeding, grunting louder now, once, twice, and again, and then painfully so. Bennet mutters an apology, and they turn, the sheets shuffling along the contours of their bodies again. She is always cold and rarely makes love above the blankets.

Cord's breathing is ragged; he's aroused and disgusted at the warmth in his groin, the heat at the back of his brain. He's intoxicated by the pain, the sex, the smell of his own blood. This is not eroticism. This is not a fantasy suddenly and unintentionally sprung to life. He thinks, You are meeting your enemy. This is the ache that has been hiding beneath your head since first jealousies forced you into battle over girls you didn't even like. It was never a matter of love; it was always a matter of want. Wanting what another had. Unable or unwilling to acquire it yourself. You're a thief. You listen to them shifting positions, muttering indecipherable words, Bennet beginning to moan and even giggle, louder, now softer, now something else, and you know what she's doing. You've been there many times. You're there with her, with them, now, and you are not needed.

The phone is wet. Although he doesn't know it, Cord begins crying when Diane begins grunting. The darkness of the room is an envelope pressing against him. He isn't sure what it means to be alive anymore; he's been completely consumed by the phone, his rage, the lovemaking that is not his and yet somehow belongs to him. He is not quite as alive as he was an hour ago when he was talking to her; he's grasped at least a partial meaning of what it is to be dead. Listening to them, and knowing Di is at the moment moving from side to side and smiling every so often, her fingernails stroking, softly scratching the inner thigh, the soul.

He knows each of the motions and all of the sounds. The bed is not large enough to contain all the pillows she keeps there. Some fall over onto the floor, others get kicked into use, under her buttocks, propping her up, or where she can hide her face, leaning over.

This is not all your fault, but it is your responsibility, he thinks. If you had ever found the handle to grab hold of your own life, to take complete control, you would not have to do this. You would not have to kill a man whose wife you have been sleeping with for more than a year in order to save what's left of your sanity. The contradiction is apparent, but there's nothing you can do.

No, wait, there is something you can do. For your own sake; not for Diane, not even for Bennet, but for your own sake. You can give him a chance.

Fumbling into the kitchen, in the dark, Cord slams into the sink and works his way to the cutlery drawer. He reaches in and grasps a knife—which instantly becomes *the* handle, this knife—and flips it casually, like a coin. He flips it, catches it gently by the blade. Heads or tails. With the expressway still under construction, it will take him almost an hour of driving to reach Bennet. So give him a chance.

Cord throws the knife again and again, over and over until his right hand is bleeding to match the left. Heads or tails. You have the fortitude for suicide, he realizes. You can drive the blade into your own stomach and carve out your nausea. That is one strength you have not neglected.

Bennet is reaching climax, groaning louder in repetitive harmony as Diane is moaning with him; sound is as ultimate a turn-on for her as anything, the noise of lovemaking, the rasps and commands and pleas. She claimed she always faked her orgasms with Bennet, but hearing her now, Cord is not so sure. Perhaps she fakes them with you too, he thinks, and is somehow relieved by the idea. It makes him feel like her husband, like the complete man he isn't. Bennet's noises fill the phone as he nearly screams, and then clamps his mouth against her flesh. Diane sighs pleasantly. The knife comes down, goes up, down, more blood on Cord's hands already, goes up. Give the man a chance. Heads or tails. One or the other. You or the husband, he thinks. One of us has to go. You or him. Him or you. *Call it.*

DADDY'S DIRTY BOOKS

Michael Garrett

Don't worry. We won't get caught, as long as we're careful. Besides, Daddy won't be home from work for a couple of hours, so we've got plenty of time, I promise. But you need to help me watch out for him, just to be safe. He's usually in a pretty bad mood when he gets home. No, I don't think he knows I've been snooping around, but he still doesn't like for me to be in the house by myself. Since my Mama left, he's been trying to find somewhere for me to go after school, but none of the places will take a kid as old as me. Yeah, you can say that again. After-school care sucks.

Is your Daddy mean sometimes? Well, you know, like yelling and hitting and stuff? Sometimes I don't think my Daddy really wants me around. Yeah, he's been in a real bad mood since Mama ran off. Your Daddy's not like that? Well, you're lucky. Yeah, I . . . miss my Mama . . . but I try not to think about her. And, boy, Daddy's dirty books can get your mind off of *anything.* Except girls. His books make you think about them *a lot.* You won't believe it, man—I swear you won't.

He hides them right in here, in his bedroom. Yeah, I know it's dark, but that's the way Daddy likes it. Here, let me turn on the light. There, that's better.

Look, he keeps them in the top drawer of this chest of drawers, way up high. Wait a minute—I've got to stand on tiptoe to reach it. He puts them down under all his underwear and stuff. I gotta really stretch to find one. . . .

Hey, I think I got one. You won't believe it—I swear you won't.

Now wait a minute. Don't be so eager to look at the beavers. No, I can't let you hold it. If something happened to this book, my ass would be grass. But don't worry. You'll get to see everything. And, buddy, I mean *everything.*

Hey, look—the lady on the cover of this thing looks like she's part of a motorcycle gang or something. Except she's naked. And she looks kind of silly with that chain around her neck. It looks kind of like a dog collar. No, I don't think chains count as clothes. She's really naked all right. But you can't see any naked parts on the cover. Sure, if they showed you the naked parts on the cover, there'd be no reason to look inside. Or, yeah, you're right—there'd be no reason to buy it, either. *Bondage Babes* is a goofy name for a magazine, though, don't you think? Do you know what it means? No, I don't think it has anything to do with James Bond. Yeah, I know his movies have some nearly naked ladies, but they don't ever look like *this.* Maybe we'll figure out what it means after we look inside. Come on, let's see. I just found this stuff yesterday, and I didn't have time to look at it before my Daddy got ho—

Wait a minute—*what was that sound?* Oh, shit, Daddy must be home early. Oh, Jesus, I can't let him catch me. Peep through the window, will you, and see if his car's outside while I put this book back in the drawer? Whew! So it's just the neighbor across the street, huh? I almost peed in my pants! Okay, I'll get it back out, but maybe we shouldn't keep it out too long. I can't take any chances. Yeah, sure, that's easy for you to say, but it's my butt that'll be in a sling if he catches us, not yours. I can't help it if I'm scared about doing this. You don't know my Daddy like I do.

No, I told you already, I haven't looked at the books yet. I just found them yesterday when I was snooping around. I never got a chance to look for stuff like this when Mama was here 'cause she was always at home. But, man, when I found these books, I almost shit! I just got to see a couple of pictures before Daddy got home. Yeah, of course, you idiot—it shows the nipples and *everything!* I swear, I'm not shitting you. I had a boner all night just thinking about it. I bet you will, too.

See? Wow, look at those boobs. I'm already getting a stiffy. Whew! Your sister has big titties, doesn't she? Have you ever seen them? Yeah, I guess it wouldn't be as much fun to see your *sister's* titties. I'd like to see your sister's titties, though. Yeah, I know. I probably never will. Well, at least I can look at *these* when my Daddy's not home. Hey, watch it! I warned you not to touch the book. I don't want any fingerprints on it. If you don't back off, I'll have to put it up and look at it after you go home, okay?

Okay. Now *I'll* turn the pages. Just relax, will you?

Oh, man! Can you believe this? No, I've never heard of these things either. Look—they're stuck right through this lady's *nipples!* Do you think your sister puts these ring-things on her titties? Maybe *all* girls wear them, you know, like regular jewelry or something. Huh? No, I've never seen the inside of a real bra before. Have you seen your sister's? Well, the next time you get a chance, look inside it and see if there's something in there that these ring-things attach to.

Here, let me turn the page.

Wow! This one's even better—look, you can even see some hair down there! Oh, man, you're really funny—did you know that? 'Cause I can hear you breathing hard, that's why! Okay, okay. I admit it. I'm sort of out of breath myself. Man, this is almost too much. The other guys would never believe this. Whew!

Now, wait a minute. Are you shitting me? You mean you've never seen your sister's titties, but you've seen her *pussy?* Come on, I'm not stupid. That doesn't make any sense. How could you see her beaver and not see her titties?

Oh, I see. Okay. I guess if she was holding the towel too high, maybe she didn't know you could see her pussy. But anyway, look at this one! Wow!

Wait a minute! Oh, shit, look what you've done—you slobbered on my Daddy's book! It's leaving a spot. He's gonna *kill* me! Wipe it off. I'm not touching your spit. Clean it up yourself or I won't let you see the rest. Shit, man, be careful, all right? Jeez, I didn't think you'd be such a klutz.

Hey! Did you hear that? I think it was . . . *the doorbell!* Oh, shit! What am I gonna do? What? Oh, yeah. You're right. My Daddy wouldn't ring the doorbell. He'd just use his key. Whew! Let me go peep through the blinds and see who it is, okay? I'll be right back. No, of course I won't let anybody in. . . .

Hey, you know who I think is out there? Well, *excuse me* for whispering, dickhead. I don't want those guys on the porch to hear me. We've got to be extra quiet so they'll think nobody's home and go away. Anyway, I'm pretty sure they're cops. Maybe they found out where my Mama went. No, it won't do any good for me to talk to them. They won't tell me anything—I'm just a kid.

See, I told you. They're leaving already. They'll come back later and tell my Daddy, though. I hope they found her. . . .

Now let's see what else is in this book.

Hey, wait a minute, though. I just thought of something. You see that bed over there? That's where my Daddy *does it* to the girls he brings home. No kidding. Since my Mama left, he brings girls here all the time, sometimes even while I'm still awake. I can hear them *doing it!* I know they're doing it 'cause I can hear the bed bouncing up and down. No shit! Well, yeah, I peeped in at them one night, but they weren't doing it then. My Daddy was looking at this lady's pussy, though. Yeah, he looked funny with his naked butt sticking up in the air, and he was looking at her real close. It looked like his face was right up against her pussy. Wouldn't it be great to look at a real live beaver close up like that? Wow!

What'd you say? No, I don't think it takes very long to do it. It doesn't take my Daddy very long. The bedsprings just bounce for a few minutes before he's through. No, I can only hear him grunting and breathing hard. The girls don't make any sounds. I guess they're having a good time, though. Why else would they do it?

What? No, I don't think this book tells you *how* to do it. It just mainly shows you pictures of the parts you do it *with*. Well . . . I'm not really sure exactly how it's done. I know, I know, you have to stick it in and all. But I don't know how many times you have to stick it in before it's done. Hey, stop asking so many questions. I don't know any more about this stuff than you do. But if you find out first, you'll tell me, won't you? Since we're best friends and all? Just remember—I let you look at this book, so you owe me, right?

Yeah, I guess it's okay if you lay down on his bed for a minute. He never makes it up anyway. So how does it feel? Yeah, lots of ladies get screwed right there where you're laying. No, I don't know where he finds them, but he sure likes a lot of them. He don't have just one girlfriend. He likes them all. No, I don't guess Mama minds. She's not here to complain, is she? Hey, I'm not Sherlock Holmes or anything. I don't know why he has so many girlfriends. Maybe after you've done it to a girl once, that's enough. I guess I never thought about doing it to the same girl over and over again. What do you think? I'm not sure . . .

Anyway, let's look at some more. Wow! Can you believe that? I didn't know a pussy looked like that close up! Sure it's for real. I don't think they use special effects in books like this. It's the real thing, buddy. *The real thing.* Yeah, I guess it does look kind of like a walnut if you look at it a certain way. Hey, did you bring your magnifying glass? Aw, too bad. Anyway, look at how the sides of it kind of poke out, like those mud flap things in pictures of old cars. Did your sister's pussy look like that? Oh, yeah, right. You didn't see that part. Then you really didn't see her pussy, you wimp. You just saw the hair!

Now, wait a minute. Put your dick back in your pants. Are you a fag or something? Sure, I like to whack off, but not in front of an audience. That's a private sort of thing. Besides, you might shoot off all over my Daddy's book, and then I'd be in *really* deep shit. Look, I'm not kidding. I'll put the book away if you don't put your dick back in your pants. Aw, shut up, will you? I'd rather look at pussies than dicks any day. Especially yours. Besides, I'd *really* need a magnifying glass to see yours.

Okay, that's better. You know, I was just thinking. I wonder if all girls put these ring-things in their titties and pussies like these girls do. Yeah, but why would they wear stuff like that under their clothes where nobody'd see it? That seems pretty stupid to me. Say, do you know anybody we could ask? Oh, come on, man, you're nuts. Mary Beth Rogers? Yeah, I guess she's a possibility. Wade told me she puts out. If any girl we know wears these ring-things under her clothes, Mary Beth probably would. But if we're full of shit and we ask her about this stuff, she'll laugh at us and tell *everybody*. No, we better ask somebody else.

Aw, come on, man. You're nuts! Danny Bonman? He doesn't know as much about this stuff as we do. He still says "dookey" instead of "shit." Haven't you heard him? Yeah, well, we better think of somebody else.

What? Now I *know* you're crazy. How could I ask my *Daddy?* We don't talk about stuff like that. And besides, if I asked him, he'd know I've been looking at his dirty books. Boy, sometimes I wonder about you. Can you chew gum and whack off at the same time? Why don't you ask your *own* Daddy? Or better yet, ask your *Mama.* At least you've still . . . got one.

No, I'm all right. I just miss her, that's all. I never thought she'd run away and leave me like that. My Daddy never loved me like my Mama did. He never spent much time with us. Maybe that's why Mama left. It's funny, he's at home more now than he was when Mama was here. But he's always bringing his girlfriends over, so I still don't get to be with him much. Shit, I don't *want* to be with him.

Come on, we better look at some more of this before he gets home. Here, let me turn the page—oh, gross! It's a picture of a *dick!* I can't believe my Daddy has a book with a *dick* in it. Yeah, sure, it's big, but it's still a *dick.* I would've ripped it out or marked over it with a Magic Marker or something if it was *my* book, wouldn't you? But look—this dick has a ring in it, too. Oh, man, that's scary. Do you think someday we'll have to put rings through our dicks, too? Maybe that's something you do when you get married. No, don't pull yours out again. I know there's a lot of loose skin down there, but I still don't like to think about putting a ring through my wiener.

This is disgusting. I'm gonna put this book back and see if I can find another one—one *without* dicks. I sure hope your slobber spot dried up good. I'll just slide this book back under my Daddy's underwear. Hey, what's this? Man, this is really weird. Come on, buttface—I'm no idiot. I know it's handcuffs. What else has he got in here?

Uh-oh. Look. It's a box of those ring-things. Maybe

they're my Mama's. Or maybe my Daddy has rings in his dick. No, I've never seen him close up. Come on, do you ever try to look close up at your Daddy's dick? I didn't think so. Wow, this is really crazy. No, he's not a cop or a security guard or anything. He reads electric meters at work. Yeah, no telling what else is in his drawer. Let me see. Here's a pair of pliers. And hey, here's a stack of pictures. My Daddy got this neat new Polaroid and—

Oh, God. Oh, Jesus. You've got to swear not to tell anybody about this. Oh, man. I feel sick. Hey, I'll knock your teeth out if you don't shut up. I can't help crying. It's my Daddy that did this stuff. Well, he must have. He took the pictures, didn't he? Look—some of them were made right here in this bedroom. These pictures are his, all right. But, man, they're really gross. No girl would let somebody do that to her. See? These girls are handcuffed to the bed so they can't move. And look at those little trickles of blood running down from the rings and how their faces are all wrinkled up. He's hurting them. *He put these ring-things on them while they were tied up!* Yeah, it feels kind of creepy to me, too, to be in this room. Sure, I bet the girls screamed, but see? He's got something tied around their mouths so they can't make much noise.

No, man. They're not just play-acting in these pictures. These are for real—can't you tell? Boy, I'm getting sick. I can't believe my Daddy would do this. I might throw up. I touched the handcuffs my Daddy used to tie those girls up with.

Hey, look, you can't tell anybody about this, okay? No, I don't know how he got away with it. Do you think he . . . *killed* them afterward? Well, you know, they would've called the cops if they were still alive when he got through, wouldn't they? Hey, shut up, will you? I can't help it if I'm crying. *It's my own Daddy that did this stuff.* He might do something to me like that someday. And . . .

Oh, shit. Why did you have to say that? No! *No!* Put that one back. I don't want to see it. The lady in that picture does *not* look like my Mama. No, you can't look at it closer. It's time for you to go home. Don't say that again. Hey, you're no detective. You don't know anything about this kind of stuff. *That's not so!* My Mama just ran off and left us. I know she did. Well, I don't know why she didn't take me with her. Maybe she'll come back and get me. But I know Daddy didn't do nothing to her. He's my *Daddy.* . . . Well, sure, the cops talked to my Daddy after she left. They still come around, too, like they just did, but they're trying to find out where she went, that's all. They don't think my Daddy did anything to her. But, yeah, I guess you've got a point. If the cops saw these pictures, they might think he did something to my mama. Yeah, I know. They might still be checking him out in secret. You know, like that undercover kind of stuff. Shit, if he hurt these other ladies, he probably hurt my Mama, too. Yeah—oh, God, I'm shaking. You're right—that one does look kind of like my Mama. It's hard to tell, with her face all twisted up like that.

Oh, God, I miss her. I can't help it if I'm crying. Yeah, I know what you mean, but if I show these pictures to the cops, Daddy'll know I'm the one that found them. Even if he didn't kill my Mama, he'd kick my butt for giving these to the cops. And if he goes to jail, what'll happen to me?

Move out of the way. I'm gonna throw up. I've got to go to the bathroom. . . .

Hey, thanks for helping me. Oh, man. Will you flush that for me? Yeah, I know I'm shaking. Wouldn't you be? I don't feel so good.

I miss my Mama. You don't know how lucky you are to have a Mama. And my own Daddy took mine away. He killed her. I know he did. That's why he hasn't missed her. And that's why he brings these ladies here. And those cops keep coming back to catch him.

Wait a minute. I've got to splash some water on my face. Yeah, that feels better.

Whew. Well, wait a minute. Let me catch my breath.

Okay. I think I know what I've got to do. I'm gonna shoot him. See? He has a gun in his closet. I found it yesterday when I was snooping around. It's kind of heavy, though. But if I hold it with both hands, like this, I can point it pretty good. No, it's *not* a stupid idea. How would you know what you'd do? Your Daddy didn't kill your Mama. And besides, my Daddy might kill *me* if I don't kill him first! He might put those ring-things on me. Don't you understand?

Oh, man. *He killed my Mama!*

Of course I'm sure. You're the one that said so in the first place. You said the lady in this picture looks like her. Why are you acting now like maybe it's *not* her? Why can't you make up your mind? You've been watching too many of those cop shows on TV. Well, maybe the cops *would* need more proof, but I know he did it. Mama would never just leave me like that. I know she wouldn't. And I think this is *her* . . . in this picture. Oh, man. She looks so sad. She looks like she's hurting so bad. I've seen my daddy hit her. He did it lots of times. I always cried when he did. I always wanted to hit him back for her. And now I'll kill him. I swear, I will.

Leave me alone, will you? Stand back. I've got to hide this gun in my room. I'll shoot him tonight. While he's asleep. I swear I will.

Back off, dammit! I do too know what I'm doing! I'm *not* crazy. And you can't stop me. Let go, you idiot! It's got bullets in it! I know it does 'cause I checked it when I found it. Now stop it, dammit. Don't you understand? Get away. I *told* you why I'm doing it, and there's nothing you can do about it. I don't care what the cops will do.

Don't try to jerk it out of my hand like that. It's dangerous. Anyway, you're supposed to be my friend. You're supposed to be on my side. Hey! Let go. Quit! Turn loose! No, wait. Don't grab it there! Watch out! *Don't touch the trig—*

RESTIN' PIECE

Nat Gertler

"Problem was that Myron died in the saddle," said the man in the cowboy hat. "Your time comes when your time comes, and when his time came, he was in *flagrante delicto,* if you know what I mean."

"Came and went, eh?" I'd paid a beer for this story. I figured that entitled me to a few questions, even rhetorical ones.

"No, that was just the problem. He went *before* he came. He was in the middle of humping ol' Maddy Conroy, used to live down on Third, when his ticker gave out on him. No surprise. Myron always had been a big beer and pizza fan, and had the gut to show it. Two-pack-a-day smoker, too. Myron used to laugh about how he'd outlive us all, but there he was, fifty-two years old, face down into Maddy.

"Now, I don't know if you've ever been interrupted just when it's gettin' good, but I have, and let me tell you that it's no fun. You walk around knowing that you got unfinished business, and you just can't rest until you drop your seed somewhere, if you get me. And it's no good taking matters into your own hand. That may release some of the stress, but it doesn't remove any of the *need.*" He stressed this last word with a poke at the table.

I knew what he meant, of course, thanks mainly to the time I'd discovered that a particular young lady had a husband, a discovery that was made at a moment and in a manner that was most inopportune.

He continued. "We buried Myron a couple days later, nice little funeral, he had some old army benefits that covered most of the cost. I was one of the pallbearers—was his best friend, don't you know?—and I could swear that the casket was shaking just a bit as we carried it, but I figured it was just one of the other guys goofin' around, and didn't give it no never mind.

"Of course, I started giving that some second thoughts when we found the dirt all pushed aside from Myron's grave and his casket empty the next day. Some folks just thought that we'd had grave robbers of some sort, but that's ridiculous, 'cause we've never had grave robbers, and even if we had, why'd they rob Myron's grave? Myron didn't have anything while he was alive, he sure didn't have anything when he was dead, except maybe that pine box, and that was still there.

"So I can't say that I was surprised when I saw Myron heading up to my front porch. Shocked? Hell, yes, I was shocked. I make a point of being shocked whenever the dead come a-visitin'. But not surprised at all.

" 'Dan,' he says, 'you gotta help me. I got the itch so bad, I mean *bad.* My soul can't rest till I get some.' He looked pretty bad, which isn't surprising, because he didn't look so hot even when he was alive, and a few days of death'll hurt even us good-lookin' folks." He elbowed me at that one, part of the comradeship that one quickly develops with the man who is buying the booze.

"'What do you want me to do about it?' I asked. I hoped he wasn't asking *me* for anything, if you know what I mean. I'm not into guys, even the ones that are alive. I may do some crazy things at times, but homo-necrophilia goes beyond even my line. Myron was never that kind of guy when he was alive, but with the desperation on his face, I wouldn't've been surprised if he'd been willing to settle.

"But he said it wasn't like that. He needed to find a lady, and in his current condition, there was no way it was going to work. Nobody'd want a stiff with a stiffy. He said that, too, 'stiff with a stiffy.' Always had a way with a joke. So he wanted to see if I could recruit someone for him, or something.

"Now, I'm always willing to help a friend, but these days I'm having enough trouble finding someone for myself—not that the girls don't like me, but, you know, all these diseases and stuff, it's just that much harder. It'd be harder yet getting someone for some-one else, and if I found someone good for him, well, once she found out what was going on, she'd probably pull out and never want to deal with me again. And if she *didn't* want to pull out, well, I sure wouldn't want to deal with her ever again!"

"Heck," I interjected, "maybe if she liked it, she'd never want you again. Maybe once you've been with a dead guy, you never go back!"

Dan grinned. "Could be right at that. Never underestimate the power of the deceased. Anyway, I tell him this. I tell him I can't get him laid. 'But,' I go, thinking of something, 'there is always another option, if you're real desperate.'

"'Damn straight I'm desperate!' he shouted. Saw the inside of his mouth when he did that. Looked kind of blue. Ugh! Anyway, I suggest to him that we go into the city, go up to Magnolia Street—there's a corner there where ladies, pros, hang out. He laughed at that—he'd gone there enough times when he was alive, didn't see no shame in going there when he was dead.

"So we headed out to the city in my limo. Oh, didn't I mention that? Yeah, I used to have a one-man limo service. Didn't make a ton, but I did okay. We got enough funerals, proms, stuff like that to make it worthwhile, and you get most of your time free. Plus, sometimes you get someone who just hit the lottery or something and wants to look the part, and they usually tip really good, because they don't know just how much of their money'll go to Uncle Sam.

"We get a hotel room, a good one. Most people never get to do one last thing for a good friend, and this was my chance. It was on my card, although if we'd thought about it, we mighta put it on his. After all, it probably takes a couple of days for them credit-card people to find out about a death and cancel the card, though it would've been fun to see what they thought when they found out that he kept using the card after he died. Maybe that'd be a new product, the you-can-take-it-with-you card. American Express, don't leave this plane without it—something like that. So anyway, we get him up to the room without anyone catching on he's dead, and then I head out to get his hooker.

"Jeez, you should've seen those girls running up when the limo slowed down. Don't know if they thought a limo meant serious money, or if they just wanted a chance to ride in the back. So I talk to a couple of the cute ones. Kind of fun not having to worry about him catching something, y'know, 'cause he's dead and it's too late for him to get anything.

"So I warn them that this client, he's a bit special, and most girls wouldn't want to sleep with him for anything. One of them actually steps back at that, doesn't want in, but this other one, she cocks a grin on her face. 'Wasn't for men like that, we'd all be out of business. You got the money, I got what he wants.' She weren't bad looking, either, looked kind of solid, didn't over-make-up. She'd clearly been doing this a while.

"She climbed in the back, and I rolled down the divider window so we could talk a mite as we drove. Real businesswoman. Talked about how she'd had plenty of guys who didn't think they could get it any other way—really fat guys, cripples, burn victims. Mostly, they treated her real nice, and she liked doing them, because it was like she was doing some good. It was usually normaller guys that made her job tough, 'cause if they couldn't get it for free, it was 'cause they were assholes.

"She said her name was Liz, which was kind of nice. It probably wasn't her real name, but at least it wasn't one of those Brandee-Candee-Dominique deals that most of those girls will try to pass off on you. It was something that you could call somebody in the middle of a sentence without feeling like a damn fool. So anyway, we get to the hotel, and I give her this pile of twenties. Wanted to be sure she felt well paid when she saw what she was getting into. Besides, she was definitely earning the money.

"So I wait down in the limo while she goes up. I don't want to be there, of course. So I'm there for fifteen minutes, and the cops pull up. I pull away then; if there's anything going on, I don't want to have to explain why I'm there with a dead guy.

"Turns out what happens is that she got into the room, and when he told her just what the situation was, she was so shocked, she screamed, 'You're dead!' But she acclimated to that—that's a pro, I tell ya—and she and Myron started to go at it. Turns out, Myron is kinda loud. So the dame next door misinterpreted, called the cops.

"Bad enough, eh? Gets worse. Cops hear that someone's being murdered in the next room, they storm Myron's hotel room. This rookie, having heard that someone was being killed and storming in to find a man on top of a woman, panics and shoots his head clear off. Wasn't hard, probably was brittle after being dead a few days.

"Nothing much came of it. When the cops found out that Myron had already been dead, they weren't sure what to do, but then they realized that if he was already dead, then the rookie didn't actually kill anyone, and it was best off being left at that. Liz, bless her soul, never said a thing. But the locals here thought it was pretty darn weird that the missing body was found in a hotel in the city. Only a couple of us went to the funeral."

* * *

The cowboy was quiet, and his glass was empty. I didn't think that those two items were linked, but I also felt that the story wasn't over, so I put some more money on the bar to get another dose of tongue lubricant.

"Waiting was tough. I knew he'd be coming around eventually, because his business still wasn't finished, and this was twice that he'd been interrupted, so he might be even worse off. I didn't sleep much; I don't know 'bout you, but I have trouble resting when I know that the dead are due to come visiting!

"It took him three days to make it back this time. Guess it took his body a while to get used to being detached from the head. There was a knock on the door, so I answer it, and there he was standing, one arm carrying what was left of his head. His face was still basically intact, so he could talk, and the first thing Myron said was 'Dan, I still got a problem.'

" '*You* got a problem?' I says to him. 'You just need to get laid. I'm the one what's got horny dead people comin' to visit at the wee hours!' He laughed at that, kinda. Guess it's hard to do a real laugh with a head that ain't attached. Or maybe it wasn't as funny as I thought."

" 'I tried everything I can think of,' he says. 'Even tried holding my head with both hands and givin' myself a hummer. But, man, I taste awful. Must be the decay, 'cause girls sure loved to lick me like licorice when I was alive.' I doubt that that was quite true, but it seemed a moot point now.

"So we sat there, thinkin' as hard as we could, figurin' a way to get him out of his dilemma. He kept shiftin' his head from arm to arm, tryin' to come up with a better thinking position, but most of his 'ideas' were merely names of women who wouldn'ta touched him even when he was alive. Let's face it, no gal would be willing to do him, and he wasn't about to force himself on anyone."

"Dead men don't rape," I said, repeating something I'd heard in a movie.

Dan blinked at that, considering it carefully. "Can't say if I know that's true. I guess there're some guys who'd resort to it if they found themselves in Myron's position. But while Myron was an asshole, and I really wouldn't recommend leaving him alone in the room with a pile of your money, he wasn't scum. Mighta gotten a girl good and liquored up before making his move, and maybe tried pretty hard to get her to turn a no into a yes, but if he couldn't, he'd just leave it at that."

I sucked on my lip for a second. I'd had a friend in college who hadn't seemed at all like an asshole, but who I later found out didn't know where to draw the line. I never could reconcile that.

He continued. "Finally, a plan came to me. It was time to head into the city again. First stop was this store on Jefferson Boulevard called Kinks and Queens. I'd never been there before, but I'd heard other people joke about it. Said they had every kind of sexual device imaginable, and I'll be damned if they didn't have even more than that. Some of those things in there, I really never want to know what a person might use them for, if you get my drift. But, hey, whatever works for folk, right? Anyway, they had this whole bodysuit made out of that stretchy rubber stuff, you know, latex. It was kind of like one of them black diver suits, only it didn't have any face opening except for some airholes. And it didn't have separate slots for the fingers and toes, just covered them all like a mitten. But it did have a tube for Mr. Johnny Wiggle, and that's what counted.

"Now, I know what you're thinking—we just gotta find someone who's into that rubber stuff and get her to have sex with Myron, and she'll never see that he's dead. But that wouldn't work, 'cause Myron's body was long since cold, so she woulda known that something was wrong right away. I'd already thought of that."

"Good thinking," I replied.

"In a messy situation like this," he said, "you can't afford to do anything but! We'd already messed up once. So anyway, he put this outfit on his body. He didn't stick his head in the head, though. We just left that in the back seat of the limo. I got a condom, not one of them lubricated ones, and blew it up like a balloon, tied it in place of the head on the rubber outfit, and Magic Markered a smily face on it.

"Couple blocks away was one of them sex show places. I don't mean a tittie bar, but one of those theater places where the girls actually diddle themselves onstage. It was pretty late, and the talent they get at those places in the wee hours tend to be, well, bowsers. So I go to the manager and tell him that I've got a bit of a special request. Try to pass myself off as a guy with a unique kink—and for $150 between the manager and the performer, they agreed to help meet my tastes.

"So during the show, I put the body on a handcart and wheel it into the theater. I laid him down on the stage, peter-up. In front of half a dozen drunks, the nude lady—said her name was Tiff Fanny, yeah, right—she rode my friend. The drunks actually lit up at that, because it was somethin' that at least they didn't see every night, a lady riding a full rubber form. She bucked and gyrated on it for only a couple of minutes. And then . . . the balloon head popped! The noise shocked her, she sat up real quick, and the rubber dick fell out. She tried to mount it again, and then she signaled for me to come over. Know what she said? 'I'm sorry, mister, but I think I broke your doll! The dildo don't stick up no more!'

"I couldn't laugh, 'cause she mighta got suspicious, but damn! It was hard holding it in. I felt tears coming out instead, that's how hard it was.

"I told her it was okay, and wheeled Myron back out to the limo. I put the body in the back, with the head—and it was smiling. Smilin', and finally quiet."

The cowboy started fumbling through his pockets. The three drinks he'd downed at my expense had had a clear effect. I thought he was looking for his keys, so I offered to call him a cab.

He laughed at that. "Don't worry about me. I live just down th' street an' over a couple blocks. I'm walkin' home. But there's somethin' I gotta show you first." His eyes lit up as his fingers landed on what he'd been looking for.

"I put Myron back in the ground, of course. That's where dead people live." He paused. "Well, they don' live, but you know what I mean. Anyway, I hit the lottery, the four number one, a week after I took care of him. I figured it was some kinda payback for handlin' the matter, you know what I mean? So I took some of the money I won, and I bought him a gravestone. After all he'd been through, I figgered he oughta have somethin' special for it."

The cowboy pulled his hand from his pocket and dropped a photo on the bar in front of me. It was a picture of a headstone, simple but nice. It was the emphasis in the inscription that made it unique.

It read: "Here lies Myron Gillis, truly *laid* to rest."

FLESH AND BLOOD

Elsa Rutherford

Papa has had a stroke, and sometimes I can go up to his room and look in on him, fluff his pillows, change the TV channel for him, do little things like that, but sometimes I just can't. It's not the way he looks lying there, partially paralyzed, in his big old four-poster that keeps me away. Or the half-shut unmoving green eye and the mouth drawn to one side, rendering his speech thick and mumbling. It's that I hate him with every fiber of my being.

It's true I loved him once, not so long ago. Loved him dearly, and was very proud of him. Everyone said Victor Courdeville had a sterling reputation as one of the finest judges ever to take the bench in New Orleans. So, naturally, I admired and respected him for that. But my feelings changed, changed drastically, after I learned the shocking truth about my own flesh and blood.

Of course I might never have known the truth if

Rusty and I had not made love that Saturday morning last summer.

It was the first time for both of us, on a morning that was as sweetly pristine and full of promise as only a Saturday morning in summer can be. In Rusty's room in the old cottage at the back of our property, where Terrebonnes have lived forever, we entered heaven with such urgency we did not care that we might have the devil to pay. And it seems to me, as I look back, that countless generations of Terrebonne ghosts must have been watching us that morning. But whether they were laughing or crying, I do not know.

Louie was up at the main house as usual, doing his butlering and trying to tell Stella Maris how to run things, and so Rusty and I were alone in the cottage. (Rusty's mother died when he was a tiny baby, leaving only Rusty and Louie to live in the cottage. My own mother died when I, too, was a baby. That's just one of the things Rusty and I had in common.)

I was used to running in and out of the cottage, had done it all my life, so I just barged on in, barefoot and carefree, and wandered through the little house looking for Rusty. To my surprise, I found him still in bed. Ordinarily, at that hour of the day, he was up and ready to start working in the garden or mowing the lawn or washing and waxing Papa's big Lincoln, his normal Saturday chores. But that morning he'd slept late and was lying in bed under a jumble of covers.

He rolled over and smiled up at me. His green eyes were shining, and his smile was as bright as the sunshine that was spilling through the windows and into the room.

"Get up, lazybones," I said, giving him a punch on the arm.

Rusty laughed, reached out for me, and pulled me down to him. I was laughing, too, my long blond hair falling into my eyes as I tumbled into the cozy nest of his bed and landed on top of him. As I fell, the full skirt of my sundress flounced out and exposed a lot of bare thigh and leg. Not very decorous for a well-bred young lady, I know, but Rusty and I had been so familiar and comfortable with each other for so long, pals since childhood, that we thought nothing of me falling into his bed with my skirts hiked up.

The smell of the rumpled bed linens enveloped me at once. It was the smell of line-dried sheets and of Rusty himself, as fragrant as ripe melons or new-mown grass. I inhaled deeply, greedily, suddenly so insatiably hungry for that smell that I wanted to rub my face in it.

Rusty and I rolled around in the bed, romping and teasing just as we'd done all our young lives, and for those first few moments our roughhousing was as innocent and childlike as ever. But when Rusty playfully snatched the covers from between us and I saw that he was naked and felt his bare skin against my own skin, my breath caught in my throat and an electric shock coursed through me. I had never seen any man or boy totally naked before, had never seen *down there.*

For an instant, Rusty appeared mortified. I think he'd completely forgotten he was naked beneath the covers and was shocked and embarrassed by what he'd done. But before he could cover himself again, something came over me and I was touching him with the tips of my fingers, beginning just below his throat and slowly tracing down to his flat, muscled stomach. To my amazement, as I trailed my fingers down Rusty's skin, I saw the organ between his legs stiffen and swell, and he made a choking sound in the back of his throat.

Before I knew what was happening, before either of us knew, I think—some powerful force had swooped down and taken control of us—Rusty was kissing me and pressing his body against mine and I was kissing him and pressing back. It was wild and strange and totally new to both of us.

Yet, in another way, it seemed both inevitable and natural, which was not so strange, given that, from the beginning, the circumstances of our lives had set us on a fateful course that had impelled us toward this very moment. No longer children, our budding sexuality was on the verge of full bloom, and indeed it was the most inevitable thing in the world that the two of us, who'd always been so close, would collide.

But natural? That, it was not. It was, in fact, wholly unnatural and a grievous sin. The straight of it is that black blood flowed in Rusty's veins and white blood flowed in mine. For over two hundred years, in what is now known as the Garden District of New Orleans, Rusty's family, the Terrebonnes, have faithfully served my family, the Courdevilles. They've attended us "from time immemorial," as Papa used to say. So Rusty and I had absolutely no business being in bed together, doing what we were doing.

We knew, of course we knew, that we were committing a terrible and unnatural sin. But just how terrible and how abominably unnatural we had no idea.

At that moment we did not care. That's the straight of it too. We did not care.

When his rigid sex touched the soft outer folds of my own sex for the first time, touching me with an insistency that was deliciously thrilling, I could think of nothing but wanting that feeling to last forever. The look I saw on Rusty's face, the look I now know was pure desire, heightened my own excitement.

I trembled and clung to him, mewing like a kitten, as he spread my legs and opened my folds. Calling out my name with great fervor—Caroline! Caroline!—he entered me. And, with one deep thrust, impaled me.

Suddenly I was dying. He was killing me. And there was nothing delicious about it. It seemed beyond belief that Rusty, my sweet Rusty, was causing me such intense pain. I struggled and cried out and hit him with my fists, but my thrashing anguish seemed only to spur him on.

At Saint Margaret's School for Girls we'd whispered and giggled about sex behind the nuns' backs, but, in truth, we were woefully ignorant on the subject, sheltered as we'd been by parents and teachers who still believed that sexual naïveté produced nice chaste young ladies. What Stella Maris had told me when I got my first period had added little to my enlightenment. She'd mumbled something about men and women sleeping together to make babies, but I couldn't see what that had to do with my bleeding and the cotton pads she'd given me to absorb the flow. I certainly was not prepared for the pain I felt as Rusty drove into me.

But then an incredible thing happened. After Rusty's initial thrusts, something seemed to give way inside me, to open up, allowing him to penetrate even deeper, and after a few more long-drawn-out seconds of agony, the pain evolved into a sensation that was mostly pleasure, tinged with just a tiny trace of oddly thrilling pain. And it came in waves. Waves of indescribable ecstasy. I moaned and bucked and clawed my nails into Rusty's back.

Time passed, aeons passed, as we rode wave after wave of pleasure, until, as I hung suspended on the crest of the highest wave, a spasm of the most intense, breathtaking rapture shuddered through me. At almost the same instant, with one fierce, final thrust, Rusty exploded inside me, his body aquiver with his own pleasure.

We lay spent at last but still holding on to each other, like survivors in the aftermath of a storm, astonished and awestruck by what had happened, and frightened by more than the bloodstains we saw on the sheets.

"I'm sorry I hurt you. I didn't mean to," Rusty said in a low, troubled tone.

I propped up on my elbow and looked at him. With his brown skin damp and gleaming like polished stone, his eyes so green, and that peculiar copper cast to his dark, kinky-curled hair, I thought he was remarkably handsome. "I love you, Rusty Terrebonne," I said, "and you love me, too. We always have and we always will."

He frowned. "I know, Caro. But we're not supposed to. Especially not like . . . this. It's wrong. Awful wrong. What if they found out?"

Which "they" he meant went without saying. "Papa would lock me up and throw away the key, and Louie would beat you within an inch of your life," I answered. "But they won't find out. We won't tell a soul."

It also went without saying that if what we'd done

ever became common knowledge, we'd have more than our fathers to worry about. A black boy who had carnal knowledge of a respectable white girl was just asking to be strung from the highest tree in the middle of the night.

"It was a mistake, and we won't ever do it again," Rusty vowed.

"No, we mustn't," I agreed.

But even as we were telling each other we wouldn't repeat our mistake, Rusty was stroking my hair and looking at me like he wanted to do it again right then, and I knew with certainty that we were totally helpless to stop what we'd begun. I knew we'd be tempted every time we were alone together and that it would be a temptation we'd be powerless to resist. And that's just how it was from that day forth.

We took our stolen moments whenever and wherever we could. In the storage room off the garage, in a bower of honeysuckle in the orchard, and sometimes, like the first time, in the cottage, and once we crept up to the attic of our ancient French manor house and did it right over everybody's head. We were on fire for each other, and our hearts and bodies demanded that we join together and worship at that fire.

Now I spend most of my days in my room. Sometimes I wander out to the kitchen to see what Stella Maris is up to, and sometimes I take little Gabriel out to our dense, rampant garden in the late afternoon, after the heat of the day has passed, and I sit on the stone bench beneath the mossy oaks, giant magnolias, and climbing vines heavy with blooms. Breathing the almost too-sweet perfume of the lush flowers all around me, I ponder many things.

I don't mind the long hours I pass in my room. I read—romantic poetry, mostly—and I take Rusty's picture from the bureau drawer where I keep it hidden and look at it, feeling both joy and shame. And grief, too. But I know that someday the grief will pass and everything will be fine again.

In my room there's hand-painted French wallpaper and antique Parisian furniture brought over by ship two hundred years ago. I have a lace-draped canopy bed that once belonged to my great-great-grandmother, or some such long-ago forebear. And it was only three months ago that I lay in that lacy bed while Stella Maris pressed a wadded towel to my lips to stifle my screams so Papa wouldn't hear—though Papa knew soon enough, of course—and Louie knelt between my legs to bring my son, Gabriel, into the world. I named him Gabriel because, in spite of everything, he seemed like an angel to me.

After Stella Maris cleaned up the baby, wrapped him in a knitted shawl, and laid him in my arms, she cut her eyes at Louie and I saw the look that passed between the two of them. From that look, I knew they knew.

When Gabriel was only a few hours old, Rusty slipped into my room. Smiling, but looking a trifle uneasy, he said, "I heard." And I knew it must have been from Louie, and I wondered what exactly Louie had said to him, but I didn't ask.

Rusty kissed me and he kissed the baby, and proudly said, "That's the prettiest baby I ever saw. Nearly as pretty as his mama."

"He's beautiful," I said, "but he doesn't look like me. He looks exactly like you." And he did. Same skin and hair and eyes. A miniature replica.

I yearned for Rusty to hold me, to lie beside me, to share the glowing warmth I felt, but I knew that was impossible and so did he. He could not stay. Not only was it highly presumptuous for a black servant boy to enter a white girl's bedroom, but to enter while she lay abed after childbirth was a flagrant violation of decency and, in this case, should he be caught, a dead giveaway.

Actually, it was little Gabriel who was the dead giveaway. Stella Maris and Louie had already seen him and drawn their own conclusions. I can't say for sure, but I think they may have suspected before. And I knew it was only a matter of time until Papa saw the baby, too.

Sure enough, Papa came to my room not long after Rusty had gone. But I don't believe either Louie or Stella Maris had told him I'd given birth. Considering the circumstances, neither of them would have been eager to give Papa the news. But somehow he knew the child had been born.

Speaking not a word to me, he strode past the bed in which I lay and went directly to the clothes basket that served as Gabriel's bassinet. The basket sat on my dressing table where Stella Maris had put it after she'd lined it with soft towels and placed the shawl-swaddled baby inside. Papa leaned over the basket, drew back the shawl, and stared down at his grandson. Then, with an awful groan, he uttered two words.

"My God," he said, and the words came out as if wrenched from his soul.

He looked over at me. Though I fully expected an outburst of anger from him—for months he'd hounded me to name the father of the child I was carrying and was infuriated that I would not—he did not appear angry, nor did he even raise his voice. He looked stricken and ill, his face drained of all color.

And he said only one more word. "Rusty." It was more than an accusation; it was a statement.

I met his gaze head-on, but I said nothing. What was there to say? Now he knew, and no explanation or confession or appeal for understanding would change anything.

He turned on his heel and went out the door, and the silence he left in his wake gusted through the room like a cold, deadly wind, whirling in my ears and raising goose bumps on my flesh.

Gabriel is a sweet baby and, with Stella Maris's help, very little trouble to tend. Louie sees to Papa, of course, just as he's always done. Except now, since Papa's stroke, Louie is more nursemaid than manservant.

Like the shadows that drift through this venerable house day and night, Louie slips in and out of Papa's room at all hours, administering Papa's medicines, assisting him to the bathroom, and fetching his meal trays from the kitchen whenever Stella Maris is the least bit tardy about it. Which, with Stella Maris, is pretty much all the time.

When the doctors proposed that Papa be moved to Tulane Medical Center for recuperation, Louie politely but firmly protested against it. The doctors, thinking they understood, offered the alternative of a small upriver sanitarium. They thought Louie did not want his employer, a respected and well-known judge, to be subjected, in his incapacitated state, to the prying eyes and unavoidable gossip intrinsic in a large facility. Therefore, the small, rather isolated clinic with its excellent and discreet nursing staff would be just the thing, the doctors said. But that, too, met with Louie's soft-spoken opposition.

He said, "Seeing as how Mr. Victor's tongue all wrenched up, I reckon I'm the onliest one that can make out clear what he's saying. And, fact is, I done been waiting on him so long he ain't gone tolerate nobody else doing it."

I was consulted on the matter, as you would expect, but I said Louie undoubtedly knew best when it came to Papa's welfare, and so that settled it. I'm sure the doctors thought it unfitting for a servant to have so much say-so, but I really didn't care what they thought. You see, I figure Papa and Louie deserve each other. If the eyes are the mirrors of the soul, then Papa and Louie deserve to have to look into each other's eyes day after endless day and face the monster that dwells in both of them.

Upon hearing Louie's comments to the doctors, Stella Maris rolled her black eyes and raised her eyebrows. As soon as the two of us were alone, she said: "I dunno why in tarnation ole Louie still wanting to run and fetch for Mr. Victor. Look to me like he be off the hook now, and he oughta have sense enough to make the most of it."

I understood what she meant, but I also understood that Papa and Louie's relationship is complicated. Even if, in one respect, Papa no longer holds the upper hand, neither is Louie in a position to abandon Papa. The yoke that binds them together is still in place, still as binding. Just more evenly balanced than before. Sin for sin. Tit for tat. Though, of course, two wrongs don't make a right when it comes to murder and deception.

Nevertheless, I realize they're bound together not only by their sins but by their long history, which is as hopelessly entangled as the tenacious ivy that clings to the outer walls of this ancient house.

Raised up from babyhood together, Papa and Louie were almost like brothers, even though one is white and one is black, a relationship that no one outside the South can ever truly understand. Yet they've never been equals. Still aren't equals. Can never, ever be equals.

But Rusty and I were equals. At least in each other's eyes we were. Rusty's real name was Russell, but his nickname was more than just a diminutive of his given name; he was called Rusty mainly because of his hair, that tight, jumbled mat of reddish-brown curls that gleamed like burnished copper when the sunlight hit it just so.

Hair like Rusty's crops up fairly often among Creoles, the mixed-blood people of our region. It's a genetic throwback. A recurring trait passed down from the days when the master used and misused his slaves as he saw fit, and an occasional coupling between the races was not uncommon. Such indiscretions were quietly and swiftly swept under the rug back then. That double standard lingers to this very day—white men with black women, you understand; the other way around was and is unthinkable. Particularly among a certain class in this part of the country, *l'ancienne noblesse,* who take a rather cavalier view of the accountability of white males.

But despite the color of Rusty's hair and the green of his eyes—indisputable evidence that somewhere in his lineage there'd been a white man in the woodpile, so to speak—he was born to Louie and his wife Colette, and, therefore, no forty-seven ways about it, Rusty was a Negro.

Rusty was born only a few weeks before my own mother gave birth to me, both of us delivered by the same family doctor, in fact. It was from Stella Maris that I heard the accounts of our births. Stella Maris is a cousin to Louie and has been our cook and housekeeper for umpteen years and, as she is fond of saying, "has seen it all," and has been known to tell some interesting tales.

As a child, I'd often sit in the kitchen with her as she went about her chores. While she kneaded biscuit dough, snapped beans, or shucked oysters, she'd tell me a tale or two.

As best I can recollect and re-create Stella Maris's words, her account of the night Rusty was born went like this: "Yore own purty mama, Miss Annabelle, helped bring Rusty into the world. She was out at the cottage half the night, holding Colette's hand, whispering couragements and mopping her brow with a cool rag.

"And when the baby come, it was Miss Annabelle who went out on the porch where Louie was chomping at the bit and tole him he done got a fine son. After that, she come back here to the big house and locked herself in her room and wouldn't let nobody in, not even your papa, and that sweet lady cried and cried till the sun come up."

"Why? Why did she cry?" I remember asking.

"Well, I reckon it might've been tears of joy over the new baby, or thinking how sweet it was gone be when her own little baby come," she said. "Or maybe it was something that run just the opposite of that. Could've been she got an ill-boding of some kind, like you do sometimes when something bad is fixing to happen."

"Yes, that must have been it," I agreed.

I understood, even then, that it is quite possible to sense danger before it occurs, to smell it in the air like the scent of rain before the storm clouds gather and the first drop falls. Of course there was another, more substantial reason that led me to believe my mother had experienced an intuitive and frightening glimpse of the future on the night Rusty was born: I knew about the tragedies that had come to pass not long afterward.

The first tragedy occurred a few days after Rusty's birth. His mother was killed in an accident—an accident involving Louie's shotgun. Stella Maris said Colette's head was nearly blown off. Left hanging by a thread, Stella Maris said. That's *what* happened, but *how* it happened, the whys and wherefores, were never clear to me. Even Stella Maris seemed fuzzy on some of the crucial details, and neither Papa nor Louie would ever talk about it.

Just a week or so after Colette's death, I was born. By all accounts, Papa was delighted with me and praised my attributes to all who would listen.

But my mother lapsed into a terrible melancholy after my birth, keeping to her bed and refusing to eat or drink and turning her head away when Papa tried to comfort her. Stella Maris stayed by her side most of the time, and even Louie, who had so recently lost his own wife, did what he could for her. But at some point, when my mother was left alone, everyone in the household thinking she was sleeping, she rose from her bed and went onto the second-story veranda just outside her room, and either fell or jumped to her death on the flagstones below. That was the next tragedy. The next sudden and unexpected death.

But it wasn't the last one that would transpire among our household. Though it was seventeen years before the next tragedy came, when it did, it was enough to drive all of us to madness.

A short time after Papa looked at Gabriel in the basket and recognized him as Rusty's child, Stella Maris came flying into my room, screaming, "Oh, Lord! Mr. Victor done got his gun and gone out to the cottage!"

Fear slashed my heart like a keen-edged knife, and I struggled out of bed and ran out of the house as fast as my weary body would go, Stella Maris at my heels.

As we hurried outside and into the yard, the distance that separated the big house from the cottage, a mere fifty yards, turned into a vast gulf that seemed to take forever to cross. I felt I was wading in quicksand, getting nowhere. But ahead of me I could see Papa, his revolver in his hand, striding up the cottage steps and onto the porch where Louie stood blocking the screened door. I saw and heard everything very clearly.

"Get out of my way," Papa said to Louie.

"No," Louie said, and he did not budge.

"I said get out of—" Papa began. But his words broke off as a face appeared behind Louie, inside the screen. It was Rusty.

I wanted to cry out a warning to him, and yet I

could not. I had gone mute and could make no sound at all.

The next few minutes passed in slow motion. Papa struck Louie, slamming him aside, and he stumbled and fell back. The screen door opened, and Papa was grabbing Rusty and pulling him onto the porch. Rusty broke free and tried to go to Louie's aide, but Papa hit him in the face and stuck the gun to his chest.

"You son of a bitch," Papa growled.

"I love her," Rusty said.

"Shut your filthy mouth," Papa told him, still pressing the gun to Rusty's chest.

Louie was getting to his feet, saying, "Please, Mr. Vic. Don't do this. We work something out."

Then I heard a loud thud. Papa had pulled the trigger.

I was close enough to see the look on Rusty's face. It's a look I'll never forget. Dazed, shocked, and yet strangely accepting, as if he had fully resigned himself to such a fate. He slumped down, and Louie fell over him, wailing and moaning.

Papa just stood there, saying nothing. But I saw the revolver fall from his hand.

I'd made it to the porch by then, and I rushed up and dropped to my knees beside Rusty and Louie. I must have been crying, because later my eyes were so bloodshot and swollen that Stella Maris insisted on putting cold compresses on them, but I don't remember shedding any tears. What I remember is feeling that I, too, was dying on that porch. Papa had shot me in the heart as surely as he'd shot Rusty.

Louie raised his head and turned to look at Papa. What he said paralyzed me.

"You killed him. You killed your own son."

I could not move. I could not breathe.

Papa's face went hard, but I saw a mistiness come over his eyes. He said, "And you killed his mother."

"She was my wife, and she whored!" Louie thundered back.

Papa shook his head. "She was no whore. It was not Colette's fault. She gave in because she was young and naive and afraid to say no to me."

"She was mine, I loved her, and you took her," Louie said, his voice no longer thundering but strained to the point of breaking. "And even when I knowed the young 'un come from you and not me, even after I made her tell me the truth . . . I still loved the boy like my own."

"I know," Papa said quietly. "But a brother cannot lie with his sister. He cannot lie with her and live. It's the law of God."

That's when I understood everything, and the whole terrible picture coalesced into stark focus: In the beginning, Papa had lain with and impregnated Colette, and that had set off a disastrous chain of events that went spiraling down through the years, bringing suffering and calamity to all who'd been caught up in it. Colette, Louie, my mother, and now Rusty. And me, too. But Papa had not escaped either. He was as damned as any of us.

Stella Maris leaned down, forcing Louie and me out of her way as she covered Rusty with a sheet, which must have come from inside the cottage, though I have no memory of seeing her go in and get it.

"Get up," she said to me. "We got to go. This here ain't no place for you."

I just looked at her. Why didn't she understand that I couldn't leave Rusty?

"Come on, honey," she said, "the baby is all by hisself, and we got to go take care of him."

She'd said the only words that could have made me go. Suddenly it dawned on me, like a revelation, that what truly remained of Rusty was not lying there in a pool of blood on that porch, but was lying in a basket, swaddled in a knit shawl, back at the big house. It came to me that I must, at that very moment, take my love for Rusty and deliver it, once and for all, over to our child, because it was in little Gabriel that Rusty would live on.

Feeling weak as a dishrag, I let Stella Maris help me up.

As she led me down the steps, she said to Papa, "Mr. Vic, you and Louie better get yo' stories straight 'cause I'm fixing to call the po-lice as soon as I put Miss Caroline back to bed."

"No. I'll call them," Papa said, and he said it firmly and resolutely, decreeing his decision, like the judge he was. Then he followed us into the yard.

But we weren't halfway back to the house when Papa collapsed. He let out one small cry and fell down on the grass.

I thought he was dead. And I didn't care. That was when I first realized that I hated him. I didn't care if he died and rotted to dust right there in the yard.

But he didn't die, of course. He'd simply been felled by a stroke. A cerebral hemorrhage, the doctors called it. The doctors arrived at nearly the same time the police did.

I found out later that Louie told the police Rusty's death had been an accident. He pointed them to Papa's gun, where it still lay on the porch, explaining that Papa had been showing it to Rusty when suddenly it went off. He said he'd witnessed the whole thing. They believed him. Why wouldn't they? It was evident that Papa was so distressed over the shooting that he'd had a stroke. Certainly there was no reason to think Louie was lying. No father would lie to protect his son's killer, would he?

Anyway, Papa was in no condition to be questioned about it. The doctors said they couldn't determine how long his recovery would take. Months, years, maybe never. They just didn't know. I decided *never* would be fine with me.

So time has passed, and we go on with our lives much as we've always done. Except that I do keep to my room quite a bit, as I've said, and it is true that Stella Maris has begun talking to herself as she cooks and cleans. Or maybe it's God she's talking to, because she's nailed icons to the walls and goes around making the sign of the cross all day long. And Louie has taken to wearing an African dashiki and a white turban, and late at night he does funny voodoo stuff, like strewing chicken bones and cemetery dirt around the yard. But as none of these things are of any great consequence, I suppose they're hardly worth mentioning.

The only real change, of course, is that we now have our darling Gabriel, and he's a true joy to us. Stella Maris sings lullabies to him, and Louie bounces the baby on his knee and, when he thinks no one is listening, calls him "little Rusty."

Sometimes I call him Rusty, too, or at least I think the name in my head when I look at him, because it does seem that Rusty has come back to me through Gabriel. Each night I take him into my bed and hold him close, and his sweet smell envelopes me. It's the smell of ripe melons or new-mown grass, and it brings back such wonderful memories that I want to rub my face in it.

Someday, when everyone else in this house is dead and gone—it's only a matter of time, for they're all getting rather decrepit, you know—then it'll be just the two of us. Just Rusty and me. Then we'll come together and love each other as we did before, fully and completely, and nothing bad will happen here ever again.

FANTASIES

Alan Brennert

She was a memory of someone he had yet to meet: her face was known to him long before he actually saw it, and when she said hello for the first time, he thought, Of course, yes; that's exactly right. She was the woman he had fantasized being with all his life, the image held behind shut eyelids as he'd masturbated, the laughter he heard in the moments before sleep. Oh, he had had other fantasy women, of course—a slutty brunette at times, an exotic Asian Dragon Lady at others—but this image, this cool, poised blonde, the epitome of class and breeding, this one had always held particular sway over him, and to find her embodied in a real person—it was incredible.

Her name was Catherine, and she was everything he had dreamed of, and much more that he hadn't: small (no more than five-two), slim (though with lovely breasts), skin as pale as champagne, blond hair pulled back in a chignon, with the easy grace of someone whose family lived in the Back Bay and vacationed every summer on Martha's Vineyard. Jack's family was not poor by any means; they were quite well off, in fact, but definitely nouveau riche: this girl was the real thing.

For her part, she saw in Jack what every other woman saw in him: a sense of humor, a hint of mischief. Eyes that glittered a little darkly, a smile that looked at times a little cruel. The bad boy you could actually take home to meet the family, because he cleaned up surprisingly well. Jack was twenty; Catherine, nineteen. They were married within six months. "You barely *know* her," his friends would say, and he'd respond smugly, "I know her better than I know myself," and change the subject.

He did not know her, of course, nor she him. He knew the woman of his fantasies and was content to let Catherine fill the outlines of that fantasy, erasing anything that strayed beyond the borders of the outline, anything that conflicted with the image he had so long desired: cool, self-assured, slightly unapproachable yet slightly seductive.

But Catherine was both cool *and* warm, self-assured and insecure, unapproachable yet sometimes quite accessible, and, like most people, more contradictory than consistent. When her father had a mild stroke, she cried in Jack's arms, overcome with grief and fear, and though Jack held her, in a clever pantomime of compassion, deep inside he was disgusted: the woman of his fantasies would have borne her pain more quietly, more *regally.* Later, whenever they made love, he sensed in her touch a longing, a *neediness,* that repulsed him. His mind would shut down seconds before his penis turned flaccid, and then her comforting words only repelled him even more.

Catherine may not have known the source of his tension, but she could certainly feel its effects. Drifting increasingly apart, they decided to have a baby, Catherine hoping a child would bring them closer together, Jack hoping privately that it would deflect Catherine's needy desires off *him.* But how to make a baby when your cock wouldn't cooperate?

And so Jack made love in his imagination, not to Catherine but to someone else. Someone taller, with long, tousled brown hair; fleshy where Catherine was firm, dark where Catherine was fair. In his mind she lay on her stomach on the bed, her ample breasts a pillow beneath her, the pink nimbis of her areolae just barely visible against white sheets. Her eyes were dark and sultry, though she wore too much eyeliner. Her lips were full and sensuous, her nose wider and flatter than Catherine's. She had a small tattoo—a pair of cat's eyes—on her back, so even when he entered from behind, he felt as though she was watching him.

She was the bad girl to Jack's bad boy. She loved sex and tequila and the occasional recreational drug; their lovemaking was fierce and passionate. After the third or fourth time, he decided her name was Margie, and at least once he had to catch himself from blurting out her name when Catherine could hear.

The fantasy served its purpose: ten months later Catherine gave birth to a beautiful baby girl. Even Jack was taken aback by the emotions he felt as he took the infant in his arms, her tiny hands waving in his face. They named her Sheila, and for a time, her parents were actually happy.

Catherine never would regain her fantasy appeal for her husband, but over the years Jack found other releases: the occasional fling with a secretary at work;

a discreet liaison on a business trip. The marriage, Jack had decided, may have been a mistake, but he enjoyed the trappings of it—the name in the Social Register, the summers on the Vineyard—too much to end it.

And there was Sheila to consider as well. Jack truly did love her, and he didn't want her to be caught in the fallout of a divorce. So he kept his affairs to himself, made love to Catherine when necessary, and enjoyed his time with Sheila. She wasn't the prettiest of children—her mouth, her nose, seemed a little too big for her face—but she was spirited, always getting into mischief, and headstrong.

And if, sometimes when he looked at her, he was bothered by something—some vague unease tickling the periphery of his conscious mind—he didn't let it bother him for long. . . .

God knows he had enough to trouble him later on, as Sheila grew older. Her terrible twos were truly spectacular: what she couldn't draw on with semipermanent markers she shredded with blunt-edged scissors she'd steal from her mother's sewing kit. By the time she was five, she was going AWOL around the neighborhood, terrorizing the dog next door, nearly getting hit by a truck as she blithely ambled across the street.

By the time she turned eight, she was getting prettier; one day Jack was watching her as she played a video game, and he noted with pleasure that her features were becoming more proportionate to her face. Her back was to him, but he saw her reflection in the television screen: dark eyes, long brown hair that always seemed rather awry, and her mouth—

Jack's breath caught in his chest. The mouth.

He *knew* that mouth.

Full lips. Lips that, in another context, on another person, he might've described as . . . sensuous. Her nose was . . . flat. Wide. He'd never thought of it before, but the nose wasn't Catherine's, it wasn't his, it—

Sheila turned suddenly, as though somehow aware that he was watching her . . . and she smiled. "Daddy?" she said. "Is something wrong?"

He knew the smile, too.

He felt cold, heavy, as though he couldn't move, couldn't get up from his chair. Finally, after a long moment, he found his voice. "No, honey," he told her. "Everything's fine."

She kept smiling. Goddammit, he wanted to say, stop it, stop looking at me like that! But he said nothing, and at length she turned back to the TV and resumed her game.

He told himself later that he was being ridiculous, irrational . . . but still he avoided looking at her directly after that, making a show of reading his paper when she spoke to him, talking to her as though she were offstage from his life, an anonymous voice in a darkened theater. It did little good. In the years to come, he saw her features—and, worse, her body—grow ever more familiar. She was a healthy girl, no question of that, a fact not lost on the boys in school. When she started wearing makeup, she wore too much, and her mother made her tone it down. Then one day Jack saw her coming home from school, and he realized she had reapplied it after leaving home in the morning. She was walking arm in arm with a young boy, her long tousled hair blowing in the wind, too much blush on her cheeks, too much liner on her eyes. . . .

She starting cutting classes and sauntering home well after midnight. Catherine would ground her, only to find her bedroom window open, her room empty. Then, while cleaning the room, Catherine found two things: a package of Trojans tucked away at the back of a drawer, and a roach clip on a shelf in the closet.

"Jack, you have to talk with her," Catherine said. "I've done everything I can." It was the last thing he wanted, but he knew he had no choice. That night she came home close to one in the morning, having done God knows what with God knows who, and Jack told her they needed to talk. She smiled, aware that a reckoning was at hand, but whose, Jack couldn't say. "Sure, Dad," she said, strutting into the living room. He followed, but she stopped suddenly and spun round; he bumped into her, and at the contact, the first touch between them in almost ten years, he felt frightened and, God help him, excited. Quickly he backed off.

"Sorry," she said with a small smile. Then she took a step closer, reached up, and straightened the collar of his shirt. "What do you want to talk about?"

He fought back his fear and said, "Where have you been?"

She smiled. Her fingers brushed the side of his neck as she drew her hand away. "You really want to know?"

No. "Yes."

She shrugged off her denim jacket; underneath she was wearing a tight black T-shirt, no bra. She turned around. "I got a tattoo," she said. "Here. Look."

She rolled up the T-shirt, exposing her back.

There, just above her left shoulder blade, was a small tattoo—of a pair of cat's eyes. . . .

Involuntarily, Jack let out a small yelp. *Oh, God,* he thought.

Sheila rolled down her shirt, turned around again, and started advancing on him. "Would it help," she said, "if I called you Jack?"

Horrified, he took a step back. "Stay away from me."

"I've missed you, Jack," she said in a quiet singsong. Her full lips were pouty. "Haven't you missed me?"

He fell backwards into a chair, regained his balance, but she was upon him. She looped her arms around his neck.

She murmured something obscene, and he felt her breath on his face.

With more violence than he had intended, Jack tore her arms away from him and jumped back. They stood there a long moment, anger building in Sheila's eyes, but Jack just shook his head. "No," he said finally, his voice flat. "I can't. You understand? I *can't.*"

She stared at him, the fury of rejection in her dark, sultry eyes, then wordlessly stormed past him and slammed out of the house.

She didn't return for three years. Oh, they knew where she was—living with this boy or that, doing drugs, even spending a few months in juvenile hall after she was caught shoplifting at K-mart. Her parents tried to get through to her—or at least Catherine did. Jack kept his distance, and Catherine never asked why. Perhaps she didn't want to know.

Then, sometime after her twenty-first birthday, Sheila seemed to turn her life around for the better. She dumped her lover-of-the-moment, somebody named Chad; checked herself into a detox center; spent time in a halfway house. Within two months she had moved back into Jack and Catherine's home; she seemed calmer, more sedate, and definitely less seductive. She wore conservative dresses and baggy jeans, and little or no makeup. Perhaps, Jack decided with relief, she just needed to work it—work *her?*—out of her system. She started taking high school equivalency courses, and in class she met a quiet, studious young man named Louis. It was a short courtship, but very chaste and proper, and within a year they were married.

Jack could finally breathe again.

He and Sheila never spoke again of that night. Of anything, for that matter, beyond harmless words and meaningless chitchat.

Sheila got her high school diploma, but before she could find a job, she became pregnant. Catherine was ecstatic, as was Jack. Sheila had embraced the same life he had, years before, made the same choices; all the craziness, thank God, was over.

When his grandson, Brian, was a year old, Jack and Catherine went to Louis and Sheila's home for the birthday party. "They grow up too fast, don't they?" Catherine said to her daughter, but Sheila just laughed and shook her head. "Actually, I'm looking forward to it," she said. "Watching him grow up . . ."

Jack glanced with affection at his grandson as the boy watched, with rapt attention, a video of *The Jungle Book,* which his grandparents had given him for his birthday. After a moment Brian turned around to retrieve his half-finished piece of birthday cake . . . and Jack looked at his eyes, really *looked* at them, for the first time.

Brown eyes that seemed to glitter darkly.

The boy smiled at him.

A smile that looked . . . a little cruel . . .

He might have been looking into a mirror. His heart pounded in his chest. And he knew then just *how* closely Sheila had followed the same path he had, how horribly alike their choices truly had been. Mouth dry, heart racing, he looked at Brian, then at Sheila.

"Absolutely," she was saying, her voice sounding impossibly distant, "I can't *wait* to see what kind of a man Brian grows into. . . ."

Jack started screaming, though he didn't know whether anyone else could hear it. Part horror, part rage, part anguish, part desire, and then he found himself rushing across the room, arms outstretched, fingers grasping—hoping that the passion thundering in his soul was merely to kill, knowing it was not.

THE SECRET SHIH TAN

Graham Masterton

Men eat the flesh of grass-fed and grain-fed animals, deer eat grass, centipedes find snakes tasty, and hawks and falcons relish mice. Of these four, which knows how food ought to taste?

—Wang Ni

Craig's father had always told him that cooking was just like sex: It aroused you. It empowered you. It enabled you to play God with other people's senses. Afterward it left you feeling sweaty and exhausted, but the first inklings of what you might cook next were already teasing you like a girl who wouldn't stop playing with your softened penis.

Tonight Craig had cooked over 112 covers since the Burn-the-Tail restaurant had opened at six o'clock, and now he was sitting on an upturned broccoli box in the back yard, drinking ice-cold Evian water out of the bottle and listening to the clattering and clamoring of dishes being washed.

He smeared his eyes with the back of his hand. He

was so tired that he couldn't even think of anything to think. But he knew that fresh carp would be delivered in the morning, and there were so many amazing things you could do with fresh carp: carp with dry white wine, horseradish, and prunes; carp with celeriac and leeks simmered in lager beer and dry white wine; carp stuffed with scallions and ham and winter bamboo shoots.

Craig didn't look at all like somebody who had been obsessed by cooking ever since he was old enough to stand on a chair and reach the stovetop. He was twenty-eight years old, as gangly as a stork, with a thin, sharply etched face and short hair that stuck up like Stan Laurel's. But both his parents were brilliant cooks and had inspired him to play in the kitchen in the same way that other kids used to take piano lessons.

His father, George, was French-Canadian, and used to cook for La Bella Fontana at the Beverly Wilshire Hotel. His mother, Blossom, was half Chinese and had taught him everything from the four levels of flame to the eleven shapes by the time he was nine. Between the two of them, they had given him the ability to turn the simplest ingredients into dishes about which *Los Angeles* magazine had said, "There's no other word for Craig Richard's cooking except 'erotic.'" The *Los Angeles Times* had been even more explicit: "This food is so indecently stimulating that you almost feel embarrassed about eating it in public."

Craig had opened the Burn-the-Tail on Santa Monica Boulevard a few days after his twenty-third birthday, and now its endlessly surprising juxtaposition of classic French and Asian cooking meant that it was booked solid almost every night, mainly with movie people and lawyers and record executives. But unlike Ken Hom and Madhur Jaffrey and other celebrity chefs, Craig had shied away from television appearances and cookbook offers. Whenever he was asked to give cooking tips, he always shook his head and said, "Ask me in ten years' time. I'm not good enough yet."

All the same, he had plenty of faith in himself. Almost too much faith. He believed that he was more highly skilled than almost any other chef in Greater Los Angeles, if not in all of California. But he had an idea in his mind of food that would arouse such physical and emotional sensations in those who ate it that they would never be able to touch any other kind of food again. He had an idea of food that would literally give men erections when they put it in their mouths, and make women tremble and squeeze their thighs together. He could cook better than any chef he knew, but until he had cooked food like that, he knew that he wasn't good enough.

He swigged more Evian. On a busy night he could lose up to three pounds in fluid. He had six assistants working with him, but his style of cooking was furious, fast, and highly labor-intensive. That was attributable to the Chinese influence: the pride in slicing marinated duck livers so that they looked like chrysanthemum flowers, and cutting sea bass into the shape of a bunch of grapes.

Tina, his cocktail waitress, came out into the yard. Tina didn't know Escoffier from Brad Pitt, but Craig liked her. She was very petite, with a shiny blond bob and a face that was much too pretty. She wore a tight blue velvet dress with a V-shaped décolletage that gave customers a brief but startling view down her cleavage whenever she bent over to serve them a drink. Tina was proud of her cleavage. She had appeared in two episodes of *New Bay Watch* and had sent pictures of herself to *Playboy*.

"Almond Head's asking to see you," she said.

"Tell him I've been bitten by a rabid dog." Craig hated it when customers asked him to come out of the kitchen so that they could congratulate him. They would kiss their fingertips and say things like, "that *feuilleté* of scallops, that was just . . . *mwuh!*" while all the time Craig knew that the *feuilleté* of scallops was not just *mwuh*. It was made from sparkling fresh scallops that he had bought himself from W. R. Merry, the exotic fish wholesalers, and had poached in eggs and cream and served with a cognac-flavored lobster sauce that had taken him three years to perfect.

"Almond Head seemed kind of insistent. Here." She handed him a visiting card. It was slightly larger than the usual type of visiting card, and printed with severe, dark letters: Hugo Xawery, The Sanctuary, Stone Canyon Avenue, Bel Air.

Craig turned the card over. On the back, four words were scrawled in fountain pen: *"The Secret Shih Tan."*

He stared at the words and found that he could hardly breathe, let alone speak. Their effect on him was the same as the words "The Ark of the Covenant" would have been on a devout Christian, if he had known for sure that whoever had written those words had actually found it.

And there was no doubt in Craig's mind that Almond Head had found *The Secret Shih Tan*, because scarcely anybody knew of its existence.

Craig had never seen a copy. It had been written only for private circulation among a privileged number of chefs; and after its publication its author had suffered such deep remorse that he had tried to retrieve and burn every copy. But two copies had eluded him, and *The Secret Shih Tan* had been reprinted in a strictly limited edition in Shanghai in 1898, under the liberal regime of the young emperor Kuang Hsü. Only one hundred days later, however, Kuang Hsü had been deposed by the Dowager Empress Tzu Hsi, and *The Secret Shih Tan,* along with hundreds of other books, had been banned and destroyed. It was rumored that a single copy had been smuggled out of China by the emperor's personal chef, the legendary K'ang Shih-k'ai, but that was the last that anyone had heard of it. As far as Craig knew, the book now existed only in legend.

Craig first heard about it from one of his Chinese uncles when he was fourteen. His mother had found a copy of *Penthouse* under his mattress. His uncle Lee had laughed and said, "At least it wasn't *The Secret Shih Tan!*" Blossom Richard had been unaccountably disgusted; and George had warned Craig's uncle not to mention it again. But later, Craig had asked his uncle what it was, and his uncle had told him.

Now here was the title again, on this stranger's visiting card, and Craig was seized by the same feeling of dread and excitement that had gripped him all those years ago when his uncle had sat smoking by the window, murmuring all those forbidden and alluring things that *his* uncle had once murmured to him, and his father before him.

"Are you okay?" asked Tina. "You look as if you've *really* been bitten by a rabid dog."

Craig swallowed. "I'm fine. Thanks. Tell Mr. Xawery I'll be right out."

"You're going to *see* him?"

"Why not? You have to kowtow to the customers some of the time. It's *their* money, after all." After Tina had bounced her way back into the restaurant, Craig went to the men's room, stripped off his sauce-splashed whites, and vigorously washed his hands.

Jean-Pierre, one of his sous chefs came in. He was plump and unshaven, and mopped sweat from his forehead with a crumpled T-shirt. "We had idiots tonight, yes?" he asked Craig, in his erratic, up-and-down French accent. "Those people on table five sent back that Columbia River caviar because it was yellow. 'We know caviar,' they said. 'And caviar is black.'"

Craig was trying to comb his hair. He was trembling so much that he had to grip the rim of the sink to steady himself.

"Hey, you're not sick, are you?" asked Jean-Pierre.

"No, no," Craig told him.

"You're shaking like jellies."

"Yes. Yes, I'm shaking." He hesitated for a moment, then said, "What's the most terrible thing you've ever done?"

Jean-Pierre blinked at him. "I don't understand the question."

"What I mean is, have you ever deliberately hurt another human being in order to fulfill a wish that you've always cherished?"

"I don't know. I stole quite a lot of money from one of my girlfriends once. Well, I say 'stole.' She kept buying me clothes and presents, thinking that I was going to marry her, but I knew I never would. She had a . . . what do you call it? A wart. Do you know, I am not fond of warts."

Craig laid a hand on Jean-Pierre's shoulder and said, "Sure. I understand. I don't like warts either."

"Are you certain you're not sick?" Jean-Pierre frowned.

"I don't know. It's hard to diagnose your own sickness, isn't it? What's sick to one person is right as rain to somebody else."

Craig dressed in jeans, a button-down oxford-cloth shirt, and his favorite sand-colored Armani jacket. Then he walked through the kitchen, turned left, and went through the swinging door into the restaurant.

It was nearly one o'clock in the morning, and almost everybody had left. The restaurant was decorated in a pale, restrained style, with lots of natural-colored woods and concealed lighting. The only distinctive decorative motif was a steel-and-enamel mural of carp leaping across the main wall, with their tails ablaze.

The man whom the waitresses called Almond Head was sitting with a young girl at table nine, the most discreet table in the restaurant, but the table with the best view. He was very tall and swarthy, with a narrow skull and ears that lay flat back against his head. His hair was jet black and combed in tight oily ripples; his forehead was deeply furrowed too. His eyes disturbed Craig more than his almond-shaped head. They were hooded and withdrawn and as expressionless as two stones. For all that they communicated, he might just as well not have had eyes at all. He wore an expensive gray suit, and his black shoes gleamed as bright as his hair. On his hairy wrist hung a huge gold wristwatch.

It was the girl who commanded Craig's attention, however. She looked part Asian and part European. She was very slight, all arms and legs, and she wore a short dress of flesh-colored silk that made her look from a distance as if she were naked. As it was, it concealed very little. Her nipples made little shadowy points, and the silk clung to her thighs as if it was trying to ride up all by itself and expose her. Her face was extraordinary. She had black hair cut in a severe cap, and beneath this cap she had the features of a sphinx—slanted eyes, a narrow nose, and lips that looked as if she had just finished fellatio. She was deeply suntanned. Her skin was so perfect that Craig found it hard to resist the temptation to touch her shoulder, just to see what it felt like.

"I wish to congratulate you on a very exciting meal," said Hugo Xawery. His voice was deep, but his speech carried no trace of a European accent. On the phone, you might have thought he came from Boston.

"You had the beef tendon," said Craig.

"That's right. It takes great skill and patience to make a piece of gristle into one of the finest dishes in the city. 'If one has the art, then a piece of celery or salted cabbage can be made into a marvelous delicacy, whereas if one has not the art, not all the greatest delicacies and rarities of land, sea, or sky are of any avail."

"Wang Hsiao-yu," said Craig. "Quoted by the scholar Yüan Mei."

"You're a very gifted man. I have searched for more than eleven years for a chef as skillful as you. Why don't you sit down? I wish to make a proposition."

Craig remained standing and passed over Hugo Xawery's visiting card. "Is it this?"

Hugo Xawery's eyes gave away nothing.

Craig said, "I've heard about it, for sure. But I didn't think there were any copies of it still in existence. Besides, it wouldn't exactly be legal to try cooking from it, would it?"

"Some things are so pure in their purpose that they are above illegality."

"You could never say that this book is pure."

Hugo Xawery gave an infinitesimal shrug. "You haven't read it. I myself have read it more than a hundred times. I know it by heart. If I ever lost it, or if it was stolen, I could rewrite it from cover to cover. It is the single greatest cookbook ever compiled. The nature of the recipes takes nothing away from its single-minded purity of purpose."

"I don't know whether everybody would see it the same way."

Hugo Xawery leaned forward a little. His watch was of a very strange design, with a brand name that Craig had never seen before. "How would you see it?" he asked.

"Academically, I guess."

"How could a chef of your brilliance read a book like *The Secret Shih Tan* and not have a burning desire to try it out?"

Craig let out a little humorless bark. "Well, you know why. The ingredients are something of a problem, to say the least. And I have my restaurant to think of, my career."

"Ah, yes," said Hugo Xawery. "Your career."

Craig waited, but Hugo Xawery said nothing more. He sat with his stone-dead eyes, his watch ticking away the seconds, one of his hands resting on the girl's bare thigh, far higher up than most restaurant patrons would have considered decent.

"I'd certainly like to see it, though," said Craig after a moment.

"You may see it," Hugo Xawery replied. "And that is a part of my proposition."

"Go on."

"You may come to my house and read it. You may read it all the way through, if you so wish. But there is one condition."

"What? That I don't steal any of the recipes and serve them up here? Not very likely! Ha!"

Hugo Xawery turned to the girl. His hand was very high on her thigh now, and his little finger had disappeared under the hem of her dress. God, she was alluring, thought Craig. She was so erotic and so vulnerable that he could hardly believe she was real.

"Mr. Richard here has named his restaurant Burn-the-Tail," Hugo Xawery said to her, almost murmuring. "This comes from the story told in the Tang dynasty of how the carp used to swim up the Huanghe River to spawn. They did well until they reached the Dragon Gate, which was narrow and turbulent, and the current was too strong for them to go any farther—that is, until one of them learned to leap."

When he said this, he turned back and stared at Craig with such an expression of power and dark intensity that Craig felt a cold shrinking sensation in his spine.

"One of them learned to leap, and so all the others followed, and as they leaped, they flew in shimmering arcs through the spray. The gods were so impressed by their beauty and their courage that they burned their tails gold and changed the carp into scaly dragons who could fly wherever they wanted. In Chinese, if anybody says you have a burned tail, it means you have a glittering future."

He almost smiled, and then he said, "Mr. Richard could be the first carp to make the leap through the Dragon Gate."

"So what's your condition for reading the book?" asked Craig. He still couldn't bring himself to say its title out loud.

"Very simple, Mr. Richard. You may read the book, but then, having read it, you must choose one recipe and cook it for me."

Craig hesitated. "Is this a joke? You're not pulling my leg or anything?"

Hugo Xawery's face made it utterly clear that he found even the word "joke" to be offensive.

"I'd be using substitute ingredients, right?"

"Do you use substitute ingredients here at the Burn-the-Tail? Do you use small-mouthed bass instead of mandarin fish? Do you use collard greens instead of Chinese broccoli? Or pig's-liver pâté instead of *foie gras?"*

"Of course not."

Hugo Xawery said, "I will provide the ingredients. Whatever you ask."

Craig smiled and shook his head, then stopped smiling.

"Very well," Hugo Xawery told him. "If you won't do it, then I will have to continue my search for someone who will. I have to confess that I am gravely disappointed. You are one of the greatest chefs whose creations I have ever had the pleasure to eat."

Tina came up and said brightly, "Can I bring you some refreshment?"

Hugo Xawery stood up. He was unusually tall—almost six feet five. "I do need refreshment, yes. But not wine. I need to have my soul refreshed. I need to taste . . . I need to taste *God.*"

Craig escorted him to the door. The girl silently followed. She brushed past Craig, and he felt as if they were both naked.

"Listen, I'm sorry I couldn't help you," he said, as Hugo Xawery buttoned up his coat.

"Don't be sorry, Mr. Richard. Only the weak are ever sorry."

When they had gone, Craig went over to the bar and asked Tina to pour him a vodka on the rocks.

"Weird people," she remarked. "That girl looks young enough to be his daughter."

"Maybe she is."

"And do you know what's strange about her? I mean, apart from the fact that you couldn't stop staring at her with your mouth hanging open?"

"Go on, tell me."

"She wasn't wearing any perfume. None at all. No makeup, either. Don't you think that's strange?"

"Maybe she's allergic."

"I don't know," said Tina. "My grandmother used to say that women can smell fear in other women, even when they're laughing and smiling and trying to show everybody that they're having a great time. That girl wasn't wearing any perfume, but she smelled of fear."

Craig lay alone that night in his pale, sparsely decorated apartment on Mulholland Drive, unable to sleep. He kept thinking of Uncle Lee, sitting by the window, smoking. He could see him now, his eyes lowered, his voice little more than a dry, crackly whisper: *"The Secret Shih Tan* was written by the scholar Yüan Mei during the Ching period. He was a great intellectual, you know, a great philosopher. For him, food was a world in itself. He loved everything about it and its preparation and the way in which it was served. He delighted in such tiny nuances as the fact that the word for 'fish' in Chinese sounds exactly like the word for 'more than enough.' He had written *Shih Tan,* a famous book of recipes that was published all over the world. But his fame became so great that he was introduced to a secretive order of chefs from the province of Shandong, on the east coast of China on the Yellow Sea. They were all master chefs. But they had another interest. Like you, they were interested in the pleasures of a woman's body."

Craig switched on the light and sat up. He kept trying to imagine what *The Secret Shih Tan* looked like, what it was like to turn the pages of the most forbidden book in the Western world.

His uncle had blown out smoke and said, "Some meat is traditionally taboo. Ch'en Ts'ang-ch'i said that you should never eat the flesh of a black ox, a goat with a white head, a single-horned goat, any animal that had died facing north, a deer spotted like a leopard, horse liver, or any meat that a dog had refused to eat."

Craig could remember staring at his uncle, speechless, waiting for the words that were almost too dreadful to think about.

His uncle said, "Yüan Mei tasted the chefs' food, and it affected him forever. After the first time, he went to a house in Jinan near the Qianmen and lay face down on the floor of an empty room for two days and two nights, eating nothing more, because he didn't want his mouth or his body to be affected by the taste of anything else until the food had passed completely through him. Only at the end of this time did he start to write a second *Shih Tan,* known as *The Secret Shih Tan.*"

Craig had swallowed. "What did he eat?"

And that was when his uncle had put his lips close to Craig's ear and fired his imagination with *The Secret Shih Tan* forever.

The Sanctuary was a large white house set well back from the road on Stone Canyon Avenue; it was fenced, gated, and almost invisible behind dark, prickly-looking shrubs. Craig drove up to the gate in his red Mercedes and pressed the intercom button.

"Xawery residence." A girl's voice, light and expressionless.

"Hi, this is Craig Richard. I'd like to talk to Mr. Xawery."

"Do you have an appointment?"

"No, I don't. But you can tell Mr. Xawery I accept his condition."

"You'll have to wait."

He waited, listening to Beck singing about being screwed up and life's a toilet and why don't you kill me. After a long while, the gates hummed open, and Craig drove up the steeply angled driveway to the house.

It was large, but it was also oddly proportioned and deeply unwelcoming. A Rottweiler barked insanely at him as he approached the porch, hurling itself from side to side on its chain. When he rang the doorbell, a small grille opened up, and he was examined for a ridiculously long time by a disembodied pair of glittering eyes.

"You satisfied?" he said impatiently.

At last he heard bolts being shot back, and the door was opened by an unsmiling Mexican in a black uniform. Inside the house, the air was startingly chilly. The floor was polished marble, and there was scarcely any furniture. No flowers, either. Without a word, the Mexican turned and walked off across the hallway, his shoes squeaking. Craig followed him, although he wasn't sure that he was supposed to. They walked all the way down a long, gloomy corridor until they reached a sunroom—or what would have been a sunroom if all the drapes hadn't been drawn. Instead, it had a kind of papyrus-colored light, as if it were an ancient tomb.

Hugo Xawery was sitting in a large armchair, reading. He was dressed in white pants and a collarless white shirt. The girl was kneeling on the floor next to him, one arm on his knee. She was wearing a plain white sleeveless dress, as square as a sack.

"Well," said Hugo Xawery. "It seems that you have changed your mind."

"As a matter of fact, no, I don't think I have. I think I was always going to have to do this, no matter what."

"Of course."

"I'd just like to know how you knew."

"What? That you were interested in seeing *The Secret Shih Tan?* I met your Uncle Lee Chan the second time I had dinner at the Burn-the-Tail. He's a well-educated man, your uncle, but he shouldn't smoke so much. It ruins the palate, smoking. I like your Uncle Lee, though. I don't like many Chinese.

We talked about your talent, you see, and the conversation went around to Paul Bocuse and nouvelle cuisine, and then to some of the great modern chefs in China. I praised your skill in using difficult ingredients and said something like 'He's probably cooked everything except the dishes described in *The Secret Shih Tan.*' That was when your uncle said, 'Yes, but he *knows* about it.' And that was when I was satisfied that I had found my man. You have only to know about it to want to cook from it."

Craig said, "I want to ask you something. Have you ever . . . well, have you ever tasted the dishes made from any of those recipes?"

Hugo Xawery gave him a closed, stony look. "What happens in this house is private, Mr. Richard."

Craig hesitated. A molting white parrot was perched in a cage, nodding at him with horrible intimacy. Craig knew that what he was about to do was wrong. It was probably the most terrible thing that he would ever do. But he also knew that if he turned around and walked out of Hugo Xawery's house without seeing *The Secret Shih Tan,* his career as a chef would be finished. He would wonder for the rest of his life what he could have done, what he could have been.

He wanted to cook a meal that would make Hugo Xawery want to lie face down on the floor for forty-eight hours, sobbing because he was digesting it and because when he had excreted it, it would be gone forever.

"Show me the book," he said in a throaty voice.

Hugo Xawery put down his book and stood up. "Very well," he said, and extended his hand. "So long as you remember what you have solemnly agreed to do."

"I won't forget."

Hugo Xawery led the way along another dark, echoing corridor until they reached a bare, marble-floored room with nothing in it but a rectangular steel desk, a plain office chair, and a gray-painted safe. A greenish bamboo shade was drawn most of the way down the French windows. Beneath the shade, Craig could see part of a patio and the feet of a stone cherub, a reminder of the world that he had now decided to leave behind.

Hugo Xawery walked across to the safe, produced two keys, and opened it. Inside, there was nothing but the book itself, wrapped in plain white tissue. Hugo Xawery brought it over, laid it on the desk, and unwrapped it.

It wasn't much to look at. A maroon fabric–bound book with a Chinese character stamped into the cover.

"No," said Hugo Xawery, "it isn't very impressive, is it? This edition was published in Paris in 1911. I've seen only one other English edition, and that was much older, and illustrated. But I don't think you need illustrations in a book of this nature, do you?"

Craig sat down in the chair. Hugo Xawery said, "I'll leave you to it. Tell me when you've had enough. My man will bring you coffee or wine or anything else that you'd care for."

He left, and Craig was alone. He sat looking at the book for a long time without opening it. The moment he turned to the first page, he would be committed. He glanced around the room. He wondered if Hugo

Xawery was watching him on closed-circuit television. Maybe he should stand up, and walk out now. There was always the Burn-the-Tail; there was always business and chatter and laughter, buying produce, devising new menus, cooking with sauces and sizzling shallots and flames.

But there was nothing like *The Secret Shih Tan;* and here it was. It was probably the only copy in America. He laid his hand on the cover. Still he didn't open it.

He knew all of the arcane secrets of great French cookery, right down to roast camel's hump, which the Algerians prepare with oil, lemon juice, salt, pepper, and spices, roasted like a sirloin of beef, and served on a bed of watercress. He knew all of the Chinese recipes that the bravest of his customers couldn't face, like *bêche-de-mer,* the sea slug, which had no flavor whatsoever and the consistency of a jellyfish; and bird's-nest soup, made out of cliff swallows' nests, a combination of bird spit, sea moss, and feathers.

But this was something else. This was the moment when food, sex, and death came together in the darkest challenge that any chef could face. Food is sex, his father had always told him. But food was death, too. Every time something was eaten, something had to die.

Craig felt as if he were standing with his toes on the edge of a terrible abyss. It was too late to turn back; and because it was too late to turn back, he opened the book.

The recipes were written with grace and subtle charm, but that only served to make their horror more intense. Craig started with the simplest of them, in the beginning, but he hadn't read more than three before he began to feel as if he were no longer real, as if the room around him were no longer real. What heightened his feeling of unreality was knowing that he had agreed to prepare one of these dishes, that he would actually be following the instructions in one of the recipes.

Young Girl's Breast, Braised

The breast should first be soaked in cold water, blanched, cooled in cold water, and carefully flattened under pressure so that its youthful curves are not lost when it is braised. Place the breast in a clay casserole. Cut two thin slices of smoked thigh meat into 1/2-inch squares and add to the casserole with 6 soaked dried black mushrooms. Make horizontal slashes along one side of each of two bamboo shoots, like a fan. These will make decorative angels' wings to surround the breast when it is served. Add salt, sugar, 3 tablespoons rice wine, and 2 slices peeled fresh ginger. Braise very gently for 3 to 4 hours. Slice thin so that each diner receives a full curve showing the shape of the breast. The most honored guests will receive a slice with a section of the nipple on it. Serve with braised asparagus and rape hearts. Breast can be served fresh, cold, or smoked.

There were over a hundred recipes in all, every one of them using male or female sexual parts, sometimes accompanied by other organs, such as liver or pancreas or stomach lining. Some of the dishes were plain—sexual interpretations of everyday Chinese dishes such as zha yazhengan, which was nothing more than duck gizzards deep-fried and served with a dip of prickly ash—a mixture of salt and Szechuan peppercorns. In *The Secret Shih Tan,* however, the gizzards were replaced by deep-fried testicles.

Woman In Man was a sausage made from penis skin and filled with a mixture of finely chopped labia, seasoned with mao-tai liquor, salt, sugar, sesame oil, and fat from the pubic mound.

There were elaborate preparations of male and female organs, marinated, steamed, and served in the act of disembodied coitus. Man Takes Many Lovers was a penis stuffed into rigidity with scores of nipples and encircled with six or seven anal sphincters, like quoits. These should be cooked in the same way as jellyfish, the book advised, and in the same way they required "spirited, vigorous chewing."

As he turned the pages, Craig didn't notice the room gradually growing darker. He was lost in a world where every meal required the death or mutilation of a human being—sometimes eight or nine people sacrificed for one tantalizing side dish.

Toward the end of the book, some of the dishes were so perverse that Craig left the table and stood on the opposite side of the room, almost too horrified to continue reading. But eventually he returned and sat down and read the recipes to tne very end.

The last recipe was the most challenging of all. It was called, simply, Whole Woman Banquet. A young woman was to be carefully eviscerated, and every organ cleaned, marinated, and cooked in a different way, including her eyes and her brains. Everything would then have to be returned to the body and her original shape restored as perfectly as possible. Then she would be steamed.

It was the footnote that riveted Craig more than any of the lengthy descriptions of how to poach lungs in the same way as soft-shelled turtle. The author Yüan Mei had written, "It is essential for this dish that the woman be as beautiful as can be found and that the chef should make love to her the evening before the banquet. The lovemaking endows both the food and its creator with spiritual tenderness and is a way that a chef can pay homage to his ingredients."

Craig closed the book. It was dark now, and he hadn't realized that Hugo Xawery was standing in the doorway, patiently waiting for him.

"What do you think?" he asked in a voice like brushed velvet.

"It's everything I ever imagined it would be."

"Did it shock you?"

"I'd be lying if I said it didn't."

"But the technique . . . what do you think of the technique?"

"Very difficult, some of it."

"But not beyond you?"

"No."

Hugo Xawery circled the table. "Have you decided what you're going to cook?"

"I don't know. You'll have to give me some time to think about it."

"Not too long. I have to find you the ingredients, you understand, and they must be fresh."

Craig stood up. "I'll call you tomorrow."

"Yes. You will," Hugo Xawery said, with an imperative tone in his voice.

"Don't you trust me?" asked Craig.

"I don't know. You could cause me a great deal of

embarrassment as well as disappointment. I've already promised this treat to several very influential people."

"I've given you my word. What more can I do?"

"You don't have to do anything more. Because I've taken one simple precaution, in case you renege on your agreement. Somewhere in one of your freezers, among the rest of your meats, there are human remains—packed, of course, in anonymous freezer bags just like all of your other meat. I'm sure the police would be interested in rummaging among your livers and your kidneys and your loin chops."

"You didn't have to do that," said Craig tersely. "I don't have any intention of reneging on my agreement."

"Let's just call it insurance. And they're high-quality remains. Even if you cook them and serve them up, they won't harm anybody."

On the way out, Craig saw the girl standing in a half-open doorway at the end of the corridor. She was wearing nothing but the thinnest of silk slips, so short that it scarcely covered her. She was watching him with those slanted, sphinxlike eyes, her skin shining smooth in the lamplight. He stopped and stared back at her. She made no attempt to turn away or to close the door.

"You like her?" asked Hugo Xawery.

"She's beautiful."

"I call her Xanthippa. Of course that's not her real name. Her mother and I lived together for a while, in Carmel. One day her mother left and never came back. So I suppose you could call me Xanthippa's guardian."

Craig took one last look at Xanthippa and then walked across the hallway to the front door, where the Mexican servant was waiting with undisguised displeasure to show him out.

Early the next morning, he found his Uncle Lee in his back yard in Westwood, hosing his roses. Uncle Lee was over seventy now, and his face was wrinkled like an aerial view of Death Valley. He wore a coolie hat and a loose blue shift.

"Uncle Lee?"

"Hallo, Craig. I was wondering when you would come."

"I've read it, Uncle Lee. *The Secret Shih Tan.* I read it yesterday evening, from cover to cover."

"Then today you will be different."

"Yes, I'm different." He watched the hose water splattering into the flower bed, and then he said, "Why did you tell Hugo Xawery that I knew about it?"

"Because *The Secret Shih Tan* is as far as any chef can go, and you would never have been satisfied with anything less."

"Hugo Xawery let me look at it on one condition."

Uncle Lee looked up at him, his eyes slitted against the seven o'clock sunlight. "Don't tell me. You have to cook one of the recipes for him."

Craig nodded. "I've been awake all night. I don't know which one to choose."

"Which do you *wish* to choose? The greatest of all the recipes or the recipe that will cause the least human suffering?"

"I don't know. It's not just gastronomy, is it, *The*

Secret Shih Tan? It has so many inner meanings. We kill thousands of people in war, and that's supposed to be moral and glorious, even though war is totally destructive. But if we sacrifice half a dozen human beings to create one of the greatest meals in gastronomic history, that's supposed to be so goddamned evil that we're not even allowed to *talk* about it."

"So which dish are you going to choose?" Uncle Lee repeated.

"I don't know. I'm still trying to work out what it is that *The Secret Shih Tan* is trying to tell me."

Uncle Lee turned off the faucet, and laid a withered hand on Craig's shoulder. "If you do not see it for yourself, then I cannot tell you."

"You can't even give me a clue?"

"All I can say is that whatever you decide to cook, you must make sure, above all, that you do it justice."

Craig didn't open the Burn-the-Tail restaurant that day, although he spent a half hour in thick insulated gloves, sorting through the foods in his freezers. He couldn't find any packages of meat that looked human, but how could anyone tell if there was one human kidney among thirty lamb's kidneys, or one escallope of human thigh among ten escallopes of veal? He would either have to throw away his entire stock or wait until he had fulfilled his promise to cook Hugo Xawery's meal.

Later in the afternoon he drove up to Stone Canyon Avenue. Hugo Xawery was sitting alone in the sunroom behind tightly drawn shades. Through the open door, however, Craig could see Xanthippa sitting on the patio under a large green parasol.

"Ah, Mr. Richard," said Hugo Xawery. "What a

pleasure to see you so soon. Have you come to a decision?"

Craig nodded. "There's no point in playing around with *hors d'oeuvres,*" he said. "I'm going to cook the Whole Woman Banquet."

Hugo Xawery's face slowly lit up with unholy relish. "The banquet! I knew you would! The greatest challenge that any chef could ever face! The greatest feast that any gastronome could ever imagine!"

"You won't be able to eat it all on your own, will you?"

"I have no intention of eating it on my own. I have . . . friends."

"Can you get in touch with them? I'd like to start making preparations right away."

"Of course I can get in touch with them. And I can procure your main ingredient, too. In fact, I have it already."

Craig looked out onto the patio. "Xanthippa?"

"Isn't she beautiful? You can't make the banquet of banquets out of inferior raw materials."

"You know what it says at the foot of the recipe?"

"About the chef making love to his uncooked banquet? Of course. And you shall. Xanthippa has been expecting this day for many years."

"You mean she already knows what you're going to do to her?"

Hugo Xawery smiled. "She lives only to serve me; she always has. Her greatest pleasure has always been to know that one day I shall ingest her. Why do you think she never wears perfume or cosmetics? She doesn't wish to taint the taste of her flesh."

"How about tomorrow evening?" Craig suggested. "Or is that too soon?"

Hugo Xawery wrapped his long arm around Craig's shoulders. "Tomorrow evening will be perfect. Expect six for dinner, including me. You can stay here tonight, with Xanthippa, and early tomorrow morning you can start your preparations. You will, of course, allow me to watch you at work?"

"You're very welcome, Mr. Xawery. In fact, I'd be disappointed if you didn't."

"How about . . . the butchery? Do you need any assistance?"

"I prefer to do my own, thanks."

Hugo Xawery gripped Craig's shoulder and stared into his eyes with such emotion that Craig thought for a moment he was going to weep. "You're a great, great chef. Do you know that? After tomorrow, your name will rank with the very finest."

"We'll see," said Craig.

Without taking his eyes off Craig, Hugo Xawery called out, "Xanthippa!"

She turned and frowned at him.

"Xanthippa, I have a surprise for you!"

The bedroom that Hugo Xawery lent him was silent and painted a silky gray. In the center stood a massive carved-oak bed heaped with Moorish-style cushions. It was a warm night, so Craig left the French windows open. The net curtains billowed silently in the breeze, like the ghosts of nuns.

Craig was sitting up in bed reading *The Secret Shih Tan* when the door quietly opened and Xanthippa came in. She was wearing nothing but a thin shirt of aquamarine linen and small brown beads around her wrists and ankles. She came across the room and climbed onto the bed next to him. She smelled of nothing but the natural biscuity aroma of an aroused young woman.

"You're reading that book," she said, although not accusingly.

Craig closed it and dropped it down by the side of the bed. "I'm sorry," he said.

"Why should you be?"

"It isn't in very good taste, is it, considering what I'm supposed to do to you tomorrow?"

"You don't understand. I'm looking forward to it. Hugo is one of the greatest men in the world. He's intellectual, he's refined, but he doesn't believe in limits. With Hugo, everything is possible. I've already had enough pleasure for five lifetimes. Why should I worry if my life ends now?"

Craig gently touched her cheekbones and then traced the outline of her lips. *Carefully remove the eyes and set aside on a dish.* Then he leaned forward and kissed her.

"You're very beautiful," he told her.

She smiled and kissed him back. She kissed him like no woman had ever kissed him before, sucking and teasing his lips and then sliding her tongue into his mouth and stimulating nerve endings he hadn't even known he had. Underneath the blanket, his penis stiffened.

Xanthippa crossed her arms and took off her shirt. She was lean and small-breasted, but her skin was so exquisite that Craig couldn't stop himself from sliding his hands up and down her bare back. Her pubic hair was shiny and black, and she had plaited it tightly and decorated it with small colored beads, so that the lips of her vulva were exposed.

She said, "Lie back . . . you can taste me first."

He lay back on the pillow and Xanthippa drew aside the blanket. She climbed astride him, with her back to him, and then she lifted her bottom so that he was confronted with her vagina. He kissed all around it, and then he ran the tip of his tongue down the cleft between her buttocks and tasted her tightly wrinkled anus. She sighed and kissed him all around his penis in return.

The room was so quiet that he heard the moistened lips of her vagina opening, like the softest click in the Xhosa language. He slid his tongue into her wetness and warmth, and tasted saltness and sweetness and something else as well, like highly purified honey. At the same time, she slowly sucked his penis, flicking it and drumming it with her tongue.

They made love for hours, and she showed him all of the tastes of love. He licked her perspiration-beaded armpits and the soles of her feet. He swallowed her vaginal juices when they were thick with early arousal, and again when they thinned out, just before orgasm. He tasted her saliva when she was excited, and again when she was drowsy. She had eaten a salad for lunch with wildflowers in it, and he could actually taste it.

Eventually, as it began to grow light, she rubbed his penis so that he climaxed into her mouth, and she drank his sperm with long, appreciative swallows. "Did you know that you can *chew* sperm and that it actually changes texture as you chew it?"

They lay together in silence for a long while. At last Craig sat up and said, "Would you do something for me? Something really special?"

"I'm yours now," she said, her voice husky. "You know that."

"Well, that's the point. I feel as if you're not really mine at all. I'm just the chef. I'm a craftsman, not a lover. If you belong to anybody, you belong to Hugo."

She propped herself up on one elbow. "So what do you want me to do?"

"The recipe says that there should be lovemaking before the meal is prepared, to give it spiritual tenderness. But I can't give you anything like the spiritual tenderness that Hugo can give you. I mean, think of it, Hugo's the one who's actually going to—"

"You think I should make love to Hugo?"

"Yes, I do."

She smiled, and kissed him. "If you want me to make love to Hugo one last time, then I will."

It was nearly six o'clock in the morning. The house was already bright. Craig stood silently outside the door of Hugo Xawery's enormous white-carpeted bedroom. The door was ajar only a half inch, but that was enough for him to be able to see Hugo Xawery lying on his back on the white silk sheets while Xanthippa rode up and down on his dark, erect penis as if she were taking part in some dreamlike steeplechase.

He didn't know if either of them knew he was there until Hugo Xawery looked over Xanthippa's shoulder toward the door and gave a wide, knowing, lubricious smile.

Craig watched his purple glans disappearing into Xanthippa's stretched-open vagina and tried to think of all the spiritual tenderness that was passing between them, one to the other. Hadn't Yüan Mei said that spiritual tenderness flows both ways?

* * *

At eight, Craig was awakened by a soft knock at the door. Hugo Xawery came in and stood over the bed. "Good morning, Mr. Richard. It's time for the kitchen."

"I'm ready," said Craig.

"Xanthippa . . . was she enjoyable?"

"Oh, she was more than enjoyable. She was a revelation."

Blood hurried down the grooves in the butcher's table, and he carefully collected it for blood puddings and gravies. His knives slit open skin and fat and sliced through connective tissue.

On the stove, pans of stock were already simmering, and the ovens were warming up. The kitchen echoed to the sound of chopping and dicing.

By the middle of the day, the house was already filled with extraordinary fragrances—frying liver, poaching lungs, heat-seared filet of human flesh—mingled with the aroma of basil and rosemary and coriander and soy sauce.

Craig worked nonstop, swallowing ice-cold Evian to keep himself going. By six o'clock in the evening he was almost ready when the Mexican servant knocked at the door and announced that the first two guests had arrived.

They sat at the long mahogany dining table, none of them speaking. The room was lit only by candles, and the plates and glasses gleamed and sparkled. The cutlery shone like shoals of fish. The sense of drama was immense.

At last, the double doors opened, and Craig appeared, in immaculate whites. Behind him, the Mexican servant was pushing a long trolley, more like a paramedics' gurney than a serving wagon.

Craig recognized at least two of the guests as customers from the Burn-the-Tail, and a famous face from one of the movie studios. They must have recognized him, too, but they gave no hint of it. Their eyes were fastened on the long trolley, with its cover of highly burnished silver.

Craig said, "I welcome you on behalf of Mr. Xawery, who has spent eleven years of his life preparing for this moment, when *The Secret Shih Tan* becomes more than a book of recipes, but a reality, which you can eat.

"I always thought *The Secret Shih Tan* was nothing more than the ultimate cookbook. But, you know, it's much more than that. It's a book of thought, justice, and devastating truth. Yüan Mei never intended that any of its recipes should ever be cooked. He just wanted us to understand what we are—that we are foodstuffs, too, for anybody or anything who finds us good to eat. He wanted to put us in perspective."

Craig beckoned the manservant to wheel the wagon right up close to the end of the table. Even though the lid was tightly closed, the fragrance of flesh and herbs was overwhelming, and one of the guests was salivating so copiously that he had to cram his linen napkin into his mouth.

Craig said, "I learned about life while I was cooking this meal. I learned about death. I learned about ambition, too, and vanity. But most of all I learned about love."

The studio director said, "Shouldn't we wait for Hugo? This is Hugo's moment, after all."

Craig took off his chef's hat. "We don't need to wait for Hugo. Hugo's already here."

With that, he rolled back the shining cover on top of the wagon, and there was a human body—glossy, plump, gutted of every organ, braised, fried, steamed, and poached, and restored to its original shape. The greatest recipe that man had ever devised. It smelled divine.

Craig laid his hand on the body's belly. "Do you see this? It was my uncle who first told me about *The Secret Shih Tan.* It was my uncle who gave me the clue to what it meant. Cook your meal, he told me, and do it justice. And this is what this is. Justice."

He turned and beckoned, and Xanthippa appeared, wearing an impossibly short linen dress, a black bandanna tightly braided around her forehead. She stood beside the body, but she wouldn't look at it.

"This is my new sous chef," said Craig. "She gave me the inspiration to cook this meal, and help in preparing it, and she also gave it the spiritual meaning that Yüan Mei demanded. Not just an eye for an eye, but a heart for a heart, a spleen for a spleen, and a liver for a liver. She was the last person to make love to Hugo Xawery, and here she is, to serve him to you. Enjoy."

Three weeks later Craig took Xanthippa to Shanxi Province in China, where the Huanghe roars and froths between two mountainous, cloud-swathed peaks called the Dragon Gate.

It was a chilly, vaporous day. The skies were the color of slate. Xanthippa stood a short distance away while Craig climbed right to the edge of the river, carrying the book.

He looked around him, at the mountains and the clouds. Then he ripped the pages out, six or seven at a time, in clumps, and threw them into the river.

He had almost expected them to catch fire, to burn, to leap in the air. But the Huanghe swallowed them and swamped them and carried them away. He tossed in the book cover last of all.

"Are you satisfied now?" she asked him. She was wearing a pink ribbed roll-neck sweater and tight blue jeans, and she looked almost good enough to eat.

"I don't know," he said. "I don't think I ever will be."

"Aren't you going back to Burn-the-Tail?"

"What's the point? Jean-Pierre is as good as I am; he'll keep it going. Once you've cooked from *The Secret Shih Tan,* how can you cook anything else?"

"But what will you do next?"

"Try to understand you."

She touched him and gave him an enigmatic smile. He could never forget that she had been willing to be cooked.

"What about the human meat that Hugo hid in your freezers?" she asked him. "What are you going to do about that?"

"Well . . . I looked for it, but I couldn't find it, and I think Hugo was lying. Even if he wasn't lying, it doesn't matter. Human meat is the very best there is. It's one thing to eat an animal. It's another thing to eat an animal. It's another thing to eat an animal that you can talk to and make love to."

Xanthippa linked arms with him and kissed him, and together they walked back down the hillside to the waiting tourist bus.

* * *

In the Burn-the-Tail restaurant that evening, Morrie Walker, the restaurant critic from *California* magazine, ordered the seared liver with celeriac. He jotted on his notepad that it was "pungent, strange . . . a variety meat lifted to a spiritual level . . . almost sexual in its sensuality.

"Without being blasphemous," he wrote, "I felt that I was close to God."

THE CONTRIBUTORS

Alan Brennert

California's Brennert is the author of six books: three novels, the most recent being *Time and Chance;* two short story collections; and one stage play, *Weird Romance.* He won an Emmy Award as writer-producer on *L.A. Law,* and a Nebula. He's currently at work on a screenplay, five original teleplays for Showtime's revival of *The Outer Limits,* and a new short story collection.

Patricia D. Cacek

Colorado's Cacek has sold over fifty stories, with recent anthology appearances in *Seeds of Fear, Return to the Twilight Zone,* and *100 Wicked Little Witches.* She says that "Metalica" was inspired by "a challenge to create an erotic situation based around an object that most women, including the author, consider a cross between salad tongs and the Jaws of Life. I think it worked."

James Crawford

This is New Yorker Crawford's second *Hot Blood* series contribution. When not writing, he spends much of his free time onstage with his community theater group. He says the idea for his latest story came to him "in a dream. It was that hour between 'I'm so comfortable I could sleep all day' and 'oh, damn, it's time to get up for work.' As I jolted awake, parts of the dream stayed with me, and after some rewrites, I had this story."

Michael Garrett

Garrett is co-editor of the *Hot Blood* series and author of the movie-optioned suspense thriller *Keeper* as well as numerous internationally published short stories. He is an instructor for the Writer's Digest School, teaches weekend writing seminars across the nation, and is a frequent speaker at writing conferences. He resides in Alabama with his wife and children.

Jeff Gelb

California's Gelb recalls that his very first serious attempt at prose fiction was an erotic horror story he wrote at age sixteen called "The Portrait," which he shared with his high school buddies during study hall. His story in this edition of *Hot Blood* was inspired by that earlier version of "The Portrait," and is dedicated to Gelb's high school and college crushes, who shall remain nameless.

Nat Gertler

California's Gertler shamefully admits that "Restin' Piece" was inspired by his being named Coitus Interruptus poster child for 1993. Besides his extensive comic book writing credits, he is the author of *Computers Illustrated, Multimedia Illustrated,* and the CD-ROM *Steel Spandex.* He has written prose for *Shock Rock 2, Offworld, Tattoo Magazine,* and more.

Lois Gresh

New York's Gresh claims she was a competitive swimmer who spent too much time lolling in the steam room. At age nineteen she met a foot fetishist who claimed to be her sole mate. Banking on personal experience, she now writes horror and twisted SF, with stories appearing in *100 Vicious Little Vampires, Interzone, Terminal Fright,* and several upcoming horror anthologies.

Bruce Jones

The California writer's most recent novels are *Terminal Velocity* and *Game Running.* Of his new story for *Fear the Fever,* Jones recalls, "When I was nine or ten, my family spent a week in the country with relatives. I slept with my brother, having shuddered through a werewolf movie on TV earlier that evening. In my dreams, I woke in the country bed beside my brother, his back to me, to find that he had sprouted coarse black hair, stank of animal odors, emanated death and hunger, and was, mercifully, still asleep. A moment later I awoke to find myself staring at exactly the same spot, and at the dark lump in bed beside me that had so hideously invaded my dream. I lay there in rigid terror throughout the night, praying my brother would stay asleep."

Jack Ketchum

New York's Ketchum is the author of *Joyride, Strangle Hold, Off Season,* and others. His short fiction has appeared in *Fear Itself, Vampire Detectives, Deadly After Dark,* and more. Of his collaborative story in this collection Ketchum comments, "Ed Lee and I always like to think about plants and viruses and big ugly bugs going around eating people instead of real guys like Jeffrey Dahmer. We figure this to be a basically feel-good story. Ed came up with it. I just got in there with my fingers and dug around."

Edward Lee

Lee is the author of nine horror novels and numerous short stories, including the Stoker-nominated "Mr. Torso" in *Deadly After Dark.* He says that no publisher thus far, however, has had the guts to publish *The Bighead,* which Lee considers the grossest book ever written. His equally gross novella, *Header,* was recently published, and the anthology *Darktide* has bought his story "The Stick Woman," which, Maryland's Lee states, "is so gross I almost threw up writing it."

Graham Masterton

England's Masterton is the author of twenty-eight horror novels, including *Master of Lies* and *Burial.* His books have had great success in Eastern Europe, and he has written a new horror-thriller, *St. Xavier's Day,* set in Warsaw. His contribution to *Hot Blood,* "The Changeling," has been optioned for a full-length feature.

Tom Piccirilli

New Yorker Piccirilli's novels include *Dark Father, Pentacle,* and *Hexes.* His most recent work is *Shards,* and he is currently working on a science-fiction crime thriller. "Call It," he says, "comes ringing directly from the cheating heart of a bad long-distance relationship, one that got a lot uglier before it was over. Nowadays even phone sex can kill you."

Wendy Rathbone

California's Rathbone has written for the *Hot Blood* series, *Writers of the Future #8, Dead of Night,* and others. Her book *Trek: The Unauthorized A to Z* was published in 1995. Of "The Sinister Woods," she says, "While visiting a small town where my mother grew up, she and I drove by a patch of woods near the town's cemetery. She told me when she was a child she always thought of that patch of trees as sinister and evil because the sun never seemed to reach through to that place and because of a bad feeling that emanated from them. From that, a setting evolved for a story about the extremes a young teenager might go to just to please a parent."

Elsa Rutherford

Alabama resident Rutherford has had work published in *Fear Itself,* and is currently serving as script consultant on a film project and teaching fiction writing at a university. Of "Flesh and Blood," which marks her second *Hot Blood* series appearance, Rutherford says, "It is my humble thank-you to Anne Rice, who has been and continues to be a literary inspiration to me, particularly her philosophy that horror and eroticism are often interconnected, and that the literary exploration of that connection belongs as rightfully to women as to men."

John F. D. Taff

Taff's work has appeared in *Shock Rock 2, Seeds of Fear, Cemetery Dance,* and others. Of his story in this book, the Missouri writer says, "I got the idea from my brother, who told me of a friend who got her tongue pierced. What do such people hope to accomplish by doing such things—by opening holes in their bodies? 'Orifice' is my answer to that question."

Lucy Taylor

The horror fiction of Colorado's Taylor has appeared in *Little Deaths, Hotter Blood, The Mammoth Book of Erotic Horror,* and other anthologies. Her novel, *The Safety of Unknown Cities,* has just been published, and she is at work on another. She calls her story in this book "pure fantasy. It would be too depressing to think that, in the name of 'love,' people actually behave in such bizarre and self-destructive ways."

J. N. Williamson

Indiana's prolific Williamson is the author of over 40 novels and 150 short stories, including the recent *The Book of Webster's* and *Bloodlines.* He says he began to create "Two Hands Are Better Than One" with "little more than a desire to place a jaded men's mag professional in the presence of photographed nudes that would blow his mind. Instantly, the challenge was: what in the world would do that?"

Stephen Woodworth

A first-place winner in the Writers of the Future contest, California's Woodworth has seen his work published in *Writers of the Future, Volume VIII, Chic,* and *Plot Magazine,* and is currently at work on his first novel. The present story, he tells us, was inspired by a peculiar conjunction of recent events, including the Bobbitt case, the U.S. invasion of Haiti, and the L.A. debut of *Miss Saigon.*